EVERY TIME YOU GO AWAY

Books by Abigail Johnson

If I Fix You
The First to Know
Even If I Fall
Every Other Weekend

ABIGAIL JOHNSON

EVERY TIME YOU GO AWAY

inkyard
PRESS

Content Note:

Some readers may prefer to know ahead of time
that this book includes references to child abuse and neglect,
substance abuse, addiction, and the death of a parent.

ISBN-13: 978-1-335-42915-5

Every Time You Go Away

Recycling programs
for this product may
not exist in your area.

For questions and comments about the quality of this book, please contact us at CustomerService@Harlequin.com.

Inkyard Press
22 Adelaide St. West, 41st Floor
Toronto, Ontario M5H 4E3, Canada
www.InkyardPress.com

Printed in U.S.A.

For Sadie

My brave and beautiful girl. Every day my life is better because of you.

And for Fanny

You sat in my lap for every book I've ever written.
I don't know how I'll write the next one without you.

CHAPTER ONE

BEFORE

REBECCA

There is nowhere else to start but with Ethan.

Ethan with his golden-brown eyes and teasing grin. He was my first friend, my first kiss, and the one person I trusted with all my secrets even as he held back so many of his.

We were kids that first day I saw him. Or I was. I'm not sure Ethan was ever a kid.

My dad scratches at the thinning part of his blond hair and bends over the griddle. "An eggplant?"

"Dad!"

"What? It looks like an eggplant." He reaches to rotate the griddle, burns himself, then yanks his hand back with a hiss. "All right, then what is it supposed to be?"

Trying not to laugh, I hand him the lobster-shaped oven mitt I got him for Christmas. "It's obviously an ice cream cone." And I obviously need to work on my pancake shapes if he guessed so wrong. Normally he always knows what I'm trying to make with mine just like I always know he's going to make his shaped like Mickey heads.

Dad—with his oven mitt on this time—turns the griddle this way, then that before shaking his head. "Sorry, sweetie. I just don't see it. Maybe if we—" He reaches past my perch on the counter to the cabinet by my head and pulls out a tiny jar of sprinkles which he shakes over half the pancake. "Yep, there it is. Ice cream cone."

I grin. "It would look extra ice cream coney with some whipped cream."

Dad snaps his fingers at me before turning to the fridge then speeds up after glancing at his watch. "And I am going to be late."

My grin slips. Summer is usually my favorite time of year because Dad is home with me all day, but since he's teaching summer school this year, morning pancakes together are all we have. Once he slips out the door with a peck on my forehead, I get to be bored—and quiet so my mom can work from the dining room table—for hours until he comes home. Sometimes I go next door to visit Mr. and Mrs. Kelly, but my mom doesn't like me going over there too often since she says retired people like to be by themselves and not entertain energetic nine-year-olds every day. When she repeated that to me just last week, I asked her if *she* was retired and my dad snorted coffee all over his pancakes.

Dad's been gone for hours now and our tiny house feels extra tiny and extra dull. My mom has already told me to keep it down three times and since she only allows me two hours of screen time a day, I end up standing on the pillowed window seat in our front room, playing a game I just now invented called Ceiling Slap. It's very complicated and involves leaping to try and brush the ceiling with my fingertips and stealing glances at the hallway to the dining room between each attempt in case my mom comes out and catches me. I'm setting so many Ceiling Slap records that I don't notice the car pulling up next door until a woman gets out tugging this scrap of a boy from the back seat. He's clutching a half-full garbage bag like everything he cares about in the world is inside it.

I immediately stop jumping thinking that the only thing I would ever hold that tightly is my dad's hand.

Mr. and Mrs. Kelly hadn't said anything about expecting company when I went over to help bake snickerdoodles yesterday, and my confused frown only deepens when they meet the newcomers on the porch and I hear the woman introduce the boy, Ethan, to his grandparents. I jerk back at that announcement, eyeing the boy anew with a stab of jealousy.

All I have left of my grandparents are photographs and wisps of memories that grow more indistinct the harder I try to grasp them. The Kellys have been honorary grandparents to me since we moved in two years ago and the sudden idea that I'll have to share them isn't exactly a welcome one.

I knew they existed, Ethan and his mom, but up until now, they'd been confined to a couple of old framed pictures on the Kellys' walls. Whenever I asked about them, they only said their daughter and grandson lived in California and they didn't get to see them often. So what are they doing here now and why isn't anybody smiling?

From my window I watch the woman hand over the garbage bag to Mrs. Kelly and try to hand over Ethan too. In the end, she has to pry his hands from her. He's skinny but strong. His mom runs her hands through stringy hair, her chin quivering so much that her entire face shakes as she says something I can't hear but makes my heart start pounding all the same. She starts to move away then, but just her, not him. And that's when my jealousy evaporates as I realize his garbage bag is a suitcase, and not the kind you pack for a weekend.

She leaves him without another look, not even when Ethan tries to run after her car and Mr. Kelly has to hold him back.

Something soft smacks me in the back and I nearly lose my balance on the window seat. I turn just in time to see my dad home already and arming himself with another pillow.

This has been our latest game for months now, impromptu throw pillow fights, and he's about to win a second point before I've even gotten a first. But instead of diving for cover behind the couch and gathering up my own ammo, I wave him off and press my ear harder against the glass, futilely trying to hear what Mr. Kelly is saying as Ethan continues raging in his arms. "Did you know the Kellys' daughter is back?"

Dad's gleefully triumphant expression fades from his softly rounded face. "What?"

I nod, my cheek squeaking against the glass. "She was just here."

Dad leans forward to peer out. "Joy was here?"

I nod. "And she left her son."

"She what?" he whispers, mirroring my position with his nose just inches from the glass. The fading sunlight turning the wavy strands of his hair to sparks of gold.

"You don't have to whisper."

He gives me a look, so I fill him in on what I witnessed. He slowly sits down when I'm done, then draws the curtains

shut, blocking the Kellys and their grandson from my pry-
ing eyes. I start to protest but he cuts me off. "Would you
want our neighbors spying on our personal family moments?
I don't think so."

I plop down beside him. "I've never seen her here before.
There are barely even any pictures of them in their house."

"Pictures of who in whose house?" Mom comes out of
the dining room with paint swatches in one hand and fabric
swatches in the other. "I didn't hear you come in."

Dad bounces up off the window seat to her. "I was just on
my way in to find you."

Like always, she stiffens the tiniest bit when his arms come
up around her, but he just waits until she relaxes before kissing her.

"Good day?"

"Mmmm," she says, resting her head on his shoulder.
"You?"

His arms tighten. "Better now."

"Now what were you saying about pictures?"

I start to tell her we aren't talking about interior decorat-
ing so she won't be interested but Dad's words beat mine.

"The Kellys. Joy was just here to leave her son with them."

Her arms lower to her sides. "Oh."

Dad nods and releases her so they can have one of those
silent adult conversations with just their eyes. I hate those.

"What?" I shoot glances between my parents. "What are
you eye-saying?"

"Sorry, sweetie, but some things are grown-up topics."
Dad stares at the closed curtains instead of me.

"But—"

"Rebecca." Mom pauses after saying my name, a sure sign that I'm irritating her. "It's none of our business." She walks over to the window and pulls the curtains closed even tighter than Dad did, smoothing out imaginary wrinkles as she does. "And I don't want you spying on the Kellys anymore."

It's not like I'm sneaking around in their bushes, but I keep that point to myself. There is one thing that I can't stay silent about though. "But his mom just left him with people he doesn't even know."

My mom, who is already moving back toward the dining room, stops. "I'm sure she didn't want to." She looks back at Dad to take over with me. He doesn't even need her prompting to pull me into his arms.

"*Left* is maybe not the right word. She brought him to stay with his grandparents because she might need some help."

Mom shifts from foot to foot, pulling at the light brown curls spilling over her shoulders. "I don't think we should be talking about this."

"Help with what?" I ignore Mom's protest, glad that my own lighter, looser curls are twisted back in a braid, and look at Dad, waiting. He's never believed in keeping things from me.

Dad considers his words. "Parents sometimes need help for different reasons. In Joy's case, she's been sick for a long time, and if she's bringing her son to her parents, then maybe she's ready to get better." Then he hugs me and after another silent-eye conversation between them, Mom sits on my other side and hugs me too. It isn't that she never hugs me, but usually, I see them coming, like on birthdays or winning a soccer game. This one catches me by surprise, and it takes me a second to hug her back.

"Just leave them be, alright?" she says. "And it's probably a good idea for you to stay away from the boy too."

My gaze travels back to the closed curtain. My fingers are itching to reopen it.

Mom starts picking up the pillows Dad threw at me, brows pinching together at the sight of a burst seam in one corner. "I've asked you so many times not to roughhouse with these pillows. The fabric is vintage and— Rebecca Ann James!" My mother's sharp voice causes me to jerk back from the window and plant my feet firmly on the floor. "I know you weren't standing on my custom cushions with your shoes on."

I glance down at my untied red sneakers and the Rebecca Ann James–shaped footprints on the cushions behind me.

Mom's lips clench around her words. "Cleaning bin. Pantry. Right now."

I start to move but Dad gestures for me to stay put, taking Mom by the shoulders and steering her back to the dining room.

"No," she says to him, her voice dropping to more of a frustrated whisper. "I can handle this."

This meaning me. I watch curiously to see how this will play out, but there aren't any surprises. Dad wins and Mom gives up. She allows herself to be gently pushed back to the dining room with one final warning to Dad to leave her pillows alone and another to me to stay away from the window, which I obey for about thirty seconds. Unfortunately, the yard is empty when I sneak a peek.

It isn't until later that night that I get another glimpse of Ethan Kelly.

The window to his room—formerly Mrs. Kelly's guest room/sewing room—is right across from mine on the ground floor. There's a monsoon thunderstorm that first night, and the rain on the windowpanes makes it seem like he's crying as he sits small and huddled on the bed.

Remembering Mom's admonition to stay away, I throw open my own window after my parents go to bed, heedless of the rain blasting into my room and soaking the floor—something I'll definitely get grounded for the next day—and tear across our connected yards in my faded peach nightgown. I tap on his window, then tap again. He finally looks up and sees me in all my drowned-rat glory.

He opens the window.

CHAPTER TWO

NOW

ETHAN

The room looks…different. Last time I was here there were little steamer trains on the wallpaper and a stuffed bear sitting on a tiny white bed. Now a bookshelf filled with thick, well-read classics stands beside a modern desk with what looks like a new laptop on it.

My grandmother, barefoot in her uniform of faded jeans and a Good & Green T-shirt, hovers in the doorway behind me, tugging at her reddish-brown braid as she waits for my reaction.

I move toward the full-sized bed and try not to look at the large black-and-white framed photos of LA on the slate-colored walls.

"We can change the colors, of course," my grandmother says. "You always loved blue, so I thought…"

"It's fine. I've got some cans of spray paint in my bag, so I'll fix it."

She twists her hands into her braid. Tight.

Look at that, I surprised my grandmother. "Grandma, I'm kidding. And I still like blue."

She exhales and then brightens at my small gratitude, the first sign that the little boy she remembered isn't completely gone. "Well, I'll leave you to get settled. Dinner is at six." From the corner of my eye, I see her turn to leave then hesitate. "Ethan?"

My grandmother's tone is all but ordering me to look at her. I consider ignoring it. She hasn't seen me in years, and size and inches are the least of the things I've gained since then. I'm still deciding when my cat pops out of my open bag and yowls at me. I rub the nearly bald patch on the top of his ancient head. "Hey, Old Man. You ready to stretch a bit?"

"Ethan, is that…a cat?"

"Well, it's not a can of spray paint."

Her expression says she doesn't appreciate my humor at the moment. "Does he have a name?"

"Probably. I just call him Old Man." I'd been rereading a lot of Hemingway at the time and when I found him on the beach losing a battle over a dead fish with a pelican, the name seemed fitting.

"You should have said something. We don't have any cat litter. Or a litter box."

I walk over to the window and push it up, then lift my cat onto the sill. "He's fine. He'll come and go as he wants."

"No, that's not a good idea. And food, we'll need to get food. I can go to the grocery—"

"Grandma, we're fine. I'll take care of his food—I always do." I take care of a lot more than just a cat or I did until my grandparents intervened, a fact my grandmother knows all too well.

She falls silent after that and when she starts eying my bag as though she's about to unpack for me, I scoop Old Man up and move toward the door, forcing her to back up.

"I'm going to take him out back, make sure he knows the best places to crap around the pool deck."

My grandmother's mouth opens. But then she closes it, considering me. "Hmmmm," she says.

"That's it?"

"For now." She retreats to the hall so I can pass with my cat. I feel her watching us though so I'm not caught off guard when she calls after me. "Oh, and Ethan? Don't you dare spray-paint my walls without running the colors past me first."

I laugh at the teasing smile on her face. Look at that, my grandmother surprised me.

The yard outside is blooming with bright, warm colors and the soft scent of the flowers my grandfather painstakingly tends. I'm not worried when Old Man takes off in murderous pursuit of a butterfly. After all the different places we've lived, I know he'll find his way back to me.

I head farther down the smooth brick path that has replaced the gravel that I remember, beneath a trellis of dripping orange petals, to a bright oasis in an Arizona desert. I stop to pull out my notebook and nub of a pencil to sketch it when something else catches my eye.

It's a credit to my grandfather that the flowers are what I noticed first and not the girl floating lazily in the pool straight ahead.

She's on her back, eyes closed, light-skinned face lifted up to soak in the warmth of the sun as her wavy hair floats around her head. She's humming but I'm too far away to make out the tune. There's a dreamy half smile on her lips, an ease to her expression that I've never even imagined, much less experienced. It has me grinding my teeth before I can recognize the sudden burst of resentment that pulses through me.

But then she lifts one arm to skim her fingers across the surface of the water, and I see the scar on her forearm. I have its twin on my arm from when I let a girl talk me into playing catch with lit fireworks...

My jaw unlocks as her name, warm and radiant as the sun, drifts up from some buried place inside me. "Rebecca?"

Her head turns in my direction, her eyes, somehow bluer than I remember, going wide. "Ethan?" The huge, joyous smile she gives me has me catching my toe on the brick as I stagger toward her.

She strokes over to the side of the pool and lifts herself up to sit on the edge, leaving her legs to dangle in the water. "I thought you weren't coming until tomorrow."

Of course, my grandparents would have told her. "Yeah, I—um, got here early." With a mental shove, I force all my thoughts about why I'm here away and let my mind fill only with her.

She scoots down a bit to make room and urges me to sit beside her, leaning away the second I do, not because we're too close, but so that her gaze can drink in every inch of me. I do the same, noticing the new curves hidden behind her simple navy two-piece. Her lower lip is fuller than the top and the prominent dimple on her left cheek flashes at me.

Her hands, more graceful but with the same always-chipped polish, lift to tug at my hair. She quirks an eyebrow at the added length brushing my collar.

"It's been a while since I cut it," I say, feeling the need to explain in case she doesn't like the change.

"I like it," she says, as though she's surprised by that fact. "I think."

I laugh, ducking my head.

Her returning smile is soft. "It's stupid, I know, but I kind of wanted you to still be thirteen."

The age we were the last time we saw each other.

I don't think it's stupid at all. There were so many nights when I wanted to go back to that time with her. I guess it's been the same for her. That's the general line of my thoughts until her fingers drift to the stubble along my jaw and my breath catches slightly.

"This is really too much though," she adds, grinning. "And what are you, six foot now?"

"Six-one," I admit, like it's a crime.

She bites both her lips. "I really want to hug you right now, but you probably don't want to get wet—"

I wrap her in my arms, feeling the water from her swimsuit soak through my T-shirt, but more than that, I feel the warmth from her sun-kissed skin, the soft sigh of her breath against my neck. And her scent, that forgotten but familiar mix of sunscreen and honeyed sunshine. The ache in my chest relaxes.

When my arms tighten, her voice half breaks. "I can't believe you're here."

I stiffen. I don't want to think about the reason I'm here,

but when I open my eyes, still holding her, I see the proof of how much we've both changed behind her.

She releases me and follows my gaze over her shoulder to the empty wheelchair on the other side of the pool.

CHAPTER THREE

NOW

REBECCA

I know he's spotted my wheelchair, and I hold my breath waiting for his reaction. It doesn't bother me to look at the sleek, low-backed chair anymore, but it freaks some people out, especially people who knew me before it became my ever-present accessory. But Ethan doesn't jerk away from me like I'm suddenly breakable. When his arms return to his sides, it's only so he can look at my face.

"I called so many times. Why wouldn't you talk to me?"

I wrap an arm tight around my waist, squeezing until the flicker of unease snuffs out. "Because we don't do that. When you're here, you're here, and when you're not…" We both just rely on his grandparents to fill us in on any major life changes. It's how I heard about his mom's overdose and that he's staying here for the next three months while she's in rehab.

"Yeah, but—"

"But what?" I squeeze tighter, needing to hold myself together when too-sharp edges begin to fracture under his pry-ing. "You had to hear it from me about the accident and the fact that I'll be a paraplegic for the rest of my life?" I shake my head thinking about everything else I can't bring myself to say. Those months following the accident were the lowest of my life. I lost everything, far more than my ability to walk, and they expected me to just get up and keep going, to be happy about successful surgeries and strides in rehab, never mind that it was more than just my body that was broken. And when I finally came home, it was worse.

"I'm sorry," he says.

My gaze, which had lost its focus, steadies on his. "I didn't need you to be sorry, I needed you to be here."

"That's not fair," he says, leaning even farther away from me. "You don't know what I was dealing with back then."

My face grows hot hearing that explanation and knowing how far short it falls. "You used to come every few months. Why didn't you come back?" And then, in a smaller voice that bleeds with hurt, "Ethan, I waited for you." So many nights I started at the sounds of cars and slamming doors outside, hoping and praying it would finally be him.

His gaze flickers, but I refuse to let him look away until he answers.

"She only brought me before when she knew she couldn't take care of me."

His mom is in rehab right now, and I'd gleaned enough from the Kellys over the years to know that she hadn't been in recovery all this time. "You're telling me she got better at that since you've been gone?"

"No, not better." The tendons in his neck grow more pronounced, implying just how not better she got. "But I showed her I didn't need looking after. I also learned how to make it harder for her to use, and when I couldn't do that, I took care of her and all the things she couldn't." He falls silent before adding, "I tried to call you and tell you before. Way before. You didn't answer then either."

I break our stare, willing the heat to trickle away from my face as unexpected guilt splashes at me. Is it wrong that I didn't want to settle for part of him? Just a nervous voice on the phone? "I thought it would be better just to wait until the next time you came back."

He snorts. "And is it?"

Not when I'm forced to think about how hard these past years must have been for him too. I'm still raw inside, and knowing he is too doesn't change that. But it does help me push the feelings back down and focus on him being here now, the way I always had to whenever he came back when we were kids.

"No," I admit. "But I wasn't exactly planning on yelling at you."

"No?" He does a better job than me shaking off the feelings he doesn't want and even manages a half smile. "And what were you planning?"

I force my lungs to empty all their air, pushing my residual anger out with it. "To be happy because my best friend was back." For now.

"Best friend, huh?"

A different kind of heat flushes my cheeks. "Well, I mean, obviously it's been a few years and we've both—"

"I'm messing with you, Bec. You're still mine too."

I face him, watching to see if his gaze will pull to my chair and then guiltily away as if he shouldn't be looking at it, but it doesn't. He just looks at it. Then me. "And you're okay? I mean, you're not in pain, like when I hugged you?"

"I'm good." I know he wants to ask more though, so I take pity on him. "I mostly can't feel my legs, but there are a few places like here." I tap the top of my right knee, then a few inches to the side. "And here."

His hand twitches toward my leg and I lift Ethan's hand and lay his fingers on the side of my knee. His skin is warm, and I jump a little from the contact, laughing at myself and at him when he jumps too. "It's okay," I tell him. It's actually kind of nice.

Ethan's hand trails slightly higher, but I can't help pushing him away when he reaches skin that I can no longer feel. Thankfully he doesn't seem to notice why I stop him, and the shy-but-real smile he gives me relaxes my unease away.

"Oh, and did you notice these?" I lift my arms to flex my biceps, loving the way his smile grows and the fact that I'd been the one to grow it. "Pushing a wheelchair around all the time does have its benefits."

He whistles. "Damn. You're more jacked than I am."

I'm clearly not, but I accept the compliment. "Hey, remember that time I beat you in that pull-up contest we had on Mr. Jimenez's grapefruit tree?"

"You went first and weakened the branch—" I pretend to look affronted at his words "—so it broke on me after one!"

I grin. "How is that factually different from what I said?"

We take turns after that, tossing old memories back and forth as the setting sun turns the pool into molten gold.

I'm weary from laughing so hard and haven't felt this alive in years, four to be exact.

He brushes the firework scar on my forearm, laughing again. "This was one of my favorites."

His touch distracts me for long enough that he looks up at me to see why I'm silent. "I was so stupid."

He turns his forearm over and holds it next to mine so our scars blend into each other. "I think of you every time I see it."

I groan even though there's a sweetness in his words that flutters inside me. "Let's maybe try something less painful for the next memory."

"I'm sure you'll think of something."

"Oh, I already have some ideas."

He laughs loud and free like he was waiting for me to say something like that. "You're the same, you know?" he says.

I quirk an eyebrow at him, unsure if I like the fact that he still sees me as a thirteen-year-old girl.

"I thought maybe you'd be different. Sad, maybe."

"Sometimes I am."

His gaze travels over my face. "But it's not who you are. You're not…" I can see him trying to think of the right word and finally settling on "…less."

Later, I'd think about that word and how it wrapped itself so tightly around my heart that I feel like it's carved into my bones, but for now, all I can do is wonder if he'd say the same thing about himself. "And you?"

He tries to lightly laugh off my question like it's a joke, but we both know it's not. "Same as I always was. Taller maybe."

We may have lost these past four years, but a part of me still feels like I know him better than anyone, and I've learned not to push. "Much taller. You look good, Ethan."

He falls quiet then, gazing back at me before delivering his own assessment. I'm painfully aware of wanting and dreading to know what he thinks. I preen and pose then, waiting for him to repay the compliment. He takes his time looking at me and I hate the way I subtly flinch when he glances at my legs. I know I don't physically look that different, but it feels that way sometimes. A lot of the time.

"You look good too, Bec. All of you."

I feel myself flinch again, but hope he doesn't notice, and force myself to grin. "Taller and smoother."

His mouth quirks up on one side. "So, tell me. What have—"

An alarm goes off on my phone and it's like a cloud has swept in to cover the sun. If I could walk, I'd have leapt up; instead I settle for lowering myself back into the cool water and swimming to the side where my wheelchair is waiting. "Sorry, I have to go." I hop back up onto the pool's edge, transfer up to the lounger, and silence my phone before grabbing my towel.

"Do you need help or anything?"

I appreciate that he asked instead of assuming I did and trying to move my chair or something. I left everything lined up exactly the way I need it. "I'm good."

"Yeah, I can see that," he says. I think he sounds impressed. "You really have to go now?"

"I'm supposed to cook dinner, but maybe we can catch up more tomorrow."

"Tomorrow?" Ethan laughs like I made a joke. "What's wrong with later tonight?"

"My mom will be home."

"Then meet me later. Sneak out if you have to. You used to know a dozen different ways to get out of your house undetected, don't tell me you haven't figured out a few new ones."

I hang my head because he's not wrong. Maybe I couldn't climb out my window anymore with an empty hamster cage in my arms and a set of golf clubs on my back, but I still remember which floorboards creak in the hall and have unconsciously memorized the exact spots and speed to silently roll over them. But just because I theoretically have thought through one or two ways to sneak out doesn't mean I will. Still avoiding his gaze, I say, "I don't do that kind of stuff anymore." I quickly finish drying off before transferring to my wheelchair, hurrying so that I don't have to worry about what Ethan might be thinking watching me.

The smile on his face falters. "Wait, you're serious?"

"Ethan." I pause and exhale slowly, thinking how best to say this to him. "Things are different now. Way more than you know. Way more than you can see."

"Yeah, but you're—"

"Different too," I say, more harshly than I mean. Of course I'm different, and not just in the obvious ways. "Aren't you?"

His expression shuts down. His eyelids lower, his face goes slack, his jaw locks. I know this look from him; I've just never seen it directed at me. It feels like being robbed, like something valuable was just taken from me.

I soften my voice. "I have to go but I'm glad you're back, Ethan." I turn my chair toward the brick path connecting our yards that Mr. Kelly laid just for me. "I've missed you."

His flat expression vanishes just as quickly as it appeared, replaced by a lazy smile that I can see right through. "Sure.

Tomorrow, whenever." He lifts his arms out. "It's not like I'm going anywhere for the next ninety days."

I wince at the reminder that this time with Ethan is no different from all the others: fleeting.

CHAPTER FOUR

NOW

ETHAN

"Heard you got a cat to feed."

"Holy—" I reflexively lurch against the hallway wall at my grandfather's voice behind me, knocking a bunch of framed photos onto the floor. Nearly every inch of their house is carpeted—including the bathrooms—so fortunately nothing breaks. I bend down to pick up the photos: mostly old pictures of my grandparents and their friends, but me and mom here and there too. "You don't need to worry about the cat. I'll take care of him."

I don't hear him moving behind me so when his arm shoots into my line of vision, I hurl myself back and throw my own arms up reflexively. My pulse stays sky-high even when I see that he was just reaching for a frame.

He freezes, his bushy gray-brown eyebrows drawing together. "Ethan?"

I shake my head, dismissing his concern, wishing I could

shake off the fear as easily. My grandfather's leathery brown arms have never been raised against me.

He gives me space, but I feel his gaze, heavy and assessing, and it makes my neck burn hot. He won't ask questions that he knows I won't answer, but he's guessing a lot right now and I let him. He can choke on his thoughts for all I care. At least I was there for her, standing between her and the angry boyfriends or whoever wanted money we didn't have. Where was he?

Before my anger can do more than simmer, I notice the bag by his feet.

"Cat food," he says, slowly shifting the bag to the floor by me as if another sudden move might make me jump again. "Used to be a stray in the neighborhood that I would feed sometimes."

I toss the bag back to my grandfather, who easily absorbs the impact like the former college football player he is. "He can't eat this kind. He's got like one tooth."

"So what kind does he eat then?"

"I told you, you don't need to worry about this."

He sighs. "Cat food costs money."

I stretch my arms out like I don't care. "So I'll get a job."

"Yeah?" His pose mimics mine. "And how are you gonna get there?"

"I've got my mom's car." Sure, there are rust holes in the floor and the brakes are kind of mushy, but it got me here. Eventually.

"That car's got maybe twenty miles left in it. Any more and we both know she'd have sold it to get high."

She'd tried. More than once. The memory makes my muscles clench as I lower my arms and stare directly at him. "You're kind of an asshole, Grandpa, you know that?"

"Don't swear in my house." My grandfather doesn't swear, ever. He used to be an asshole in every sense of the word, even my grandmother will say that—she'll even use the word. Now he's a deacon at their church and leads a weekly Bible study at the prison where he was once an inmate. He lives by the "there but for the grace of God go I" mentality. Based on some of the stories I've heard, and the track mark scars I've glimpsed on his arms, I know he believes that. But it just pisses me off to follow his conclusion that mom and I didn't get that same share of grace.

"Or what? You'll kick me out? You're the one that forced her to send me here."

His voice rises for the first time. "We didn't force her. She had a choice and she made it."

A choice. Right. "I never should have called you." I try to shoulder past him, but the hallway is narrow and he doesn't let me by.

"The way I see it you should have called long before that night."

My voice drops and I stare him straight on. "You don't know anything about our life. Or me," I add, thinking about Rebecca's words by the pool. She's right; we are different now. "I'm not a little kid anymore. If I'd called before, you'd have just tried to take me away sooner." They'd tried to get custody of me before, but Mom always squeaked by—I learned quick how to lie to anyone who came around asking questions about how we were doing. Besides, there was only one person in our family with a serious record and I was looking at him. "I asked you for money because she finally agreed to check into an actual rehab. I didn't ask you to pack up our apartment while she was still in the hospital and tell her you'd only help if I came here."

Even now I feel sweat prickle my skin at the thought of him walking through our front door and holding his breath when the sour, vomit-laced air hit his nose. Her dried pool of sick had still been on the floor in the living room that doubled as my bedroom.

Here we are, days later, the soft scent of fresh roses drifting from a vase in the dining room. I can't argue that the accommodations aren't better. Still, he has no idea how much worse things would have been for her without me, how much worse they will be if I'm not there when she gets out.

"Joy's been my daughter a lot longer than she's been your mom. And struggled with addiction since she was younger than you." I hear his throat constrict around the words, but he pushes through. "We've been down the money road with her and the promises road too. I've prayed for her every day of her life, and I'm gonna keep praying for her, but we weren't about to leave you there on her say-so. Right now she recognized that the safest place for you is here and not somewhere that taught you to flinch when a man reaches past you." His voice starts to shake with anger before he gets a hold of it. "We're trying to do what's best for you. And her. But help for her can't come at your expense."

My hand closes in a tight fist. "You know for years now I've been helping her a lot more than she's been hurting me."

"No, Ethan. I don't know that." Instead of saying more, he reaches into his pocket and tosses something metallic toward me. I catch it easily thanks to all the hours he spent throwing spirals to me.

"What is this?" I'm dumb, ask almost any teacher I've ever had, but I've rarely felt stupid until now. He can't be serious.

"Starting tomorrow, you can come work for your grandmother and me at Good & Green, Monday through Saturday, hauling plants, laying sod, whatever the job is that day. You pay for your own gas, insurance, any food you eat outside of this house, phone, movies, whatever else you want to do. The rest will go toward paying us back for your car."

Something claws at the inside of my throat as I stare down at the keys in my hand. My Doc Martens are more duct tape than leather at this point and he's just given me a car.

"Only one thing I need you to promise me."

I'm almost relieved that he's being upfront about the catch.

"We all agreed that you'll stay here for the next three months. You're right that you're not a kid anymore, but you're not an adult yet either, not for another year. Your grandmother and I want you to consider staying here until you are." He interrupts my scoffing. "And we want you to get your GED."

I outright laugh this time. "Anything else? Maybe I'll apply to Harvard while I'm at it."

He's dead serious when he says, "I was thinking maybe you start with one of the community colleges around here."

"Oh, so now I'm staying here for *years*?" I laugh again. "What makes you think my mom is gonna leave me here? She always comes back for me."

His head dips as though he can't look at me anymore. "Not this time."

My smile freezes on my face. "And why's that?"

"Because she knew the deal. We promised to take care of her back rent, the hospital bill, and you if she completes ninety days."

"She will," I say in a voice gone strained as doubt creeps in.

"She checked herself out of rehab last night."

CHAPTER FIVE

NOW

REBECCA

I am *not* running away from Ethan Kelly. I'm not. But I know that's what it must look like to him. My mom used to have to track me down for dinner when we were kids, and I made that quite the task for her, hiding in bushes, sprinting around corners, and pretending not to hear her. Now I do the job of pulling myself away from my friends for her.

I'd meant it when I told him things were different.

The second I wheel up the ramp and through my back door, I toss my towel in the general direction of the open laundry room, then hurry into the kitchen, which isn't really accessible despite the limited changes Mom was able to make on our one-income budget while I was in the hospital recovering.

Cooking a full meal on my own is something new I'm trying, more of a last-ditch effort really. Before the accident, we had a routine: Mom, Dad, and I all sitting around the table together, no devices, no TV. Dad would ask us a million questions about our days and Mom came to life in a way she always seemed to struggle with on her own. So. Dinner… which I'm really going to have to hurry on if I want to surprise her when she gets home.

I lock my wheels before shifting up until I'm sitting on the wheel closest to the counter. It gives me the few extra inches I need to reach into the upper cabinet. My balance is a bit precarious whenever I do this, but I manage. A few more tricks and only the tiniest burn on my forearm and I have rice on the stove and chicken in the oven.

I have time to rinse off in the shower—my hair already hates me from the amount of chlorine I expose it to on a near daily basis, but we've reached something of a truce as long as I rinse it out before it can fully dry.

Back in my room, I pull out easy clothes, a short olive green sundress, then throw everything, including myself, onto my bed to finish drying off and dress.

"Keri? Rebecca?" a man's voice calls out.

"Just me!" I answer, heading to the kitchen to get the rice before it boils over. John, Mom's boyfriend of over a year, barely beats me there.

John is a big guy. We have tall doorways in our kitchen and he still has to duck when he walks in. He grins back at me, but falters as he sees the food. "You're cooking?"

"I thought it'd be a nice surprise." I'm zigzagging around the kitchen as I talk, pulling out dishes and silverware. "Are you dropping something off or can you stay? I'm making a Creamy Chive Chicken recipe that I saw on TikTok and it's probably mostly edible. And," I add, slipping into an infomercial voice, "I can guarantee it won't give you salmonella."

Mostly because I for sure overcooked it. John looks less than enthused by my sales pitch; in fact, he looks slightly uncomfortable at a dinner invite he now knows he can't turn down.

I start talking at John the second he sits. "So get this, Ethan's already here." John's discomfort vanishes and his suddenly wide-eyed expression matches mine exactly. I have to ignore the sharp twist of my heart whenever he does stuff like that, match my emotion without any kind of prompting. My dad always did that too.

"Ethan-Ethan? I thought he wasn't coming until tomorrow?"

"I know." He helps me start setting the table. "Surprised me too. He seems different. More different than I was expecting." My movements slow. He'd said I didn't know what he was dealing with... Would he ever tell me? I clear my throat when I realize I've paused for too long. "And tall. Really tall."

John's deep brown skin wrinkles between his brows. "Oh no," he says, hanging his head in his hands. "Layla's only six. I'm not supposed to have to deal with this kind of stuff yet. I haven't read the right books. Um…okay." He straightens up, looking very serious, for John anyway. "You see, there are these things called hormones—"

I shove hard at his massive shoulder and succeed only in rolling my wheelchair back a few inches. John laughs. "Okay, so he grew up well. He's not the only one." John still doesn't know how to give me a compliment without being weird about it, so he pats my head, deliberately awkward. I pull away before he tries to ruffle my hair.

"Right. Thanks."

"I'm just saying…"

I'm saved by Mom bursting through the door.

Slim and pretty in her gray pencil skirt and steel blue silk blouse, her curls are pulled back into a soft twist with tendrils slipping free against her pale face. I can see, like actually see John's heart skip a beat when he spots her. That should make me happy, shouldn't it?

"You weren't waiting long, were you?"

I'd started to turn back to the table, so at first I think she's talking to me and my chest swells with unexpected happiness. But when I spin to face her, I see she's gazing up at John.

"Bec's been keeping me company. And, um, cooking."

Mom glances over at me for the first time. Like always, her glance bounces away as quickly as it touches me. It feels a little like dying of thirst just as I reach the edge of a river.

"Oh, Rebecca." She slips free of John's embrace and smooths her skirt. "I thought you'd still be swimming."

"I finished early and decided to make dinner." I wasn't expecting clasped hands and exclamations of delight, but something more than the awkward glances she and John keep exchanging would have been nice. "I already invited John to join us if that's the problem...?"

John gives her a "tell her" look, but it's only after I say, "Mom?" that she answers.

"The Sandovals finally approved my design for their primary bedroom. They invited John and me to Ruth's Chris Steakhouse to celebrate. I think he wants to talk to me about a commercial job for his new hotel."

"Hotels. That's great." I take a shallow breath. "The Sandovals. Good job."

I don't know who the Sandovals are any more than she

knows that Ethan was coming back. But John does. We talk
to him way more than we talk to each other. But I thought
tonight could be different. Not heavy or hard or anything
important, but a start. I'd hoped anyway.

She glances at me, then at the food on the table, the single chair and the space for my wheelchair. Then she looks to
John, in such a familiar move that my throat squeezes like a
fist. She wants him to intervene, to smooth everything over
with me like Dad always did.

I think I might be sick if he does.

"It's just that it might be an important dinner."

Unlike this, she means. I just cooked my first full meal
since the accident and she hasn't even asked why.

"A big project right now would be good. With college ex-
penses coming up…"

The sick sloshing in my stomach gets worse.

Cal State University Northridge is one of the most
wheelchair-friendly colleges in the country, which is the reason Mom says she insisted I apply and, even after I got my acceptance letter, still asks me for updates constantly. But that's
not the real reason. I know with every passing second she
spends staring at the table instead of looking at me.

"You two should go. I'm feeling kind of tired actually. Not
really up for eating anyway."

"Rebecca, you need to eat," is what she says.

Eating is not what I need, but it's the practical thing so
that's what she focuses on.

I agree to eat, whatever she wants. I'm very convincing so
she eventually drops the issue.

She promises to be home early, but I'm not surprised when

a text comes in—from John—letting me know they are going to catch a late movie and I shouldn't wait up.

I'd put all the food away hours ago, so I'm in my bed in less than ten minutes, and I lie there with my eyes and ears wide open waiting for her.

I turn my head to the side, away from the door. I'd forgotten to close the curtains before getting into bed so I can see straight across to the Kellys' house and Ethan huddled over the desk typing on a battered laptop held together with duct tape.

My heartbeat picks up as I think about that first sight of him earlier, the way he'd said my name like it was special, beautiful. I hadn't felt that way in years and he gave that back to me in an instant.

That feeling is long gone now as I wait for Mom to come home. I hope in vain for a light tap to sound on my door, even if it's only to poke her head in and assure herself that I'm safe in my bed, but what I get instead is a text.

Mom:
I'm home.

I pull my blankets up even higher, wanting to hide from so much more than the boy next door. It's no good though. Every time I open my eyes I see the open curtains. I'm the worst at sleeping even on good nights, and this is not a good night.

I hate the fact that I'm thinking about how easy it would be to just walk over there and pull them shut. I could be back in bed in a matter of seconds. Instead, I loll my head to the right to where I'd left my chair. I'm thankful for my chair, I am, but that doesn't stop me from wanting to hurl it across the room, set it on fire, and leave the smoking remains on a train track sometimes.

And I still have to close the curtains.

Sitting up, I slide to the edge of the mattress, lower my legs off the side and, leaning forward to shift my center of gravity, transfer into my chair. I settle my feet on the footplate and then I'm pushing over to my window, tugging at my curtains and not even noticing at first that Ethan isn't at his desk anymore. He's at his window too, not to draw curtains, but to climb out after the bag he's already dropped to the ground.

CHAPTER SIX

BEFORE

REBECCA

Ethan's mom was gone for a month that first time.

Thirty whole days and I think we spent nearly every one of them together.

I let him carve his name in my tree house and he drew me a picture that we planned to paint on the walls.

We swam in his pool so much that my fingers and toes stayed pruney even while I slept.

I showed him how to cut through our neighbor's backyard when we heard the ice cream truck and he showed me how to catch a stray cat with a box and a can of tuna fish.

He made me let the cat go and I wasted what turned out to be our last week being mad about it. I was just getting ready to forgive him when his mom came back.

After a brief argument on the porch between Joy and Mrs. Kelly, Ethan heard his mom's raised voice calling for him—half the neighborhood heard her—and he came running.

He was gone for six months.

The next time she drops him at his grandparents' house, the Kellys aren't home, so he has to sit huddled on the front steps of their porch alone for hours. Well, he's only alone for one. I take him my very last Halloween candy bar, a Butterfinger that I've been saving.

It's one of the only times we ever talk about his mom.

"Why did your mom leave you with your grandparents?"

He shrugs, nibbling at his half of the bar while I've already finished mine.

"Don't you know?"

He shrugs again and this time his shoulders stay up high by his ears.

"My dad said it's 'cause she's sick. Does she go to the doctor?"

It's hard to tell if he shrugs or not with his shoulders up so high.

"No, she said she doesn't need doctors, she just needs to be by herself for a while. She always gets better."

I work at the candy stuck in my teeth. "But then she gets sick again?"

His shoulders completely cover his ears at this point. "She tries not to, but it's hard."

"Are you gonna get sick too?"

He shakes his head violently. "I didn't like being sick like that. It made me throw up and then it made my mom cry and bring me here."

"How come—"

"I don't want to talk about my mom anymore." He draws his knees up to his chest, hiding all but his eyes from view.

After that we started planning different ideas to paint my

tree house and I told him it could be his tree house too. His shoulders stopped hunching up and the next day he showed me the snow globe his mom had gotten him from the Santa Monica Pier. He said she was coming back for him, swore it fiercely, and even then, a part of me hoped he was wrong.

Over the next few years, Ethan came in and out of my life in bursts. I'd get weeks or months with him at a time, but she always came back, and he always left. I told myself that I was the one thing he would have taken with him if he could, and in his way, he told me that too.

Every time he left I found a flower on my windowsill. Sometimes it'd be a single pink bougainvillea from one of our neighbors' yards or a tiny golden sunflower. And when there were no blooms to pick, he would draw them for me. The real ones withered, but I have a shoebox under my bed full of flowers scribbled on receipts or napkins that never will.

Back then I hated Ethan's mom for the wrong reasons. Not because she neglected and endangered him, but because whenever I saw her, it meant that I was about to stop seeing him.

As suddenly as he'd show up in my life, he'd be gone just as quickly.

And he never said goodbye.

CHAPTER SEVEN

NOW

ETHAN

I can't find my cat.

I'm crouched and searching under the bed when I hear Rebecca's voice from outside my open window.

"You're leaving." It's not a question.

I swear and turn around so fast I almost lose my footing. Straightening, I avoid meeting her gaze as my eyes travel past her to a packed bag on the ground beside her.

"Just like that? Were you even going to say goodbye? Or was I going to wake up to another note?"

How many of those did I leave over the years? Hastily scribbled flower sketches meant to say what I didn't have the words for then any more than I do now.

She doesn't wait for my answer, just spins her chair around.

"Wait! Rebecca, wait." I scramble out the window, swearing when my foot catches on the ledge and sends me sprawling into a hedge of rosebushes below. Faint red lines appear up my forearms as I jerk away from the thorns, and a small dark shape shoots away.

I turn my anger on the cat. "Now you show up?"

"You have a cat?"

"I have an Old Man and he's an asshole who likes to randomly attack things, people. Butterflies." Except he doesn't *look* like he's about to claw Rebecca's face off when he jumps up onto her lap and bumps his head into her hand.

"Doesn't seem like an asshole to me."

"Yeah, well, he's probably still confused by the new location."

Her mouth twists. "Guess it's good he's going back with you then. Here." She scoops up the cat, ready to be done with this night and me.

Instead of taking Old Man, I move around to get in front of her. "Stop for one second and let me explain."

"Explain what? That I happened to see you leaving otherwise I wouldn't have gotten this touching goodbye moment?" She makes a disgusted sound in her throat. "You're here one day and I'm already sneaking out for you. Look, I'll make it easy for you. It was good seeing you again, Ethan, better than good." Her voice cracks. "I kind of thought you'd stay longer this time. Every time you go away—" She lifts one shoulder along with one corner of her mouth. "But I get it, okay? Now take your cat."

"No, you don't." And she should, I realize. "I don't know what I was going to do about saying goodbye because I hadn't thought that far. All I know is that my grandparents just told me my mom checked herself out of rehab and took off."

Rebecca's expression shifts from hurt to concern as her hand reaches out for mine.

I shift away, not wanting her to touch me when I know I have to leave. I step back so she doesn't have to tilt her head so far to meet my gaze. "They didn't even tell me when it happened so now she could be…"

"Anywhere. I'm sorry, Ethan." She takes a deep breath. "So you're what, going to find her?"

"What else can I do?"

"And you have a lead? Someone who saw her?"

I shake my head as various "anywhere" possibilities splash vividly across my mind. Anywhere means way more to me than it does to Rebecca.

"You know a place she'd go? Someone she'd stay with?"

My hands are in my hair, half pulling, half pushing, but the thoughts that keep coming are each worse than the last.

My mom walking alone down a street toward the wrong person.

My mom choking on her own vomit on the floor while some asshole trips beside her.

My mom on a metal table with a sheet drawn up over her.

"All day out there on her own. It's too long, too long."

"I know, but Ethan…" Her voice is a caress. I stop pacing and look at her. "I don't think you should go."

I feel that too, not soft but stinging. "What?"

She wheels closer to me and Old Man abandons her lap for my windowsill. "Hear me out, okay?"

That's what I'd asked from her and she'd still tried to leave. There's a part of me that wants to throw her own actions back at her. It's what I would have done before, and it's a near thing now, but I don't.

"How are you planning to get there?"

I pull my new keys out of my pocket and explain about the car my grandfather is going to let me work off.

Her eyes are sad when she returns my gaze. "You're going to take a car you haven't paid for yet?"

My jaw clenches and I stare down at the keys to a vehicle that suddenly feels like a payoff. I wind up and hurl them through my open window, earning a yowl from Old Man as they whizz a good foot away from him. I'm not about to hurt my cat. He jumps down outside and makes his way back to Rebecca's lap.

"So I'll take the bus."

Her eyes don't leave my face. "You have enough money for that? What about a place to stay once you get there? And food? And what about him?" She starts petting Old Man. "Will they let him on the bus? What about—"

Her questions fly at me like arrows I can't deflect and as each one pierces me, I get angrier. When I sneer it's not meant for her, at least I don't think it is. "Stop! Okay? Stop. I don't know. She's my mom. She's gone and if I'd been there I could have stopped her. You don't understand. It's—"

"Your fault?" Rebecca's smile slices across her face like a blade.

"I didn't mean it like that." Except maybe I did. I feel vicious right now and I don't want to be that way around her. None of this is her fault. "You haven't told me much about two years ago."

"And I'm not going to now." There's a rasp in her voice

that tells me she might never share everything about the night her world changed forever. "But I do understand and you know it." She understands that kind of guilt in a way that I pray I never will.

I feel like I should say I'm sorry, but I don't. I look away from her gaze that has grown way too steady on mine. "Look, I'll figure it out. But I have to find her. I have to—"

"Go? How do you even start looking for her with no money, no car, and no place to stay?"

An angry sound tears from my throat. Rebecca wheels closer to me. Or she tries. The brick walkway stops and she's forced to, as well. Her hands tighten until her knuckles turn white on her push rims, but that's the only giveaway of her true emotions.

Automatically, I move to close the distance she couldn't and I drop to sit on the brick beside her, my shoulders even with her waist. "Bec, I don't know what I'm supposed to do. I can't do nothing."

"I'm not asking you to. But taking off like this?" She shakes her head. "That doesn't help either of you."

"I don't care about me."

Her eyes flutter, almost shutting, and her knuckles turn even whiter. "Yeah, but I do. So if you have to find her, I'll help you."

CHAPTER EIGHT

NOW

REBECCA

I'm not thinking when I slip back in through my front door, not like I need to be. I remember the creaky floorboards but not the oversized vase Mom recently added beside the entryway.

I bump it with my front caster just enough to send a possibly-not-too-loud clang echoing through the house. I have barely a second to convince myself that I'm still in the clear before the vase topples into the wall with a definitely-heard-by-everyone crash.

"Rebecca?" Mom's voice calls from down the hall, then louder as I hear her hurried footsteps. "What happened? Are you okay?"

My head whips around and my heart starts thundering. "It's fine! I just dropped something. You don't have to—"

But she's too fast and I'm not nearly fast enough. I'm lunging back to close the still-open front door when she appears in the hallway. I awkwardly click it shut and freeze.

Her dusty lavender robe hangs loose as she processes the sight of me by the door.

"It's not what it looks like," I say, then spot a clump of spilled pampas branches stuck to my wheel and quickly throw it at the vase beside me. "I mean it is, but I can explain."

The moonlight filtering through the curtains shows her blink. "You snuck out?"

I can't tell if it's anger or incredulity I hear in her voice. I point my thumb over my shoulder toward the Kellys' house. "Yes, but I was only over—"

"You snuck out."

Not a question this time and based on the tremble in her words it's a lot more than an angry parent I'm facing. My mouth falls open at the picture of—I don't even know, worry?—she's presenting me with. "I'm sorry?" I say, like I'm reading from a script I've never seen before. "I didn't plan it. I was just—"

"No!" She raises her voice. "You don't do that. You don't get to do that ever again."

I don't understand the tears that suddenly spring to my eyes as I wheel toward her. I'd never do that again. She has to know that. I need her to know that like I need my next breath. "Mom, no, I wasn't—"

"Stop it." She slices her hand through the air to cut off my protests.

"I was only next door. At the Kellys." There. Her eyelids flicker. She wasn't expecting that and the surprise emboldens me to go on. "Ethan's back," I say in a voice barely above a whisper. I told John the second I heard Ethan was coming, but despite the handful of quick conversations I've had with her in the days since then, I haven't brought it up.

The truth is I don't share things with her. I barely did before the accident and I never do now.

Except I don't have a choice now, not if I want to banish that haunted look from her face.

"I found out a couple of days ago and saw him for the first time this afternoon. It was a lot," I say, dropping my gaze and tugging at the hem of the oversized sleep shirt I'm wearing—one of Dad's—before trailing my fingers to the frame of my wheelchair. "He knew about everything here but it was still—" I fumble around for the right words and fail "—a lot. And he has a lot going on too. At least I think he does. Which is why I snuck out. I needed to talk to him tonight before he did something not great. But I shouldn't have snuck out like that and I'm sorry." I finish my eloquent speech and look up to find that she's staring unblinkingly at my T-shirt with barely an indication that she heard me.

"Mom?"

Her eyes flutter as she sucks in a breath. I think for one hopeful moment that the hurt I see flickering across her features is about me keeping this huge, important person who's suddenly back in my life a secret from her, that she's going to express worry about the type of person he might have become or the potential hurt he may cause me and ask how I feel seeing him again after so much has changed.

I want her to ask with a longing so deep it almost pulls me from my chair as I lean toward her. I want her to care. She doesn't though. Because she's punishing me too, in her own way.

Tonight, for example, she walks right past me and chains the door before snapping the deadbolt shut.

"I don't want to go back there, Rebecca. Bed checks throughout the night. But I will if I have to."

I blink away a hot, half-formed tear as anger begins to take over the hurt. "Why would you when you've gotten so good at sending texts?" I meet her steady gaze with my own suddenly hard one. "I know I messed up tonight but you wouldn't have even known about Ethan or any of this if I'd been quieter coming in."

"John told me about Ethan."

I frown, the heat cooling behind my eyes in an instant. "When?"

"The same day you told him."

Ice crystalizes in my belly, chasing the burn away and leaving an empty chill behind. "Then why didn't you say anything?"

She stills, glancing at my T-shirt again before turning away and adding in a broken voice, "Because in a few months it won't matter. Even if he's still here, you won't be."

Then she's gone, retreating back to her room before I can move an inch toward mine.

CHAPTER NINE

NOW

ETHAN

I'll help you.

Rebecca's words from last night are all that keep me from taking off the next morning. They keep me stoic when my instincts are the opposite all through breakfast with my grandparents. And now that I'm officially wearing my Good & Green polo at my first worksite, they're the only thing keeping my thoughts from crushing me.

Mostly.

"This sucks."

The guy shoveling gravel beside me laughs. "But that view," he says, gesturing at the dying mall the city is desperately trying to resuscitate with new landscaping.

I bark out a laugh, then laugh harder. Then I'm laughing so hard that the guy, Neel, has to ditch his shovel to steady the wheelbarrow I'm close to dropping.

"Hey, I'm funny, but I'm not picking this up if you spill it all over the asphalt."

Sweat stings my eyes as I rub the tears away and try to get myself under control. It wasn't even that funny. Maybe I just have heatstroke or something. I'm definitely delirious. Probably because it's a million degrees out—slight hyperbole—and I've been wheeling eight tons—not hyperbole—of gravel into parking lot islands for the past six hours.

At least I haven't been working alone. Neel's about my age, strong and smart enough to use one of those squishy bandana things that looks like you wrapped up a long hotdog and tied it around your neck. I'd silently laughed at him when he soaked it and put it on earlier, but his warm brown skin hasn't been dripping sweat like mine has and I'm starting to feel like the stupid one for turning down his offer to use his backup. I'm feeling like the stupid one for many, many reasons.

"You know it's not always shoveling gravel in parking lots."

"What, this is just my grandfather's way of welcoming me to the job?"

Neel snort-laughs. "Probably."

Great. I'll be sure to thank him later for the breathtaking backside view of the former JCPenney that we're looking at all day. Truly majestic.

Equally majestic is the other guy with us, our supervisor, Eddie. He's older, probably in his thirties, with a patchy blond beard and a shaved head that isn't fooling anyone into thinking he's not prematurely balding. He's technically in charge of the project, which as far as I can tell means leaning against the truck and yelling at Neel and me anytime we stop moving for more than thirty seconds.

Following my line of sight, Neel says, "Eddie's alright. He

puts on a show for new employees, but he'll lighten up after a few weeks." He side-eyes me. "If you last that long."

My throat goes dry at the thought of being here for weeks. I never had a choice when I was a kid. She'd slip up, do something that messed me up, then panic, drop me with my grandparents, and stay gone just long enough to convince herself that it would never happen again. But that was years ago and that cycle of slipping—sometimes diving headfirst—followed by guilt-driven abandonment and finally stretches of peace ended once I stopped doing whatever she said no matter how messed up she was when she said it. Now I was the one taking care of her, keeping her slips at bay as much as possible and helping her get back up when I couldn't.

She's never gotten up on her own without me or at least the inescapable knowledge that I needed a clean mom. This time there's no reason for her to try.

"Hey, man, are you okay?" Neel eases the shovel from my hands. "You look kind of pale."

I try to clear my throat, then try again. "Yeah, I think maybe the heat is getting to me."

"You want to grab some water and go sit in the shade for a few? I can make sure Eddie doesn't give you any crap."

I reach for a water bottle and take a healthy swig. "No, I'm good." I have to be. Rebecca was right about all the flaws in my non-plan to find my mom. I can't just take off, which means I have to make this work here, for now, until I figure out where to start looking. And, I realize with a small smile, I'll get to have Rebecca by my side the whole time.

"The magic of water," Neel says with a grin. "You already look better."

"Yeah, water," I mumble, then at another yell from Eddie, we get back to work.

The grueling task of shoveling gravel while being baked alive keeps me slightly pissed off for the rest of the day. Neel cuts me some slack but not Eddie. In fact, the latter pulls me aside once we get back to the Good & Green building. With his thumbs shoved into his belt loops, he makes a show of looking me over, unimpressed.

"You think I care that you're their grandson? I don't. I care that you're strong, work hard, and don't pull any attitude with me." Eddie sucks at the gap between his front teeth. "As far as I can see, you're O for three today, kid."

It's hard not to laugh at him, really it is. I'm grateful though. His posturing is exactly what I need right now.

He leans into my personal space. "Did you hear what I said?"

"Yeah, man, I hear you. And I appreciate it. So much. In fact—" I glance from side to side as though to ensure no one is nearby and listening before leaning a little closer to him "—the truth is, I have a real people-pleasing complex. I probably won't be able to sleep tonight knowing I let you down. So if you could, you know—" I turn and look at him over my shoulder "—pat me on the back and tell me you believe in me that would… Hey wait!" I call when Eddie makes a disgusted sound in his throat and strides away. "How am I supposed to sleep tonight?"

"I'm guessing just fine," says a voice that makes me smile, a true smile, before I can even turn around to see Rebecca leaning out the driver side window of a white car, the frame of her wheelchair in the passenger seat.

My smile grows as I stride over to her. "You're early."

A hint of pink colors her cheeks. "Oh yeah, I had to—"

"I'm not complaining." And not just because we're going to start figuring out where to look for my mom.

The pink deepens a little as she hears the compliment in my words. "So first day, huh? Should I ask?"

I squint at her in the glare of the setting sun and move a little closer. Just a little. Every part of my body aches and I've got blisters on my hands because I decided I didn't need the work gloves my grandmother left me this morning. "Well, I made a friend," I say, gesturing in the direction Eddie went. "So there's that."

Her mouth quirks. "I saw. Gold star for you."

"And there's you. I didn't know you had a car."

"It's my boss's car. I only get to drive it when I'm running an errand for her. She's a wheelchair user too, obviously." She gestures at a lever beside the steering wheel that connects down to a metal plate over the pedals. She pushes her sunglasses up to keep the breeze from blowing her curls into her face. "Listen, about last night. I—"

"Was right. I didn't get to say it then, but you were. Taking off isn't going to help me find my mom. I know I got mad, but I just couldn't think, and you did. So, um. Thanks."

Rebecca stares at me and I come close to wiping at my face thinking there must be something on it. "Ethan Kelly. Wow." She half laughs, half exhales. "You would never have done that when we were kids."

I still kind of want to wipe at my face. "Done what?"

"Admitted you were wrong and thanked me for pointing it out."

I crack a smile. "When we were kids it was usually you wanting to do the stupid stuff."

"Stupid? Don't you mean fun?"

My answer is to lift the hem of my shirt revealing our one and only attempt at becoming tattoo artists.

Her cheeks flush redder than before as her gaze traces the faded and wobbly sun on the right side of my abdomen. "I was hoping it faded away maybe?" She bites her lip in a way that catches my eye. "Though I kind of feel like that one's on you. I mean you knew I couldn't draw."

I lower my shirt and pull my gaze away from her lips—had they been that full when we were kids? "Drawing and stabbing me a million times with a safety pin you dipped in ink are two different skills. That was kind of your selling point if I remember." Well, that and even at twelve, I was not about to pass up the chance to have her hands on my skin for that long. Or mine on hers. "Is yours still…?" I hadn't thought to look for the tiny sunflower I inked on her lower back yesterday.

"Barely." She slumps slightly. "I told you you weren't sticking the pin deep enough."

Before either of us can say anything else, the door behind me opens to let Neel out, carrying a huge pot of white star-shaped flowers with red centers. He makes a cartoonish course correction when he sees Rebecca, and heads straight toward her.

"Hey, you."

"Hi, Neel," she returns brightly. "Is that my order?"

Neel brings the pot up to her for inspection. "Hoya carnosa. And if Amelia doesn't like it—"

Rebecca sighs. "She'll send me back out until she does." To me she adds, "Amelia's my boss and she's kind of…"

"Picky," she and Neel say at the same time, and then share a smile that I'm not even a little bit a fan of.

"She uses them for design inspiration," she continues. "Amelia's a jeweler by the way, did I tell you that? I mean we both are."

She had not—of course, we had gotten interrupted by the pool…and again right now. I side-eye Neel. I didn't realize they knew each other.

"Wow. That sounds so much cooler than what I'm doing." I rub at the base of my back which is sore from shoveling and Neel answers for her.

"It is. You should see the shop where she works. It's this old converted airplane hangar out by the citrus groves. Get her to take you sometime."

Rebecca gives me a smiling nod. "Sure, anytime."

I wait for Neel to leave once he's got the flowers loaded in the back of her car and then realize he's waiting for me to leave. I duck my head to hide my half smile. Yeah, that's not going to happen. "Hey, man, give us a minute, would you?"

"Oh," Neel says, backing up a step. "Right, sure." Before he leaves for good, he steps right back up to Rebecca's side of the car, forcing me to move back. "If Amelia doesn't like the Hoya, text me and I'll bring something else over."

"You know you don't have to do that kind of stuff anymore," she says, lowering her voice in a way meant to include only the two of them.

"Just like you don't have to come pick up orders yourself anymore." He grins as he backs away. "And yet…"

Rebecca's gaze lingers on Neel's retreating form a beat too

long before returning to me. "He's really great," she says. "You guys are going to like working together."

"Yeah." But I don't want to talk about Neel. "So when can we start? You aren't on dinner duty again tonight?"

A new expression passes over her face, but it's gone too quickly for me to figure out what it means and then it doesn't matter because she says, "I'm all yours."

CHAPTER TEN

NOW

REBECCA

We meet in front of Ethan's grandparents' house. It's going to be a pretty night, clear sky, lots of moonlight, and even a soft breeze that makes you think there's no better place to live than Arizona in the late springtime. For two whole months, it is kind of perfect.

At least I have the Kellys' pool. I glance sideways at Ethan. Maybe that isn't the only thing I'll have this summer. If his mom stays gone.

That's not a kind thought and I feel mostly bad for having it.

We're walking through our neighborhood—well, he's walking, I'm rolling—heading up toward the park where we always used to hang out without exchanging a word about our destination. I've long since abandoned the sidewalk—too many driveway dips and besides, the streets are as quiet as we are.

We don't really start talking until we're surrounded by

grass and a few trees sprinkled between the playground and the pond, and even then there's a moment of awkwardness when Ethan abandons the sidewalk and heads downhill toward the wide stretch of grass beneath what used to be our tree. He takes a few steps before realizing I'm no longer beside him.

My smile is stiff when I trail my gaze from him back up to the sidewalk. "My shoulders aren't the biggest fan of wheeling up and down grass slopes." It's on the tip of my tongue to add a "sorry," but I catch the apology and lock it behind my teeth, holding it squirming and wrestling to break free. It's not an easy thing to suppress, that constant feeling that I'm holding people back or making things harder or less simply because I'm there. I don't know that I'll ever banish it completely, but I've been trying so hard not to voice it constantly. Instead, I nod toward a nearby bench. "This okay?" I wheel up to the side and lock my wheels. He doesn't miss a beat before joining me and relaxing against the curved back.

"Way better than rough tree bark anyway."

Maybe, but I can't stop one last longing glance toward the tree, which he notices.

"If it's not weird I could carry you over to sit on the grass sometime or push your chair or…" He lets his words trail off. "I don't know. Is that stupid?"

The tightness in my face eases at the care I hear in his voice. "No, it's sweet. And maybe. Sometime." I miss the grass but I'm not sure how I'd feel about him carrying me. Right now it's enough just sitting beside him again. I breathe in and let the warm, sunbaked air blow the lingering discomfort away. "How many days do you think we've spent out here?"

"Never enough," he says too quickly, then ducks his head with a laugh. "It doesn't feel completely real yet, does it? I mean I keep expecting to glance over and find you gone like I made you up or something."

"Same," I say, without a hint of the laughter lightening his voice.

He looks at me, a quicker but no less complete survey than the one he gave me at the pool yesterday, and once again it leaves a warmth in its wake. This time his attention catches on the ring on my right hand.

"Did you— Is this one of yours?"

"This used to be a hex nut." I hold it up for him to see better.

That warmth inside sparks to life when he takes my hand and runs his fingers over the raw opal I'd set into the top. "Seriously, you made this?"

I lift my chin, more pleased than I expected that he's impressed. "It's one of my more recent pieces. Not bad, huh?"

"Bec, it's amazing." He kind of scoffs and releases my hand. "How'd you get into it?"

"It's this whole thing with Voc Rehab—sorry, vocational rehabilitation. When I turned sixteen and wanted to get a job, my mom found out about the program and they helped connect me with Amelia and her amazingly accessible workshop."

"And you love it," he says, studying my face. "Your left dimple still digs into your cheek when you're trying not to smile too big."

"I kind of do." I lose the fight with my dimple. I can feel him looking at me, as I tell him about my first awkward attempts in Amelia's shop when it was still a daily battle not to focus on all the ways my disability made things harder, but how now I'm even starting to take my own commissions.

"Damn, I missed you."

"Yeah?" I let my shoulders perk up. It's a nice compliment and he should know that. "'Cause I didn't miss you at all."

His mouth lifts higher. "You did."

That is very, very obvious.

But I need to remember that he's not staying, he can't.

"So," I say, no longer fighting a smile that's fading all on its own. "How do we find your mom?"

His smile vanishes too. "She could be anywhere."

"Well, I guess we can start with calling the rehab center. Maybe she left some information? A forwarding address or something?"

Ethan doesn't look optimistic. "I'll call, but she wouldn't have."

"But somebody had to pick her up, right?"

His shoulders straighten ever so slightly. "Maybe. She was working at this secondhand clothing store, Buffalo Exchange on Melrose."

"So a co-worker? Okay. That's good. Ethan, it is," I add, resting a hand on his arm when he doesn't look up. "I'll call them tomorrow and see what I can find out."

He stays silent and my heart aches for him. I have my own issues with Joy, but I don't want anything bad to happen to her. I don't think Ethan could ever get past that.

"They don't open until ten. Won't you be in school?"

I shake my head. "I got all my credits in early so technically I graduated last semester. Nothing but an extra-long summer for me."

His mouth quirks. "I think I got you beat. See they don't actually care if you go to school after eleventh grade." A flutter of distress beats through my chest, but he only shrugs. "It was never really my thing anyway. My grandparents are already on my case about getting my GED but…"

I seize onto those words and barely keep myself from seizing onto him too. "That's a good idea, you should look into it. I can help you study too. There are practice tests and all kinds of guides we can get online. It'll be just like Mr. Zabell's English class and you got your best grade ever that semester."

"Yeah maybe." But Ethan's smile is all surface. His mind is only half here with me and I think I understand why.

"And I'm gonna make sure you find your mom too."

Ethan draws in a deep breath, so deep it stretches the fabric of his T-shirt. Then his gaze lowers to my wheelchair and my stomach drops realizing I was wrong about his train of thought. "When I heard you'd been hurt, and your dad—"

I suck in an involuntary breath and cut him off. "We don't have to go into any of this."

"But I need you to know—"

"I know, okay? And I'm sorry about getting mad by the pool yesterday." Panic starts to hitch my breath faster. "Of course you couldn't come. It was stupid of me to want something I couldn't have."

"I wanted that too, but we're here now. If there are things you should know and things I should know…?" His voice drops lower and softer making me bristle in response.

"Why can't we just skip over everything that happened while we were apart?"

"You're the one who said we're different. Shouldn't we understand why?"

"Even though it's ugly, and it hurts?" I shake my head. "'Cause I don't want to be any of that to you."

"You think I do? That I want you looking at me with pity 'cause I dropped out or disgust because I—" He chokes off whatever he was about to say, clenching his jaw tight. "I'm not proud of all of the things that I did."

My gaze locks on his as flashing emergency lights and the piercing squeal of tires claw their way through my mind. "You didn't do what I did."

He stares right back. "Are you sure about that?"

I shudder, my insides raw and bleeding from memories that are never truly staunched. "Then why make either of us relive it?"

"Because I know some of it already," he says. "And so do you."

I bite my lip and flinch away because he's right. Somehow knowing we each only have secondhand information about the other is worse. I can hear the unspoken question in his head when I finally meet his gaze again. *What? Do you just want me to say it?*

I try to remember the brave kid I used to be, the one who ran through the rain the first night I saw him and basically demanded he be my friend. I release my lip. "What do you know?"

"I know there was a party and you were drinking."

Party. Drinking. Those two words shred through me. "A

lot. I was drinking a lot. And…" I dig my teeth back into my lip, hard enough to change the reason behind the tears stinging my eyes. "There was an accident."

CHAPTER ELEVEN

BEFORE

REBECCA

Sweat prickles between my shoulder blades as I drag my paint brush down the inside of my tree house wall, trying to stay within the mural outline Ethan spent the last few days sketching. We have the shutters on the two windows open, hoping to coax a breeze through, but so far the summer air has been still and stifling for weeks now. But for some reason, I'm still smiling. Actually, for an Ethan reason. A buzz of happiness tingles inside me when I realize that it's been over five months and he's still here. I'm starting to hope that we'll not only finish painting the tree house, but we might even get to start seventh grade together.

I went into each wall of the tree house almost like a dare, a project that would inevitably get cut short by his mom showing up. But Ethan started drawing and she didn't come. We argued over paint colors and she didn't come. We dragged up drop cloths and brushes and spent way too long repositioning tape. And she didn't come.

So one day we started bringing our idea for the first wall to life; a wintery forest full of majestic stags; great, slumbering bears peering out from behind snow-heavy branches; and a single solitary lamppost. I held my breath the entire time, but we finished it and, when there was still no sight of his mom, started something completely different for the second wall, a beach view with a blazing sun in the corner, endless rippling waves, and the silhouette of a man fishing from a small boat surrounded by shark fins.

I'm breathing easier today despite the heat as we're painting delicate stars for a night's sky on the third wall. After this one, we'll only have the last wall left to do. Ethan's stressed about the design, tearing up sketches before even showing them to me. Nothing feels tight in my chest as I stare at that blank wall though. For a change, I'm not worried about the time we have left, hoarding it like some kind of dragon with its gold. We'll get there.

"Oh, is it a dragon?" I say out of nowhere.

"Is what a dragon?" Ethan doesn't lift his brush from the asteroid he's painting.

"Your idea for the last wall."

"Do you like dragons?"

"Not especially."

"Then why would I draw you a dragon?"

He's finishing his asteroid, ready to move on to the small boy standing atop it, so he can't see me grin. I told him to pick something entirely for himself to put on the last wall since the other three at least started from ideas I had (something wintery, the sea, the stars) but I like that he's still thinking of me too. "Am I at least close?"

"No," he mumbles, and then sighs. "And I haven't even settled on anything yet."

I grin wider. "You will." Then return my focus to the wall, leaving him to stare at me this time. It takes him a beat to start painting again, but when does, he seems lighter, like my confidence in him has helped create some of his own.

I return to my job of painting the moon's base coat—Ethan has to come back after me and add all the craters and shading—while simultaneously inching the battery-operated fan more in my direction with the tip of my toe without him noticing.

He notices. He puts down his brush and fully aims the fan at me. Then he goes back to painting again.

"Aren't you hot?" I can see damp spots on his T-shirt so I know he is.

"My mom and I never have A/C so I'm used to it."

I lower my own brush and immediately scramble to the fan, lifting it to blow directly in his heat-flushed face.

"I don't need it," he says, moving away.

I refocus the fan on him. "You should get used to having things you need."

A non-heat-related flush starts to creep up his neck and after a moment he swipes the fan from my hands, but instead of pointing it back at me, he drags his paint tray right beside mine and sets the fan down so that it's hitting us both.

His flush makes its way to me when our shoulders touch.

I pretend to paint after that, but mostly I just run my brush over the same area and think how he smells exactly like summer. It's nice feeling this close to him, so nice that I can't help wanting to feel closer.

"How come you don't talk about your mom much or your life when you're with her?"

Ethan's shoulders hunch up, tensing. "There's nothing to talk about."

"There must be something. I tell you everything that goes on with me when you're gone."

"That's because nothing ever happens to you." His brush jerks and accidentally swipes indigo over one of his stars. Then he's grabbing his rag and rubbing way too hard on the wall, smearing the two paint colors into a streaky brown mess.

"Stuff happens to me," I say, a slight break in my voice. The last time he was gone my hamster, Fredrick, died. I cried for three days and again when I told Ethan about it.

"I didn't mean it like that." But he's not looking at me and I start running my palm back and forth over my shorts.

"Then why did you say it?"

"Because I don't want to talk about my mom, but you keep pushing. All the time." His voice is getting louder and more sweat has started beading up on his forehead. His eyes are bouncing around the tree house as though the walls are about to start closing in on him and suddenly I feel like the one being squeezed.

"Then we won't talk about her," I say, trying to hold my breath in as if that act alone could possibly keep her from taking him again.

He makes an angry sound in his throat and throws the rag down. "This is ruined."

And when he leaves—because Ethan always leaves—I don't know if he means us or the mural.

CHAPTER TWELVE

NOW

ETHAN

When Rebecca invited me to stop by her work during lunch the next day, I don't know what I was expecting her workshop to look like. Maybe like an actual jewelry store or something with lots of glass windows and black velvet everywhere. Not this.

Nestled back from the road between two citrus groves, it's a hangar, like the kind where you keep planes and stuff, only smaller. The rippled metal siding is covered all over with huge painted flower motifs; not realistic flowers, but almost prehistoric. I stop to get a closer look, admiring the skillful brushstrokes and envying the artist who got to make them.

I'm still smiling when I walk up the ramp and open the door using a long, flat handle on the left side by the hinge rather than on the far side like typical doors. Pushing it open I realize how this would be a lot more practical to use if I were a wheelchair user.

Inside is loud. There's the hum of a swamp cooler fan,

whirling motors, grinding machines, and clanking tools. It takes a minute for my eyes to adjust from the bright sunshine outdoors to the relative darkness of the hangar. I see Rebecca first. She's got her curls twisted up and held back by a red bandana and glowing golden light illuminates her face as she leans over a table, pouring molten metal into a small mold with tongs.

She spots me then and when I smile, impossibly, her face lights up even more. Relief hits me hard that she's not feeling too awkward after the park. She only shared a glimpse of that night with me, but I wasn't sure until now if she was regretting even that little bit.

She gives me the one-second signal with a gloved finger and I look around.

The hangar isn't as big as it looks from the outside, or maybe it's all the equipment that makes it look smaller. The workshop is divided into two sections: one side has all the machines and complicated-looking equipment, and the other side is mostly thick wooden tables with tons of small drawers, like apothecary cabinets, and a glass-framed office in the corner. Vices are bolted in between more cabinets and lots of small tools and files hang—not too high—on peg board–covered walls above them. Everything smells like pennies.

"Hi, sorry." Rebecca wheels to a stop beside me. "I lost track of time. Please tell me I didn't leave you standing there your whole lunch break."

I pretend to glance at the watch I'm not wearing. "I probably have a couple minutes left."

Rebecca laughs. "Want to spend one of those minutes on an abridged tour?"

I don't really follow all the names of the machines she points out. There are chemical baths and saws, mini drills, and something that looks like a pasta machine on steroids that stretches and flattens metal instead of dough. It's cool and kind of overwhelming. Not to her though. Her fingers glide lovingly over everything we pass.

"This one is called a ring resizer and has all these cone-shaped holes at the base. I can press a ring into it and it'll taper, which is great for adding inlay bands. Then—" she moves over to a thin tapered rod with a lever "—I use this guy to stretch the ring back out." Grabbing the lever, she pulls it and the rod splits into sections. "Cool, huh?"

"Very." Everything is accessible too, either on a lower-than-standard tabletop or with plenty of clearance on either side. She gets really excited when she leads me to one of the worktables and the piece she's currently working on.

"So this one started its life as a couple of hex nuts, one gold and the other silver fused together, and I even left some of the angled edges on the outside 'cause I think it suits the client." She offers it to me and close up I can see wavy lines etched deeply around the band that make me think of the waves in LA and the sunsets here. I turn it around in my fingertips, feeling the little grooves and how perfectly smooth the inside of the ring is. "It's like two places at once." I drag my awed gaze away to look at her. "How'd you do that?"

"She practically locked herself in here for a week is how," says a woman from behind us in an acid-yellow wheelchair. The first thing I notice about her are the tattoos covering her deeply tanned arms; they look exactly like the prehistoric flowers painted outside.

"It was not a week," Rebecca says to the woman I'm guessing is her boss, Amelia. Then to me, "It wasn't."

I'm very aware that I'm being studied by a woman holding what looks like a blow torch. I reach out and set the ring back on the table. "It's impressive."

"That's because I taught her." She cocks her head at me sending her short, Bettie Page–style bangs shifting across her forehead, before extending her hand. "Amelia Huerta-Peck."

I shake her hand. "Ethan Kelly."

"Oh, I know."

I fail to decipher whether that's a good or a bad "oh, I know" then turn back to Rebecca. "It's one of the coolest rings I've ever seen."

Rebecca scoops the ring back up and holds it out to me on her palm. "Good. Because I made it for you."

I freeze in the loud and suddenly too-warm space. "Seriously?"

"Well, yeah." Rebecca reaches for my right hand and works the band over the knuckle of my thumb. It's a perfect fit. "I have a good eye," she says with a self-satisfied little shrug. She seems to realize that she's still holding my hand and lets it go suddenly. "You don't have to wear it all the time or at all if it's not your thing or whatever. I mean not everyone likes to wear—"

"It's my thing," I say. "It's exactly my thing." I've never been into wearing anything besides clothes, but as soon as the cool metal slides on my thumb, metal that she shaped and designed for me before I'd even come back, I know it's perfect.

Her chest rises and lowers with a sigh of relief. "Good, because I actually did spend close to a week designing it and if you hated it I don't think I could have sold it to anyone else and then Amelia would have to threaten to fire me again and she already does that enough."

"No, not fire." Amelia leans toward Rebecca and puts an arm around her shoulder. "Dock your pay for the materials and time, oh yeah, but I wouldn't fire you for that."

"Hey, I'll pay for the ring," I say, praying she didn't use anything more expensive than hex nuts because Old Man needs to eat and I'd kinda not like to be in debt to my grandparents any more than I already am. "Unless it's really expensive in which case I hate it."

"All it cost was my time. Besides it's a gift, you don't pay for those."

I nod like I know all about gifts.

"Hey." Rebecca angles her head at me, all hint of a smile gone from her face. "Where'd you go just now?"

I suck in a huge breath. "Nowhere I want to stay."

"Then come back." She leans forward, angling to watch Amelia retreat back into the office before turning a beaming smile on me. "I'll even give you a present."

I hold my ringed hand up. "Another one?"

Still grinning, she moves the heavy apron she's wearing to the side and reaches into her pocket for a piece of paper. "I spoke to Cindy Wu this morning, you know, the manager of Buffalo Exchange on Melrose? Super nice lady. Kind of a stickler for rules though, so it took me close to an hour before I got her to give me these."

I take the paper and open it to reveal a list of six names and phone numbers. Stunned, I look up at Rebecca to see her all but shimmying from her success.

"Cindy said those are the people your mom is closest to at work. So if she called somebody, there's a good chance it was one of them. I haven't had a chance to—"

I cut off her words as I half tackle hug her. My heart is pounding so hard I can't even speak.

"You know, a thank-you would have been fine."

No, it wouldn't have. I wouldn't have thought to call my mom's boss and I most definitely wouldn't have said the right things to get her to give me these names.

"Oh, hey." Rebecca's voice comes soft and soothing as her arms wrap around me. "You're gonna find her. It's gonna be okay."

I release her to settle back on my heels, letting one hand slide down and linger on her arm so as to not fully break the contact between us. "I mean I already struck out with calling the rehab center. They just kept saying they weren't allowed to give out information regarding former patients. But you..." I hold up the paper. "I wouldn't have anything right now if it weren't for you."

"Ethan—"

"No, I mean, I feel like I've been this shit friend to you. I didn't even say goodbye when I left the last time and we both know I would have taken off again the other night if you hadn't stopped me."

"You told me you were planning to say goodbye."

"I told you what I wanted to be true. The truth is I don't think I could have faced you. All those other times I left, I didn't have a choice. This time I did and I was still going to do the wrong thing." Shame weighs my head down.

"You always could have said goodbye, done something

besides leaving those flower sketches on my windowsill. Do you know how much I started to hate waking up to those?"

No, I didn't.

She draws in a breath, waiting a beat and almost shaking herself before saying, "I don't know what you want me to say here, that it was okay that you took off like that all the time when we were younger or that I'd eventually forgive you if you'd done it again the other night? I can't say that to you."

"I'm not expecting that. But I can't undo what I did either."

"No, but you can mean it when you tell me you won't ever leave like that again. When you go this next time—" she tries to shrug, but the gesture looks strained "—promise me more than a flower?"

"I promise," I say, even as a sliver of guilt coils inside me. If it comes down to my mom needing me, I'm not sure if that's a promise I can keep. "Then we're good? You're helping me find my mom and I'm helping you with…what? Shouldn't you be getting something out of this too?"

She gives me the strangest look, almost like I hurt her feelings, and wheels back a foot. "How very transactional of you, Ethan."

I reach after her, resting my hand on the frame of her chair. "I meant that I can do something for you too. Isn't there anything you need or want?" Something sparks in her eyes, a flash that she tries to conceal but too late. "Anything, Bec. Say the word." She bites her lip and I can't help moving closer even as her hesitancy sends a trickle of nervous energy through my bloodstream. "It's not illegal is it?"

"Nothing illegal," she assures me, but I have too many memories of us skirting that line as kids to take her word for

it now. "There are just a few things I think I want to do before summer ends. I guess you could tag along."

"What kind of things?"

Her smile creeps back. "You never used to ask when we
were younger. What happened to the kid who was up for
anything?"

He grew up with a mother whose entire life was lived
that way. It wasn't as fun when you didn't know where you
were gonna sleep at night. But I'm not ready to tell her that
so instead I remind her about my tattoo. "He let a cackling
twelve-year-old ink a wobbly sun on his back and has been
wary ever since."

Rebeca leans toward me bringing a whiff of honey and
sunscreen with her and I know I'm about to agree to anything she asks. "I'll meet you at your pool after work and I
promise to let you help me with the first nonillegal item on
my list. Deal?"

"Deal," I say, waiting for a shiver of apprehension that
never comes.

She moves to the entrance then looks back at me when I
don't follow her. "What?"

I shake my head and join her, pushing open the outside
door for us. "Just thinking about how I was never worried
about anything when we were together as kids. I thought that
might have faded, but…"

She hesitates and I see her throat move as she swallows.
"Ethan Kelly. Are you trying to tell me I make you feel safe?"

There's an intensity in her glance that's making me feel a
lot of things, too much and all at once, so I step out into the
fresh air and suck in a deep breath before glancing back at her

over my shoulder. "Maybe ask me again later tonight, yeah?" I wait for her to return my half smile before adding, "And after your thing, I could maybe use some company for these calls in case I start to say the wrong thing."

Rebecca pushes down the ramp, the incline temporarily allowing her to outpace me. "I think you underestimate yourself."

I jog ahead to pick up a tiny branch from in front of her, surprised how natural it feels to scan the road for rocks or small stuff when I'm with her. "But you'll be there? With me?"

Her eyes trail the branch as I toss it away and when she looks at me again I feel like I just lifted a car or something. It's a nice feeling.

"There's nowhere else I'd want to be."

CHAPTER THIRTEEN

NOW

REBECCA

"So that was Ethan." Amelia is waiting for me back in the shop right by the door when I get back inside.

My face flushes a little. "That was Ethan." I move to the lathe and the meteorite I'd left in there earlier.

"He's cute."

"I know." Safety glasses, safety glasses...where...?

"He's *really* cute."

"I know." I add a singsong tone to my voice, and finally find the glasses...in the pocket of the utility apron I'm wearing.

"Oh, I know *you* know." Amelia glances back toward the entrance. "I'm trying to decide if he knows."

"If... What?" I spin to face her.

She waves me off until I turn back to the lathe. "Childhood friends reunited after years apart, each having overcome their own personal tragedies, and discovering that time has made them both superhot."

I audibly groan.

"What?"

I can hear the laughter in her voice as I reach to turn on the lathe, but instead of ending the conversation, she just raises her voice to compensate for the machine noise.

"You know this means he'll either be the greatest love of your life or the one you end up warning your granddaughters about."

"Those are my only two options, huh?" I'm only half paying attention to her though. Meteorite is hellishly expensive and Amelia really will take it out of my pay if I ruin this commissioned wedding band. I don't want to take off too much and now I'm worried that I should have used a collet instead of a three-jawed chuck to hold it in place.

"You should have used the collet," Amelia says. "You're putting a lot of pressure on those three points. And yes, those are your only options."

I ignore her and pray that the tiny piece of meteorite hangs on just a little longer… "Ha!" I present her with the machined-out—and still intact—meteorite. "You do not, in fact, know everything."

"Next time use the collet."

Embarrassment tugs my chin down a fraction. "Yeah, I know." It's mostly luck that it didn't crack.

"I'm just saying to keep an open mind. You're not with Neel anymore, right? Or are you? I can never tell."

"We were barely together and we both agreed we're better off friends." That's maybe stretching the truth a bit. We never had an official conversation about what we were. The lines between friendship and more-than-friendship just blurred a few times—okay more than a few times. And blurry was really kind of amazing for a while.

Neel was the first guy I felt comfortable being with after my accident. I didn't have a million insecurities racing through my head when we kissed. I just got to want someone and feel wanted in return. Neel treating me like I was exactly enough, more than enough, helped put that broken part of me back together and let me feel whole, at least in that way.

But blurry wasn't good for either of us in the long run. It turned into too much and at the same time not enough. Thankfully, we stopped it before either of us got hurt and our friendship is stronger than ever. And if he occasionally gives me a blurry look, I know he doesn't really mean it any more than I do. It's just a bit of the past forgetting that it doesn't fit with our present.

Amelia offers little pointers here and there as I continue working with the meteorite, but mostly she questions me about Ethan.

"So how much are you already in love with him?"

I side-eye her. "He's been back for less than a week."

Amelia stares at me, waiting for an answer.

"And he's not staying."

"Why? Because that's what happened when you guys were kids? You did notice he's not a kid anymore, right? Maybe he'll get to make his own decisions this time."

I bite back a response about how Ethan decided he was leaving again before he even came back. There's no point in expecting anything to change just because we're older. The door pushes open again and I don't appreciate the way my heart rate picks up as I turn thinking—hoping?—it might be Ethan coming back.

Mathias, Amelia's husband, strolls in with a squirming toddler in one lean, tattoo-sleeved-and-freckled arm along with lunch for his family in the other. Luis squirms even more when he sees Amelia and practically dives out of his father's arms the second he's within her reach. She covers the squealing baby's face with kisses then gives Mathias an entirely different kind of kiss, the kind that makes me suddenly very interested in the file I'm holding.

"You want to go see your Be-be?" Amelia's voice takes on the quintessential baby talk style as she expertly wheels toward me, alternating her arms so she's always securely holding her son. "Tell her all about how you're going to be a big brother."

"No!" My gaze bounces back and forth between them as I reach for Luis and happiness bubbles up inside. "Seriously? Wait, wait. When?"

Mathias rubs Amelia's stomach. "Little Accident is due in, what, eight months?"

"Seven and a half, and I don't like that name," she tells him.

"I thought it was Little Life Destroyer you didn't like?"

"Oh wow," I say. "So you just found out. Am I the first to know?"

"Everything looks good so far." Amelia exchanges a soft smile with her husband that is almost more intimate than the kiss I'd witnessed earlier. "But we want to wait a little longer before telling people, you know?"

Amelia's spinal cord injury, a little higher than mine, doesn't have any bearing on her ability to get or stay pregnant. Still, women miscarry early on for all kinds of reasons. But another baby! And Luis is just over a year old.

When Mathias takes Luis into the office to eat, Amelia's hand absentmindedly falls to her belly and a little smile plays at her lips. "I should be scared and overwhelmed and worried about a million things, and I am, but also—" her hand rubs a small circle "—I can't wait to hold Little Accident."

"I heard that!" Mathias calls.

Amelia drops her head in her hands. "Problems for future me. At least I have you here. When I'm a wheeling whale you'll practically have your run of the place."

A sharp stab of panic jabs inside me thinking about how far away from here I'll be by then if my mom has her way.

Amelia misreads my reaction and points a finger at me. "No boys when I'm not here."

"Ha. Ha."

"And especially no way-too-cute-boys-who-you-are-already-way-too-into."

"Thanks, Mom." Amelia has four younger sisters and sometimes forgets that I'm not one of them.

"Wait," she says, her eyes going wide as though she's just remembered something vitally important. "Wasn't he your first kiss too?" Amelia's grin grows to show all her teeth when I still and don't answer. "In your tree house. It was raining too, wasn't it?"

Okay, I had obviously told her that story way too many times. "I don't really remember." Lies and she knows it. It had just started raining. And the sunset was magic. We might have been the most awkward thirteen-year-olds on the planet but somehow the kiss wasn't.

"Makes you wonder what the second kiss will be like," Amelia calls over her shoulder as she leaves to join her family.

I roll my eyes at her back even as I'm smiling, grateful to be thinking of something significantly more pleasant than possibly leaving for college at the end of the summer. As far as first kisses go, it hadn't been too bad. And I would be a liar of epic proportions if I said I hadn't thought—briefly—about what it might be like to kiss Ethan again, now, with his longer hair brushing my cheek and his hand lifting my jaw…

Amelia drops something and the metal clang off the concrete floor sends the fantasy screeching to a stop.

We aren't those same kids in my tree house and we never will be again.

And Ethan's already got his bags packed, ready to leave the second we find his mom.

CHAPTER FOURTEEN

NOW

ETHAN

When I get back from seeing Rebecca at lunch, Neel has his earbuds in and is absentmindedly hauling plastic pots full of plants and trees from one side of the massive warehouse to the other, occasionally doing little dance moves that look kinda familiar but also not.

"What are you listening to?" I ask after he takes a bud out.

"Irving Berlin." He grins and does a quick soft-shoe ending with the tip of an invisible hat. "He scored some of the greatest musicals of the early twentieth century."

"Never heard of him."

Neel lets his knees slightly buckle as though I've wounded him. "Here." He presses the bud into my hand. "Listen to 'The Best Things Happen When You're Dancing' and tell me you don't feel a little bit like Danny Kaye."

I shake my head again. "Who?"

"Amazing dancer and comedian." He hurries my hand to

my ear and then waits with barely suppressed excitement for my reaction.

My nod and half shrug don't deflate him when I hand the bud back. "Yeah, it sounds like some of the movies my grandmother watches. Not exactly my thing."

Neel snaps a finger and points it at me. "Rebecca used to say the same thing and now she loves Old Hollywood nearly as much as I do. I'll start you with a playlist then give you a couple of movies to watch. You, my friend, are about to be singing a much better tune."

If Rebecca's as into it as he says then it can't be that bad. "Sure, I'll check it out."

Neel grins. "Good man. Now go grab a plant and check the clipboard, will you? Eddie said to start hauling, but I don't know how we're supposed to be sorting them." Then he's off spinning with a potted tree and dipping it like it's his dance partner.

I hesitate at the chart on a clipboard showing how we're supposed to organize everything then glance up the stairs to where my grandparents have their respective offices. Through the big, windowed walls I can see my grandmother pacing with a phone clamped between her ear and shoulder while she frantically digs through a mess of papers on her desk. In contrast, my grandfather is sitting almost perfectly still at a drafting table, his hand moving a pencil in sure, steady motions across a sheet of tracing paper, flipping it back and down again as he compares it to another page beneath it.

I wonder if he's designing anything like his backyard. I squint, but all I see are basic shapes. I could go up there and ask about the plant sorting Neel and I are supposed to be doing in order to get a closer look at his design, maybe even watch him working on it up close for a minute, but I can't bring myself to take a step. We've barely spoken since I found out they hid my mom checking herself out of rehab—like I'm still a little kid—and I'm not in a hurry to change that no matter how curious I am.

So not only do I ignore the chart and start setting up groupings of my own, I get Neel to follow my instructions, passing them off as my grandfather's.

Waxy leaves brush against my cheeks as I lower a poufy bush to the ground, careful not to crush any of its tiny golden flowers, and pull out my phone to text Rebecca.

Me:
Are we meeting by the pool tonight and then going somewhere?

She responds right away.

Rebecca:
Is that your way of asking what you should wear?

Me:
I don't know...yes?

Rebecca:
All black and a ski mask.

I laugh a little too loudly.

"Hey." Eddie snaps his fingers in front of my face, drawing my gaze away from my phone screen. "I'm not paying you to make phone calls."

"Not paying him, Eddie," Neel calls, grunting as he drops his pot. "You work here, same as us."

"Shut up, Neel." I get a surge of satisfaction when Eddie's voice rises an uncontrolled octave before he can bring it back down again. "I can write you both up."

I raise an eyebrow at Neel. "Can he?"

"Nope." Neel's voice echoes around the warehouse.

Eddie turns all kinds of red as his lips tighten over his teeth before barking out a pointless command to get back to work.

I take pity on the guy and wait till he's gone before laughing.

My phone buzzes with another text from Rebecca.

Rebecca:
Come on, you knew that was a joke.

Rebecca:
Fine, I'm wearing a swimsuit. You should too. We can cool off and be suitably attired for my plan and your calls.

Even that indirect mention of my mom acts like a firing shot at a race and instantly my brain is off, churning up image after image of my mom on the stained carpet of our apartment because I wasn't there to stop her when I should have been, and reshaping the memory so that she's crumpled up on a new floor and this time no one comes, no one finds her, no one saves her and I have to watch helplessly as her breathing gets slower and slower until—

"No," I breathe out, blinking hard and panting as hot fists pound against the inside of my ribs. I force my gaze to my phone, rereading Rebecca's texts and urging new thoughts to chase away the old. Cool water, Rebecca in the pool, droplets clinging to her skin and the way her lips lift in a soul-warming smile at the sight of me.

It's like I can feel it now.

My expression must shift from torment and fear to something more open and happy because Neel comes to a stop beside me.

"That's what I need." He gestures at my phone with his chin. "Is that your girl?"

"Just a friend." I give Rebecca's text one last glance, before repocketing my phone.

"Rebecca?"

That brings my head up.

Neel just shrugs. "You just got here. How many friends could you have?"

He's got me there. I pretend to start counting on my fingers. "Well, there's Eddie…"

Neel laughs.

Thinking our conversation is over, I bend down to lift the yellow-flowered bush again and head back to my last cluster only Neel walks with me.

"But you guys were close before?"

"Me and Rebecca?" I almost snort but hold it back. I can't remember a single day here that she didn't fill in one way or another. "Yeah, we were close."

"But that was years ago. You were kids, right?"

I halt in the process of setting the pot next to a tall spindly tree. "Yeah. Kids."

He nods. "Okay, just checking." And then he turns, heading back to haul more plants.

It had been on the tip of my tongue to ask why he was so concerned, but I'm not an idiot—dumb but not an idiot, at least not about that. There's definitely something going on there, or at least there was. So he likes her. Why shouldn't he? Yeah, sure, things in her life are different now, she's different, but not in a way that dims any of those vital parts of her, at least not that I can see. Can I blame Neel for seeing that too?

I glance over at Neel again, trying to imagine what Rebecca might see. Tall, with thick dark hair and matching deep-set eyes, slim and just this side of lanky but not an awkward bone in his body—even dancing with a plant he seems completely at ease in his own skin.

I'm not at ease with anything. And it's not like I can offer her much. It's the same as when we were kids and we both knew I could be gone at a moment's notice. Except it's almost worse this time because we're both actively working toward me going away as soon as we can. Knowing I'd be leaving Rebecca was always the worst part of coming here, a phantom pain that promised to swoop in and nearly smother whatever happiness I felt from being reunited with my mom. It hasn't even been a week and I already know this time is going to kill.

None of this makes Neel's interest in Rebecca feel awesome. "Who did this?"

I start at the sound of my grandfather's voice and turn away from staring at the back of Neel's head. His face is flushed as he walks through the stacks I'd arranged, jerking up a pot here and a pot there before realizing that nearly every one of them is misplaced.

Neel shoots me a sharp glance, and while I wouldn't mind letting him share in the blame, my mouth has other ideas.

I wait for my grandfather's stern expression to settle on my indifferent one and say, "That would be me."

CHAPTER FIFTEEN

NOW

ETHAN

Rebecca beats me to the pool.

I'd been half-prepared for this since my grandfather kept me late to go over all the plant sorting I have to redo tomorrow, but I still stop short seeing her cutting through the water. *Yeah, Neel, I definitely can't blame you.*

But I can cannonball right beside her.

She's sputtering when I surface and shake my hair out like a dog. "You know there are other ways to enter a pool."

"Yeah? How do you get in?" My grin sinks off my face the second the words are out. "Sorry. I didn't mean to say something stupid. I wasn't thinking."

"It's okay," she says, in a tone that makes me think she actually means it. "I get in the same way I get out, except, you know, in reverse." She smiles at me, then we move down to the sunken bench in the deeper end, which felt a lot bigger when we were kids. Now it's practically impossible for our thighs not to touch once we're sitting side by side, a fact that I seem to be a lot more aware of than she is.

Noticing my downward glance, she says, "Can't feel it."

"Right. Is that okay? I mean do you want me to move?" I have no idea if that bothers her or not and I don't want to make her feel uncomfortable. I'm already pressing myself into the side wall when she points out across from us.

"Would you? Because it would be great if you could just tread water right in front of me the whole time we're talking." She bats her eyes at me, all sincere innocence.

My mouth lifts up just as hers does. "Actually—" I deliberately scoot closer until I'm half sitting in her lap "—this feels like a good compromise to me."

She shoves me off into the deep end.

I return to my seat beside her. "So you don't—"

"Care if your leg is touching my leg that I mostly can't feel? No, I would tell you. I have this cool thing called a voice. It works great."

"Okay, good." I deliberately drape my leg over hers.

She laughs. "Um, no."

"Just checking." There's a pause and I twist my new ring around my thumb, loving the way the water droplets run through the groves. "Still can't believe you made this." But what I mean is that I can't believe she made it for me. "And the workshop is pretty cool."

She smiles softly without looking at me. "It is." Then turns to meet my gaze. "Good & Green is great too."

I'm still a bit sunburnt from my first day and my shoulders are aching from all the hauling today. When I don't respond, Rebecca nudges me.

"What? Not feeling so great to you?"

"I got in some trouble with my grandfather." I slump in the water, enjoying the coolness on my overheated skin. "I was supposed to sort all these plants in a specific way."

She waits a beat. "And?"

"I didn't."

"Wow," she says, mirroring my slump. "That's a great story. I mean, I feel like I was actually there."

"I remember hating that about you," I say, eyeing the stretch of smooth water in front of me. "You've always been the person in my life who pokes and prods." I'm fully aware that I could just swim away from her and end this whole conversation. Not because anything awful happened with my grandfather—it didn't—but because I'm not used to talking about stuff that happens with me.

A second later, she's straightening. "Well, don't worry, I'm older and wiser now. I'll take what I can get and leave it at that."

I think about that comment long enough that I feel her draw further away from me. The thing is, I'm not worrying. There's not a single part of me that wants to bolt from this pool. Angling my head to meet her gaze, I just start talking. "It was stupid. I didn't want to do what he wanted, so now I have to go in early tomorrow and redo it all. But it wasn't even about the plants. I'm angry at them and I don't care if they know it this time," I say, surprising myself when the words keep coming out. "When I was little, I never knew what was going on with my mom. They kept so much from me and nobody listened when I tried to tell them what I wanted."

"To go back to her?" There's a hint of something in her voice, worry maybe?

"To never have left her alone in the first place." The tendons in my neck tighten to near pain. "You know why it's been four years since I came back? Because I got big enough to do actual damage with the bat I slept with, smart enough to keep her from finding new *friends*—" I sneer the word "—after I fended off the old ones, and old enough to say no when she tried to send me away."

I don't realize I'm shaking until I feel Rebecca's hand on my arm. Unlike when my grandfather reached for me, I don't jolt away. I could never confuse her touch with another's.

"We don't have to talk about this," she says. "Just 'cause I shared a little doesn't mean you have to. I really won't push like I used to."

"Yeah, well. I guess I'm different too." At least a little. I didn't tell her everything, far from it—it's the end I don't want anyone ever knowing—but this part feels safe. "Since you're helping me find her, you deserve to know some of it."

Her head dips and her cheeks pink. "I'd help you anyway, even if you told me nothing."

"I know." An odd mix of anticipation and reluctance swirls through me. I want—no *need*—to find my mom, but at the same time I know I'm nowhere near ready to leave Rebecca yet. "It's the same reason I bought this." I reach up behind me to the bag I'd dropped earlier and pull out a ski mask.

CHAPTER SIXTEEN

NOW

REBECCA

I stare at the black knit ski mask hanging from Ethan's hand and the somehow sheepish yet defiant look on his face and burst out laughing. "You really would commit a crime with me, wouldn't you?" Something aches inside me for just a second, but I tuck it away along with the mask. "Well, you don't have to worry. I'm not interested in playing Bonnie to your Clyde. I've just been realizing how different things are going to be when summer ends and how I don't want it to go out like this." A very different kind of ache pounds through me, cold and familiar and much harder to ease.

"Out like what?"

I lift a hand from the pool and watch water drip back down into tiny, dissipating ripples on the surface, then let my hand drop with a much more satisfying splash. "I never used to feel like I was just watching my life go by, but that's all I do now. I barely make ripples, let alone a splash."

Suddenly I'm the one feeling sheepish, and I try to slip

lower into the water so there's less of me to see. The last person I mentioned this to was Neel and he just didn't get it. The three months we let things be blurry were usually spent alternating between Gene Kelly and Bollywood movie marathons, kissing on his couch, and the occasional ice cream run. I kind of miss the kissing but the rest wasn't enough. He never would have shown up with a ski mask. But Ethan did, I remind myself, sitting up straighter and turning to him. "We used to splash all the time."

His answering laugh is low and soft. "We did more than splash, Bec. Caused a few tsunamis maybe."

"We had fun though, didn't we?"

He tries to hold back his smile. "So what kind of splashing did you have in mind?"

I grin. "Actually you gave me the idea. What do you say to revisiting a faded classic?" I drop my hand below the surface to brush along my lower back over the tattoo that you can barely make out.

Ethan's body relaxes as he takes my meaning and laughs. "Right, sure."

"Why not? Stick and poke tattoos are really common and I'm sure you can tattoo me a better flower now."

"I definitely couldn't tattoo you a worse one." Then his laughter dies. "You're serious."

By way of answering, I push up onto the pool edge then lean way back to pull my own bag to my lap and start emptying the contents one by one. Paper towels, rubbing alcohol, a thin marker, tattoo ink and needles, gloves, Vaseline—

Ethan's hands stop me. "Okay, okay, you're serious." He pushes his wet hair back from his face. "But wouldn't you rather have somebody who knows what they're doing permanently mark your body?"

I shrug one shoulder. "You never got my sun redone by somebody who knows what they're doing." A fact that had given me an absurd amount of pleasure when he showed it to me the other day.

He frowns hard at me like I've made him realize something he didn't want to. Is it that bad of an idea? Ethan and I used to come up with the wildest stuff to do and I hadn't fully realized how much I missed that until he came back. Before now I'd been all talk and barely that, but today I literally borrowed Amelia's car and bought tattoo supplies. And I really hope that wasn't all in vain.

"I'm still gonna make those calls with you no matter what you decide about the tattoo, okay?"

Ethan doesn't stop frowning. "I know that."

"Then why are you still making that face?"

"Because," he says, climbing out of the pool and drying himself off, "I'm afraid you're somehow a worse tattoo artist than you used to be, but I've never been able to say no to you and I'm not about to start now. So what are we doing first, calls or needles?"

The answer is both, which ends up working out a lot better than I expect since I have a very effective method of distracting Ethan whenever he starts getting frustrated with his mom's former co-workers.

There's a reason why his tattoo is still visible all these years later and the one he gave me isn't; I have no problem breaking the skin.

The hardest part, besides watching Ethan's expression fall more and more with each dead end, is just figuring out how we each need to sit for me to reach him well. I basically sat on him when we were kids, but despite Ethan's gallant offer to use him as a chair again, I opted for pulling two lounge chairs together and carefully leaning across his lap. It's a balancing game all around, between distracting him, keeping my lines straight, and, you know, keeping my actual balance while still being close enough to see what I'm doing.

Ethan's, um, not a scrawny twelve-year-old anymore, and seeing him with his shirt off feels all kinds of different now. Touching him too.

Maybe he's not the only one who needs distracting.

We get a hit on the fourth number: a guy named Theo admits to picking up Ethan's mom from rehab, driving her to a nearby motel and, reading between the lines, staying with her only to wake up with his wallet cleaned out the next morning.

"She left a note," Theo says, eager to put a shine on an unshineable deed. "She promised to pay me back as soon as she gets settled."

Ethan's hand tightens around his cell, which is on speaker between us. I'm trying not to touch him more than necessary, but we're still aware of each other, or at least I'm aware of Ethan. He's tense; over the fact that I'm hearing these not-so-great-things about his mom? The fact that he didn't hang up and leave shows me he's changed a lot more than just physically.

"But did she say where she was going?"

Theo makes some wishy-washy sounds. "I'm not sure if I should be talking about this stuff to her kid. How old did you say you were again? 'Cause I mean she's only..." His voice trails off as though considering for the first time that the co-worker he picked up from rehab who fleeced him while he slept might not have been completely honest with him.

Ethan gives me a look like he's about to lose it with this guy. I jab with the needle, forcing him to bite his lip or else yelp, and then take over the call. "Hey, Theo? Hi, I'm Ethan's friend Rebecca. He's gonna go in the next room really quick so none of this has to be awkward."

The hell I am, Ethan mouths at me.

I roll my eyes at him then address Theo again. "Okay, he's gone. Where did Joy say she was going?"

"Well, um. She was really grateful to be out of the place, if you know what I mean." He laughs and I scrunch my face, carefully focusing on the tattoo and avoiding Ethan's gaze.

"Uh-huh, but, she did say something about somewhere you both could go?"

"Not really, unless you mean La Jolla?"

Ethan and I exchange glances, but I keep my frustration from my voice. "La Jolla?"

"Yeah, I guess she still had some friends in the area. I don't really like the beach though, you know? Like all that sand?"

"Yeah, sand is the worst. What's the name of her friend in La Jolla?"

"She didn't say. Hey, what did you say your name was again? You have a really nice voice. You're over eighteen, right?"

And that's goodbye to Theo. I suppress a shiver of disgust and lightheartedly say to Ethan, "So you call all the guys from now on."

Ethan's laugh is humorless and then it turns into a grunt when his abs shift under my pressing needle. "Sorry about that. Also, are you aiming for my kidneys with that thing?"

"You moved, not the needle. And stay still, I'm almost done." He's still after that. "But we got a lead. I'll have to shower longer than usual tonight, but...yay?"

He nods, careful not to move anything else. "Yeah. I remember a few people from when we lived in La Jolla. I'll get started on a list of names."

I let out a soft sigh that causes goose bumps to appear on Ethan's stomach. "Okay then. We've got our next move." I know that means Ethan is one step closer to leaving, but he's still here now and, his tattoo is... "Done!" I sit back, smiling at what I think is a fairly decent tattoo. "What do you think?"

Ethan hunches to see and then makes a noncommittal sound in his throat.

"Oh, come on. It's way better than it was."

"I think you mean way darker."

"Better."

"Darker." But this time he's smiling. "Your turn."

I use all the hot water that night and even contemplate staying under the cold spray, but I know it's not worth the time it'll take my body to warm up afterward. The internet said showering after a stick and poke tattoo is fine and as I stare at the tiny petals of the forget-me-not Ethan inked a few inches above my right hip, I really hope that's true. Not that I'll be forgetting the experience anytime soon no matter what happens to the tattoo.

Ethan had been so careful, barely touching my skin as he

bent over me until I had to take his hand and press until the needle pierced through. Me and needles are old friends and I welcomed the slight twinge of pain from each poke. Sensations of any kind have taken on new meaning for me, and I was grateful for even this small hurt.

My tattoo turned out much better than his, but there was never any doubt about that. Still, he seemed happy and I know I am.

It's so much better to splash.

Still in my towel, I'm wheeling down the hall toward my room when Mom comes out of her office, both of us surprised to see the other.

"I didn't know you were home."

"Just," she answers, but her makeup is washed off and she's already changed into leggings and a T-shirt.

"I was swimming next door," I add in a rush, not wanting a repeat of the last time she caught me in the hall. Not that I'd been late or even close to it this time, but the phone calls and doing both our tattoos had taken longer than I'd expected. A combination of disgust and cold shower chill shakes through me remembering the conversation with Theo.

"What's wrong? Are you having leg spasms? Does something hurt?" She starts scanning me in a very clinical, diagnostic way that I remember too well from when I'd first gotten home from the hospital. Back then our lives had been a constant revolving cycle of appointments: physical therapy, doctors, specialists, school administrators, insurance people, on and on. We spent more time together that first year than I think we had the preceding fourteen combined.

One would think it would have brought us closer, but it turns out you can do a lot without actually talking.

"I used up all the hot water. And then some. I'm fine though."

She frowns. "That's not good for you, Rebecca. With your circulation, it takes you longer to thermoregulate than it would someone else. I read an article last week about—"

"Mom, I'm fine." It was mostly a Theo shiver but I can't explain that to her.

"Was it the pool? Are you getting cold over there? Because maybe swimming so much in the sun isn't a good idea."

It was a recommendation by the physical therapist she found for me, one that took me a while to warm up to since swimming, like everything else in my life post-accident, was different. But I love it now.

"I can look into finding a covered pool. Even a temperature-controlled one."

I pull away before she can rest a hand on my forehead, feeling done with people touching me like I'm still a patient in a hospital. "I said I'm fine. Why won't you listen to me?"

She lowers her hand in a jerky motion and I regret the harsh tone.

"Sorry. I didn't mean—"

"If you're fine, you're fine." Then she starts to walk past me to her room. "Make sure you hang up your towel."

"Mom, wait."

She stops, but only half turns to face me.

"I didn't eat yet and since there was nothing in the fridge I'm guessing you didn't either. Maybe we could watch some

HGTV and order takeout from this new Thai place Neel told me about?"

She hesitates and I let myself feel a flicker of hope before she shakes her head. "No, you need to get to bed and warm up. Order whatever you want and I'll bring it in to you when it gets here."

When I finally get under my covers, I stay the kind of cold that heat can't thaw.

CHAPTER SEVENTEEN

NOW

ETHAN

Neel can't get over the fact that my air conditioner works.

He adjusts the vents in the car for the third time in as many minutes, leaning forward and aiming a blast of chilled air so that his jet-black bangs blow straight up off his forehead. The grin he flashes me is so blissed out that I can't help but laugh despite the fact that I didn't want company.

We're on our way to drop off an order for Rebecca's boss. I offered to go alone, but since I'm new, Eddie decided I needed to be shown the ropes. All I really want to do is show Rebecca the list I made and hope she knows some sort of magic to turn my names—sometimes not even full names—into phone numbers, email addresses, or at least social media profiles. My google searches led me nowhere.

Neel sighs happily beside me.

"I take it the A/C doesn't work in your truck."

Neel laughs harder than I did. "My truck is a classic. A

perfect mix of luxury and beauty in its day and perfectly restored down to the whitewall tires…"

"But?" I glance over at him when I stop at a red light.

"But I'd have to sell a kidney to afford adding A/C to a 1953 Chevy 3100."

"Sucks," I say.

"Nah, it just means I'm twice as hot when I drive it. Plus, it's easy to put Rebecca's wheelchair in the back."

My hands tighten around the wheel at the casual way Neel says her name. "You guys are good friends…?"

Neel half smiles as he gazes out the window. "We used to be more than friends, but it didn't work out the way I was hoping. I don't really know what happened. She kind of pulled away? I feel like there could still be something there, you know? I mean we talk a lot but…" Then he frowns. "Actually now that you mention it, we haven't been hanging out as much lately." He turns his frown on me. "Not since you came back."

I guess we have been together every day since I got here. "She's been helping me with a problem."

His frown smooths away. "Oh yeah? What kind?"

I shoot him a cutting glance before returning my eyes to the road. "The personal kind."

Neel holds his hands up in surrender. "Oookayyy," he says. "Just make sure you're helping with hers too."

My gaze snaps back to him. "What are you talking about?"

Neel gives me the strangest look. "She didn't tell you?"

I widen my eyes in annoyance at him, deeply disliking that there could be something that Rebecca shared with him but not me.

"You know, with her mom?"

I obviously don't know, but I don't feel like admitting any more to Neel so I give him a slow half nod like I finally realize what he's talking about.

He relaxes beside me. "Maybe you can get her to talk more than I can. She's so good at deflecting, you know?"

Are we talking about the same person? Rebecca used to always tell me everything. I never minded because it helped fill the gaps I didn't want to. My brows pinch together though; our conversations since I've been back have revolved around me. I come up blank on her mentioning her mom. Something is clearly going on and she is just as clearly not telling me about it. She told me about the accident, why not this?

When I turn in and park in front of the jewelry shop, Neel pauses before getting out. "Hey, there's nothing going on with you and Rebecca, is there? 'Cause I'd appreciate the heads-up."

In an instant, I'm thirteen again and I've just kissed Rebecca for the first of what I hope will be many, many times. Only, it didn't work out that way. My mom came back right after. Shame clenches inside me when I remember leaving Rebecca a flower instead of a goodbye that time too. I'd thought I'd be coming back, that I'd have a chance to make it up to her, but that didn't happen either. First because my mom was in a good place for longer than usual, and then because when she fell, I didn't let her send me away so she could fall further.

It wasn't any different now, just because there were moments—more than a few—that made me wish it could be.

I straighten and face him. "No, there's nothing going on.

I'm just getting used to being back is all. We were close before, as kids, you know? I guess I'm feeling protective maybe?"

Neel's frame relaxes and one hand slides in my direction. "If
it helps, I care about her. I'm not messing around or anything.
And besides—" that thin smile is back on his face "—she's not
thinking about getting back together. Or if she is, she's hella
good at hiding it."

Right.

"It could be worse," he adds, as we carry our pots up the
ramp to the front door. "It could be Eddie who likes her."

I laugh with Neel when we go inside, but the sound feels
forced even to my ears.

"What's so funny?" Rebecca asks when she comes over.
I don't know if it's the fan or what but I catch a hint of her
honeyed sunscreen mix and wonder if it spins Neel's head as
much as it does mine.

"Oh, you know," I say to hide the effect her presence is
having on me, "just the idea of Eddie ever knowing the love
of a woman."

"Hmm those for me?" Rebecca eyes the plants we're holding.

"No, we just like to carry them around with us now, kind
of like plant dads." Neel sets his pot on the nearest table. "Cute
right?" When he grins at her, she doesn't look uncomfortable
or like she's hella hiding anything. My head spins again, and
not in the good way.

"Where do you want the rest?" I heft my pot higher in
my arms, feigning that it's heavier than it really is. Rebecca
frowns but points toward Amelia's office. I stride across the

shop before Neel can grab his and follow. *Take your shot, man, just don't make me stand around and watch it.*

I head back outside while they are still talking to grab the remaining plant, ignoring the sound of Rebecca's laughter that chases me out.

CHAPTER EIGHTEEN

NOW

REBECCA

Neel grabs a wheelie stool and sits down next to me. "So that's the famous Ethan."

I give him a look. "Hardly famous."

"You've talked about him a few times."

My cheeks grow warm. Had I? "Seems like you're the one talking about him now."

Neel's mouth quirks. "That is an excellent point." He spins on his stool showing off his sweater vest that makes him look completely throwback cool, like James Dean meets jazz. The boy has style.

I compliment him aloud to change the subject. "You like?" He stretches out the hem. "It was my grandfather's, my dad's dad. I got a ton of his old stuff when he passed away last year. Never thought I'd be wearing any of it, but I feel like it works for me."

"It definitely does."

Neel's smile is one of genuine pride. "I've got some cool

traditional Indian clothes from my mom's side too. I've been messing around with ways to blend the two styles together, like maybe a kurta with some saddle shoes?"

I nod. I'm not exactly sure what a kurta is, but I bet Neel looks great in it. He's quick to return the compliment as soon as I pay it.

"I told you that you look good too, right?"

I laugh. "Many times." Neel is a walking, talking ego boost.

Neel uses his toe to slide his stool in front of me so we're knee to knee, not touching, but close enough that my gaze flicks down to the scant space between us. "So I'm thinking two people this good-looking should be going out again soon."

"Oh, you are?"

He shoves his hands in his pockets and drags his foot across the floor like he's an old-world aw-shucks cowboy as he drawls, "It's just that we had such a swell time last time."

I laugh which makes him grin.

"Kiwanis Park has their movies in the park all summer and they're doing a Gene Kelly tribute this month starting with *An American in Paris*. They did something similar last year and it was really cool."

The skin above my hip itches, reminding me of my still-healing tattoo and how good it felt to do something like that again. "I guess it has been a while since we hung out." Since Ethan got back specifically. My face grows hot and I try to hide it by focusing on the ring I was working on. What was with him just now? He barely acknowledged I was here. Did he get another lead on his mom? My throat goes tight at that possibility.

"Um, hello? Rebecca?"

My gaze snaps to the door as it opens and Ethan steps inside. I look away quickly and see that in my distraction I've nearly ruined the space I'm channeling for an inlay on the ring. "What? Oh, sure, we can hang out this weekend."

Neel tucks his hands into the pockets of his sweater vest and scrunches up his face. "Right, but how about—and stay with me on this—instead of calling it hanging out, we call it a—"

"Did you ruin my ring?" Amelia calls out.

I jump, automatically hiding the ring with my hands even though she's nowhere near me. "No."

"Did you almost ruin my ring?"

So much for hiding. "Define almost."

I hear her sigh from across the shop. "You know I could find a new nursery to order plants from, one without cute and distracting delivery boys."

"Nah, you'd never do that," Neel says, elbowing Ethan when he joins us. "You heard her call us cute, right?"

"I heard her call us boys," Ethan says in a flat voice, earning a laugh from Amelia that cuts off when she has to answer her cell.

Amelia's call is short and she beckons me over after directing Ethan and Neel to relocate the plants in, what seems to me, a pointless task.

"What's up?"

She smiles at me, the kind that shows all her teeth and is the opposite of endearing.

"Oh no, what?"

"Mathias's mom needs me to pick up Luis early today."

"Okay…?" I'm not seeing the need for the scary smile yet.

"I was thinking maybe you could get a ride home with…" She lifts her chin toward Ethan and Neel.

"Oh, um…" My mind is whirling ahead to logistics about transferring and my wheelchair and a million other things that, as Amelia knows, I constantly have to think about with new situations. But that's not the main reason I'm hesitating. Ethan is still being weirdly standoffish.

"You know," Amelia says, giving my chair a gentle turn toward Ethan and Neel, "some girls wouldn't hate being trapped in a car with a couple of cute guys."

"I thought you said they were boys."

"To me, they are, but I'm not single and seventeen." She gives me another shove but I grab my push rims, bringing my chair to a sudden halt, and turn to look at her over my shoulder.

"Does Mathias's mom really need you to pick up Luis?"

"I would never do that to you," she says in all seriousness before a sly grin creeps back up onto her face. "But sometimes God provides."

CHAPTER NINETEEN

NOW

ETHAN

For some reason, Rebecca is really, really happy to see my 2012 Chevy Impala parked outside. I'm guessing it's better than Neel's sweltering truck.

Then, as I watch her transfer into the passenger seat, I realize how much easier this must be than in Neel's higher truck. Despite how much we've been hanging out lately, I haven't gotten to see her do this yet. Not that I stare and gawk or anything, not that I have time to stare or gawk. She lines her wheelchair up, lifts her left foot off the footplate, and, bending forward, shifts right over. She hooks an arm under her legs to swing them in and she's done.

I know it's not easy, but that's how she makes it look.

Neel springs into action after that, taking her chair and popping off the wheels and even folding the back down to stow it in the backseat before hopping in beside it. He's obviously done this a lot. I make a mental note to learn how to do it myself as quickly as possible.

"This is nice," Rebecca says, running her hand over the dash then along the fabric of the bench seat.

"Did you notice the A/C?" I turn the knob so the chilled air is blowing fully at her. I think I hear Neel mutter *dick* from the back seat and I crack a smile. Before I can say anything else to Rebecca, Neel is there, leaning forward over the seats and blocking my view of her. He stays there the whole way back to Good & Green, making her laugh with inside jokes and "hey remember that time" stories. I barely get a word in before he's grabbing her attention back; it shouldn't bother me but kind of does.

When I finally pull up beside Neel's truck, I'm more than ready to be done with him, except even then he doesn't leave. He gets out but goes only as far as Rebecca's window and gestures for her to roll it down.

"So tonight in the park, you, me, and Gene Kelly?"

My hands tighten on the wheel and I stare straight ahead out the windshield. Why is he doing this in front of me? My finger moves to the passenger window button and I genuinely contemplate pushing it.

Rebeca runs her palms back and forth over her shorts. She did that sometimes when we were kids, not often, but I always knew it was a sign of discomfort. She's really trying to hide it with Neel though. After glancing quickly at me she says, "Can I get back to you? I'm kind of helping a friend with a project and I don't know how much time it might take."

Neel makes the briefest of eye contact with me before offering her his fist to bump. "Sure. I'll text you later."

The second we pull away from the curb her hands are back

on her shorts. Is that because she's upset that my "project" is keeping her from going out with Neel?

"Thanks again for the ride," she says.

"Sure."

"Everything okay?"

How the hell am I supposed to know? According to Neel, she doesn't tell me anything anymore. "Yep."

Her eyes flash angrily in my direction. "What's with you today? You barely looked at me when you came in the shop, said next to nothing on the drive here, and now you're Mr. One-Word Answers?"

Before, when she'd get worked up like this, she'd pull her knee up against her chest and wrap her arms around it. She can't do that now and I can feel her frustration grow.

"You don't have to bail on Neel this weekend for my sake."

"I thought you needed my help?"

"I do, but it doesn't always have to be about me and my stuff."

For some reason that comment makes her look very tired all of a sudden. "Your stuff is kind of everything right now."

How am I supposed to know if that's true when I don't know what is going on with her?

"I'm just saying that if something else was going on, you could talk to me about it. Maybe we try your next thing when we're *not* on the phone tracking down my mom. Give me a chance to help you for once." I don't mean for that last line to come out heated but it does and her response is just as biting.

"Can't help me when you're gone, can you?"

I turn my head to fully stare at her. "Are we gonna go there again? 'Cause I'm gonna need to pull over if we are."

Her cheek puffs as she exhales. "No, I don't want to go there. I just want…"

"What?" I say, trading quick glances between her and the road. Now that Neel's opened my eyes to how much she may be holding back, I'm desperate to hear her answer.

"…to talk about something else." And there's the deflection Neel mentioned.

I'm already making her do something hard by helping me find my mom, so it's not exactly fair to make her do anything else right now.

"Okay," I say, no longer fighting to keep anger from my voice. "What do you want to talk about?"

She's white-knuckling the seatbelt. "Anything else? Something about you?"

Something about me. My words come out before I can yank them back. "I used to have this dream about coming back here one day. It'd be years from now and you'd be all grown up, in college or something, but somehow I stayed a kid. And you'd be nice to me and everything, but you'd have this whole other life that I didn't fit into no matter how hard I tried."

She twists sideways to face me, the seatbelt going slack in her hands. "What a horrible dream."

I shake my head, my gaze on Rebecca but seeing the slightly older, dream version of her. "It wasn't so bad."

She studies me. "So you never grew up? Never got to start your own life, just watched everyone around you do what you couldn't?"

"Not everyone." I slow down at a light. "My mom didn't change either."

She bites her lips. "That's not a good dream, Ethan. I hope you had other ones, that you have other ones."

Her words make the small car feel crowded and stuffy. It's growing dark outside, and hot air made sickly sweet from the citrus trees baking in the sun all day rolls inside when I lower the windows.

"Oh, sure, tons." Not like she means though and we both know it. My dreams are finding my mom and trying every day to make sure she has another. It's not a bad dream.

Her gaze drifts away from me and settles on a book I left on the floor. Before I can stop her, she reaches for it.

"What's this?"

A rhetorical question since the title is right there on the cover. "Some book I found on that bookcase in my grand-parents' living room. I ran out of ones to read in my room."

She starts flipping through it. "Gardening and botany? You read this?" There's a little gasp when she turns another page and flips it to show me. "Did you do this?"

This is a sketch of a prairie smoke bloom, a reddish-pink wispy flower that I now know is in the rose family, is native to North American prairies, and grows best in full sun. "It's just a sketch."

She laughs. "Can't see your grandfather loving you doodling all over his book. Please tell me there's a flip book anima-tion with Old Man in here somewhere." But her quick flip-ping soon slows as she realizes I wasn't just absently sketching. She finds more flowers with little notes about their growth patterns and what zones they thrive in, other pages where I squeezed in full landscapes. "Ethan," she breathes my name. "These are beautiful. And so detailed. You were good before, but this…" She brushes her finger over one. "It almost looks real. You have to show these to your grandfather."

"Yeah, I don't think so." I ease the book from her hand.

"But he could help you, you're obviously interested in this."

"I don't want his help. I can only think about finding my mom right now. I'll think about what comes after that… after that."

She sighs, just slightly, but nods. "I just want you to know it doesn't make you a bad guy to want something for yourself beyond protecting your mom."

Her words bounce off me.

"And when is after?" Her voice is quiet like she's not sure she wants me to hear her. "After you find her? After you go back to LA so you can watch her every day? After she gets clean?" She reaches for me when I grip the steering wheel hard, her words as soft as her touch. "After she stays clean for a year? Five years?"

I shrug off her hand. "Why are you asking me this? You think I know? That I have any clue?" I jam a hand into my pocket and pull out the crumpled piece of paper that's somehow supposed to help me find my mom. "That's how close I am to after." I throw the paper down between us, turning away again as she picks it up. I don't want to see the look on her face when she reads the fat lot of nothing I have to go on. I spent hours trying to remember my mom's friends from La Jolla and then match names to the memories. The problem was that I was just a kid and sometimes I only knew first names or even just nicknames. I don't know if any of them still live there—most of my mom's friends were pretty transient—or are even still alive.

I hear the paper opening and I tense more with each crinkling sound until it's all I can do not to snatch it back and just take off. That was my go-to as a kid, and as slowly as she's opening it, Rebecca's at least half expecting me to bolt too as she smooths the paper out on her thigh and skims the paltry list I came up with. "Okay, so we begin with the names you know, track them down, and if they haven't heard from your mom then maybe they'll be able to fill in some of these gaps." Her brow pinches as she points to the name at the top. "Bauer? That's where you want to start?"

I nod. "I don't know his actual name, but they were together for a while when I was like ten, used to bring me old paperbacks every time he came over, and then he'd send me down to this cafe where he worked to read while they got high."

I swallow as those last few words slip out before I can stop them, but Rebecca doesn't turn a pitying gaze in my direction, she doesn't turn anything in my direction, just nods and makes a note on the paper.

Start with locating the cafe.

I smile at the road. "Remember how when we were kids and my mom would leave me with my grandparents and I just knew that whatever you were doing, wherever you were, you'd come? It's not fair to still expect you to do that. Or to get mad that you have other people in your life. You should. I want that for you and I need to remember that better." I reach to take the paper back, setting it facedown on the dash. "I can work on finding the cafe this weekend. You should go hang out with Neel, go watch a movie or whatever." I mean to sound easy, encouraging her to go out with Neel, but there's a strain in my voice that she must hear. "He still likes you, you know."

One palm rubs over her leg. "We're just friends now."

"What happened with you guys anyway?"

"Nothing *happened*, we just—I don't know." More running her palms over her shorts. Her shoulders start shifting until she's practically squirming beside me. Wow, she does not want to talk about this with me. I consider tormenting her a little longer but decide to be merciful.

"Bad kisser, huh? Yeah, I could see that."

The squirming stops instantly. "What?"

"Too much tongue, am I right?" I shake my head. "Some guys can't take a hint."

Her lips tighten and I know she's trying not to smile. "Actually, he's a really good kisser."

"You know he's not here, right? No need to spare his reputation on my account."

She gives up fighting that smile, but it stays soft with barely a flash of dimple as she runs a finger over her lips. "Maybe it's all those old movies he watches, but there's a reason women were always swooning in them."

"You swooned?"

She nods. "This one time—"

"Ah, ah, ah." I wave her off with a hand. "I heard enough earlier from Neel about you two."

She shrugs. "You asked."

"And now I'm un-asking." I coast to a stop at another light, sending the paper sliding toward the windshield. Rebecca reaches for it but I stop her with a hand on her arm. "Just leave it."

She frowns. "Why?"

"Not much to go on, is it?" I know I encouraged her to ditch me this weekend, but the truth is I don't know what I'm doing without her.

"We found Theo, didn't we?" She grabs the paper, refolding it more neatly than I had. "Now we find Bauer, and then whoever after him and whoever after that."

I stare unblinking at the red light, not moving even when it turns to green. There aren't any cars to honk behind me, but I don't know if I would care in that moment if there were. "I'm scared, Bec," I say in a quiet voice. "If we can't find her or we do but she's…"

Rebecca slips her hand into mine. "We'll find her. And it'll be okay."

I cling to her hand and her words as we drive home. We won't stop. She said it so many times in so many different ways, and each time I believe her a little more. It's gonna hurt when I leave her. It's already there, that feeling like I can't take a deep enough breath, but what else can I do?

I help her put her wheels back on her chair when we get home and close the door after her once she transfers over.

"So I'll come over in a couple hours and we'll start cafe hunting, okay?"

"No Neel?"

Her shoulders drop a little and I can't tell if she's bummed to be missing a date with him or what. "I've seen every Gene Kelly movie with him at least a dozen times."

"Well then maybe we can also figure out our next tattoo or whatever?"

It's probably just the streetlight flicking on but it's like her whole body lights up at my question. "Yeah?"

"I mean I've got to do something with that ski mask, don't I?"

"Oh, we are gonna have so much fun until summer ends."

It's not until after I watch Rebecca go inside her house that I realize I never asked her what happens after the summer.

CHAPTER TWENTY

NOW

ETHAN

Two hours come and go, but Rebecca doesn't show.

I text her after three hours.

> **Me:**
> Still coming over?

> **Rebecca:**
> Can't. My mom came
> home early.

> **Me:**
> She won't let you
> go next door?

> **Rebecca:**
> I didn't ask.

> **Me:**
> So ask.

> **Rebecca:**
> I'll just catch you tomorrow.

Tomorrow? I glance out my window and can see the light still on in her room. I keep looking until I see a shadow shift behind the curtains. She's right there, sitting on her window seat.

> **Me:**
> I'm coming over.

> **Rebecca:**
> Have fun with that. My mom doesn't
> open the front door after nine.

> **Me:**
> Who said anything about
> the front door?

I don't wait for her response before shoving open my window and crawling out, careful not to get sliced up by the rose bush this time. I grin when my phone buzzes in my pocket several times in quick succession as I cross the space between our houses and then I'm tapping ever so lightly on Rebecca's window.

She throws back the curtain almost immediately, and then, with a skill honed to perfection over her childhood, silently opens her window. "Go home," she hisses.

I grin in response and match her volume. "How come you were the only one sneaking out to my window when we were kids?"

"'Cause you were afraid your mom would come looking for you and leave if you weren't tucked safely in your bed."

My grin falters. I'd never thought of it exactly that way before but she's right. I had this thing in my mind about needing to stay right where she left me. My grandparents couldn't even get me to go to school at first until my grandmother came up with the idea of me leaving a note with the school's address on my bedroom door just in case my mom showed up.

Not really a concern anymore though. I didn't even think about it this time.

"Guess I'm the rebel now." I brace my hands on the sill, ready to climb in until Rebecca flattens her hands on my shoulders.

"What are you doing?"

"Coming in."

She locks her elbows, preventing me from moving even an inch forward. "Um, no you're not."

I frown at her. "You used to come in through my window all the time."

She frowns back. "Yeah, used to. You don't see a difference now?"

I stare down at her, taking in the curls she has piled on her head and the oversized Aerosmith T-shirt she's wearing—one of her dad's—and the long stretch of bare legs folded on the window seat beside her.

I lift my hands from the sill, the exact opposite of what I

want to do. "Guess we're not exactly playing Pokémon any-more."

She widens her eyes as if to say, *You're just now getting that?* "And if my mom heard anything and found you in my bed-room? Not good, Ethan. Majorly not good."

Just then Old Man jumps up on the sill from outside and quickly claims a spot on Rebecca's bed. She doesn't even bat an eye.

"He gets to come in?"

"He comes in all the time. He knows how to be quiet."

My cat stares at me and swishes his tail, gloating. "What if I promise to be quiet?"

"Ethan." She gives me a look that's equal parts frustrated and pleading.

"And stay outside," I add. "Plus if we hear anything, I can dive into these sky-flowers and she'll never see me. You can even give me a helpful shove."

She sighs. "You have to promise to be so quiet."

My grin bounces back and I move to sit on the sill. "It was the chance to push me out the window that won you over, wasn't it?"

"Yes, but I better not need to."

"You won't." I shift, ducking my head a little so it's more technically inside than out, causing the wood to creak.

Rebecca's curls whip around as she turns to face her closed bedroom door. She stays frozen like that for several seconds, straining to hear anything before relaxing and turning back to me. She holds two fingers up in front of my face. "I've al-ready had a not-so-pleasant encounter with my mom over being out late with you and I'm not looking to have another."

I reach for her hand and gently force a finger down. "One, you're technically not the one who's out. And two—" I slide my hand until the next finger lowers "—it's not even ten o'clock. On the weekend."

Her gaze lowers to where I'm basically holding her hand and color tints her cheeks in a way that I could so easily become addicted to. When I show zero interest in letting her go, she frees her hand.

"It's a thing, okay? My mom freaks if she finds out I went out without telling her." She hunches in on herself. "I don't need to do that to her again."

"So the last time you officially snuck out…?"

Rebecca draws her lower lip between her teeth and tugs at the hem of her T-shirt. "Was two years ago. To go to that stupid party with people I don't even talk to anymore." A warm breeze, heavy with the promise of rain, wraps around me and she watches my hair brush against my cheek before I can tuck it back. "It's funny." She half smiles as her eyes fill with unshed tears. "But it was only the second time I'd ever been drunk. Both times were pretty horrible."

"When was the first time? It wasn't when I was still here, was it?" I feel like I would have known even if she hadn't told me and I can't imagine why she wouldn't.

She shakes her head, rubbing her palms back and forth on her thighs. "Sorry, but you only get one story tonight."

I don't prompt her, just wait and eventually I'm rewarded when she opens her mouth.

"At the party, one of my former friends got worried when I lost my balance and cut my head the tiniest bit." She pushes her hair back to reveal a thin white scar disappearing into her temple. I don't halt the impulse to reach forward and trace it and she doesn't draw back from the contact. If anything, she leans into my touch. Her eyes bounce between mine as she keeps talking, watching for flickers of reaction, but I don't give her any.

"I guess it bled a lot and she wanted to leave with me but her boyfriend wanted her to stay so—" her eyes stop bouncing and lock on mine as my hand stills, still touching her but no longer moving "—he took my phone, called my house, and scared the hell out of my parents with a story about me drunk and bleeding on the floor of some stranger's house. I don't know what happened here but my dad showed up alone and drove me home." And here is when she reaches up to draw my hand away, not wanting to accept any kind of comfort when she adds, "We didn't make it, obviously."

Rebecca's dad ran a red light. According to my grand-parents, he'd never gotten so much as a parking ticket before then, but for some reason, he tore right through the inter-section that night. No one else was seriously injured but Re-becca was thrown from the car and her dad died instantly.

I tell her I'm sorry, twisting my hand in hers to twine our fingers together.

Holding her now when I failed to then.

CHAPTER TWENTY-ONE

NOW

REBECCA

"Are you going to tell me what we're doing today?" Ethan asks, stuffing one of our last In-N-Out fries into his mouth as we idle in the parking lot.

It's Saturday, the sky is perfectly clear, the sun is blazing, and we just demolished a couple of animal-style burgers and chocolate shakes. I had him wait in the car earlier while I dashed into Walmart for supplies and he keeps leaning over to try and peek inside the bag at my feet.

I smile around the straw of my milkshake and push him back. "What, you don't trust me?" When he straightens, I catch sight of his list of names just barely sticking out of his pocket. Somehow, I ended up completely monopolizing the night before at my window and we didn't even talk about finding his mom. I wait for more than a prickle of guilt to stick me, but all I keep coming back to is that when I peeled back another layer of my past, someone was there to hold me for the first time.

"Considering the last time we did something on your list you ended up stabbing me a million times with a needle, not so much."

"You know it's not an actual list, right? I'm just coming up with stuff in the spur of the moment."

"Wow, why am I not comforted?" He offers me a fry.

"How's it healing, by the way, your tattoo?"

"Better than the last time." Ethan lifts his shirt to show me and it's not half bad. You can definitely tell it's a sun now. "Let me see yours."

I shift as much as possible and push the edge of my shorts down just enough to reveal the flower he tattooed. "You can say it. It looks a million times better than the one I gave you."

"I worked on the better canvas," is his response. And when I glance up at him I think I catch the tiniest flush in his cheeks. Mine warm too and I cover the tattoo again before clearing my throat.

"So did you bring your ski mask?"

He side-eyes me and then leans in so fast that way more than my cheeks heat, his arm reaching...past me to open the glove box and reveal the ski mask inside.

"Wait, you weren't kidding about the ski mask?"

Ethan and I stare up at the two-story Spanish-style house— the very locked two-story Spanish-style house.

"It's not technically breaking in," I tell him, wheeling up the driveway. "I just don't have a key."

"That's the actual definition of breaking in," he says, but he follows right beside me. "Who even lives here anyway?"

I thought it was fairly obvious. There's a funky terrazzo tile walkway leading up to a front porch and a fountain against the wall with a stone dog peeing into it. The walls on either side are painted with brightly colored flowers and best of all there are no steps to get inside.

"This is Amelia's house?" He answers his own question after all. "These murals look a lot like the ones covering the outside of your workshop. Does she paint too?"

"Her husband, Mathias. Want to see his studio?"

Ethan's head snaps in my direction, unable to hide his excitement at the prospect. "Can we do that? Can we do any of this?"

"They went to visit friends for the weekend and won't even know we were here." I move to the garage door and punch in the code on the keypad. "Voila!"

I let Ethan give himself a tour of the garage-turned–art studio since I wouldn't know what I was looking at anyway. There are walls of paint and canvases, brushes and scrapers and all kinds of things that I don't know the names for. Maybe Ethan doesn't either, but it doesn't stop his grin from growing the more he looks.

"I would kill to have a space like this," he breathes some minutes later.

I close the garage door to block out the heat and sigh happily as the A/C kicks on. "I'm sure he'd let you come by sometime. I'll have to introduce you guys."

"Yeah?"

"Yeah. Mathias is really cool." I plop my bag on a counter next to a giant paint-stained utility sink.

"Will he still be cool after he learns we broke into his house?"

"He'll never know." I'll tell Amelia, of course. She'll be

happy I did something fun. I slowly remove the contents of the Walmart bag one by one. And this will be fun.

Ethan comes closer, but his footsteps slow as he sees what I brought. "That's just for you, right?"

"What? There's no needles."

He narrows his eyes at me. "You tried to get me to do this when we were kids and that was one of the only times I said no to you."

"Yeah, but you're not a kid now," I say, opening the first box. "And you also don't care what Laura Sitton thinks about you anymore, so…"

He leans against the counter beside me. "I had a crush on her for like two days."

I scoff. "Okay, sure."

He picks up a bottle of electric blue hair dye. "This is gonna stain everything…and…" He eyes the sink and floor and all the years of paint staining them. "Right. At least tell me it washes out?"

"Okay. It washes out." It does wash out, but it's more fun to make him sweat.

His face scrunches up in a comically pained expression. "Fine but you're first this time."

I shimmy at his consent. "I'm so glad you're back."

He gives me a crooked smile. "Yeah, me too."

The sink is a little high for me to reach the faucet comfortably, so it works out for me to lie on the counter and have Ethan wet my hair. He does a good job, running his fingers through the long curls without snagging, and I tell him so.

"I've washed my mom's hair a bunch," he says, turning off the water. "It's a lot nicer when there isn't vomit dried in it."

I sit up slowly, taking the towel he offers me. It had been a nice moment, sweet even, but I guess just for me. I didn't have anything negative to compare it to. "You should have said something. I could have figured out another way." Or thought up something different for us to do.

"It's not like that," he says, moving to stand closer to me and reaching out to brush at a loose tendril of wet hair. "I mean it's not the same." He frowns softly. "I wasn't thinking about anything besides you." He lowers the strand and steps back just as my pulse kicks up.

As kids, he was always thinking about something else. We could be having the best day ever and I'd still feel like he was only half there with me. My heart begins beating faster when I realize I haven't felt that at all with him today. I drop my gaze to his chest, taking in the faster rise and fall, and my heart starts galloping.

He really means it. He was just thinking about me and breathing that little too fast because of it.

I suddenly feel like I'm sitting a hundred feet off the ground instead of just a few.

Ethan must feel it too because he takes another step back along with a deep breath. "Guess it's my turn, yeah?"

I don't even know what kind of sound I would make if I tried to talk, so I just nod and scoot down to give him room at the sink.

He dunks his head under the faucet and after that we take turns scooping the hair dye out of the jar and working the color into our hair. There aren't any mirrors in Mathias's stu dio, so we help each other catch any spots we miss. Slowly, we get back to the lighter mood we came in with. My heart-beat still likes to speed up whenever his hands linger on my skin too long or I have to lean in close to him, and it's some-how scarier than it was before because I know I won't get to have it forever.

"Alright," I say, setting a timer and placing my phone down. "Now we wait." Ethan is sitting beside me on the counter, his hands curling around the edge on either side of his legs and almost but not quite brushing mine. "You could look around more."

"Or?" He angles his head at me, bringing our faces closer together. There's a drip of blue dye inching toward his eye-brow and I lift my hand to thumb it away in possibly the stu-pidest move I've ever made.

Because I have to lean closer—scary-heights, heart-hammering, too-warm, too-much-but-nowhere-near-enough close. And Ethan is right there, leaning too, the hand between us turning to ghost up to my side.

I have maybe one moment to decide, to meet him in the middle and let us fall together or pull back and grab onto the edge for dear life. I know what I want—I can practically taste it—but I also know how it feels after the impact, to be left alone and hurting.

There's no room for wanting there.

Instead of reaching for his face, I shift to his pocket and the paper I saw earlier. "We could work on this."

Ethan doesn't breathe at first, still staring at me before forc-ing his gaze to the paper. The hand that was almost wedged between us moves to take the paper, then he's nodding and standing. "Yeah, that's a good idea. Not sure how much we can find in forty-five minutes, but yeah. That's definitely what we should do."

Turns out we could do a lot in forty-five minutes, like find out the cafe Ethan remembered is still there and even owned by the same couple, a Mr. and Mrs. Dos Santos who ran it when Bauer worked there. Mrs. Dos Santos remembered Bauer and felt bad about having to fire him.

"Don't have a lot of rules but not coming to work high is one of them."

"So you let him go?" I asked.

"Shame. He was one of our best line cooks too."

"And his real name was…?"

"Stephen." Her voice shifts and the first note of suspicion enters it.

"Right." I mime for Ethan to write that down. "I always forget that."

"Who did you say you were again?"

I hadn't. She'd been chatty from the start and I'd just bluffed my way through the conversation until we landed here. "Just an old friend. I'm hoping to track him down."

There's silence from her end of the phone and I don't look at Ethan, not wanting to see his expression when I'm about to blow it here. "You don't sound grown up enough to have old friends, honey."

I close my eyes, unsure how to answer her.

"Mrs. Dos Santos?"

I open my eyes at the sound of Ethan's voice.

"Who's this?"

"I used to sit at your counter all the time as a kid, reading paperbacks. You always brought me free fries. Sometimes a slice of pie."

"Oh, I do remember you. Scrawny little thing you were. But you don't sound so scrawny anymore."

"He's not," I say, earning a laugh from her and a raised eyebrow from Ethan.

"Well, good for you, sweetie. I bet he's really handsome now too."

Ethan smiles waiting for my answer.

I smile right back. "Yes, ma'am. Though the blue hair is something of an acquired taste."

He laughs, light and easy and safe.

"What was that last part?" Mrs. Dos Santos asks.

"Nothing." Ethan touches his hair and examines the blue that comes away on his fingertips. "I'm hoping you might know how I could get in touch with Bauer or maybe you know someone who does?"

"Well, now, I heard he was working at another restaurant a few years ago. In fact, I think he's still there."

I grab Ethan's arm in excitement. "Nearby? In La Jolla?"

"Oh yes, now what was the name again...?"

CHAPTER TWENTY-TWO

NOW

ETHAN

After being back in Arizona for a couple of weeks, I'm starting to settle into a routine. My grandparents and I mostly avoid each other except for two events that have been sacrosanct since I was a kid: sitting down together for dinner during the week and going to church on Sunday mornings. Dinner has been increasingly awkward and brief, but I don't mind going to church. There's always been something appealing to me about a group of people getting together to all study the same book that people have read for millennia. And, at least during the service, my grandmother can't try to talk to me. She gave me more than a look when I came back with blue hair yesterday, but I haven't given her a chance to ask me about it or anything else.

We're probably halfway through a sermon on the eighth chapter of Romans when my phone buzzes and, with a start, I recognize Bauer's number. When we'd called the restaurant Mrs. Dos Santos remembered, all we'd had to do was mention her name and they gave me Bauer's cell. I left a message yesterday but didn't really expect him to call me back, at least not this quickly.

I all but bolt out of the sanctuary, a blue-haired streak, not even giving my grandparents a second glance as I hurry into the narthex.

"Hello?"

"Ethan?"

"Yeah. Thanks for calling me back. I wasn't sure if you'd even remember me."

"Joy's kid, sure, I remember you. How you been?" It's loud wherever he is, lots of voices and clattering.

"Um, fine, yeah," I say, caught off guard that he's asking about me.

"Listen, I'm in the middle of a shift. We're about to start prepping for the lunch rush, but I was thinking we could set up a time to really talk. Maybe even get together?"

"I'm not living in California right now, but I'll be quick," I promise. "It's about my mom."

I don't think I say it in any special, revealing way, but Bauer swears softly then I hear him yell out that he's going on break. The noise from his end of the phone gets briefly louder then it's gone.

"She dead?" He asks it bluntly, evenly, and I nearly drop my phone because it's too easy to imagine that reality.

"No, she was in rehab but she checked herself out and no one's been able to find her."

His sigh is long and drawn-out and I tell myself it's relief I hear, but I don't really know.

"Have you seen her? Or maybe she tried to call you?"

There's a sound from his end of the phone, a match striking and I picture him leaning up against the outside of a brick wall with a cigarette in one hand and running the other through his lanky brown hair. "I haven't seen Joy in years, not since you guys were living above that diner over on Hermosa. You were what? Ten, Eleven?"

"Twelve," I say. I'd been small for my size until I hit fifteen and shot up.

His laughter fills my ears. "That's right. I was gonna take you to see an Angels game for your birthday and you got sick before we could even leave, remember?"

"Yeah, I remember." My mom had had that look in her eyes for days, the one that told me she'd be high the second we drove off. So I'd made myself sick instead, downed half a bottle of apple cider vinegar and threw up all over the place. I missed the baseball game, but my mom couldn't get high that night. As far as birthdays go, it wasn't my worst.

He laughs again before sobering. "I'm sorry I didn't stick around to take you another time."

Yeah, me too. The guy after him introduced my mom to a whole new world of shit.

"Is there anyone you can think of that she might have reached out to?"

There's a pause. "Aw, kid, I wish I could help you. Maybe, maybe she doesn't want to be found right now? There were times in my life when I didn't." I have no doubt about that, but her wants rarely match with anything good for her. "But I can ask around, okay? I still know where to find a few people from back then."

"That'd be great, thanks."

He makes a sound in his throat, dismissing my gratitude. "You know I've been meaning to track you down, you and your mom. I—ah, wasn't a great guy back then." He laughs a little. "I'm nothing special now, but I haven't hocked my kid's bike for a fix or anything."

"You never sold my bike."

"No? Well, I guess that's something."

There's a pause that makes me wonder why I'm still on the phone. I should probably hang up, slip back into church, and hope my grandparents don't ask too many questions about who I was talking to. Instead, I say, "So you got a kid?"

Another laugh that dissolves into a cough. "Can you believe it? Got the minivan too. I mean the kid's not exactly mine, but I'm claiming him. Stayed sober for two years before his mom agreed to marry me and now we got our first one together on the way."

Jealously spikes through me hard and fast and I can't answer him. He and my mom were in the same place not that long ago, spiraling around the same endless cycle and dragging anyone who cared about them along for the ride. How is it fair that he got out and she sank deeper? Bauer says something, but I'm so tangled up in my thoughts that I miss it.

"Hello?"

"Sorry, what?"

"I said you still reading?"

"Oh yeah, I'm still reading. All the time."

"Good, good. Don't ever stop, you hear me? Books are the keys to the world."

"Right."

"So you're not in California. Where'd you end up? If it's not far maybe we can still—"

"It's not a great time for me right now."

"Okay, yeah. I get that. You'll let me know when that changes?"

"Sure. And you'll call if…?"

"Anything I find out, I'll call."

We hang up and I linger, staring down at my phone. I tell myself it's possible that he's lying about having his life together, but I can't think of a reason he'd need to lie with me. I know I should be glad for him, glad for the kid he'll bring more than books to now, but all I feel is resentment.

I look up when the door opens, not surprised to see my grandfather has come looking for me.

He walks right up to me, concern etched on his features. "Is it your mom? Is she alright?"

I slowly lift my gaze from my phone and my first instinct is to throw his concern back in his face and see how he likes it when somebody keeps things about his family from him, but I know just how messed up that is. They kept stuff about my mom from me all the time, even now they didn't tell me when she left rehab. And maybe it's because I just got off the phone with a man who may have actually succeeded in turning his life around or the fact that I'm in a church, but I don't feel like being angry right now. My grandfather looks as small as I've ever seen him in that moment. He looks afraid.

"It wasn't her," I say. "If I hear from her, I'll tell you."

CHAPTER TWENTY-THREE

BEFORE

REBECCA

I flop over dramatically on the grass in Mr. and Mrs. Kelly's backyard and squint up at the hazy pink sky still edged with gold and orange from the setting sun. "This is the most bored a human being has ever been." A second later a thin paperback gently hits me on the side of the head and I shoot to a sitting position to glare at Ethan. "Um, ow."

He doesn't look up from the book he's reading. "I gave you *The Old Man and the Sea*. Less than a hundred pages."

I rub my temple. "Still not awesome trying to catch it with your head."

He smiles, then turns another page in a book so thick I don't even bother to read the title. He looks like he's nearly a quarter of an inch into it, worse, he looks like he'll gladly keep turning pages until curfew. No, thank you. He's been extra tense about leaving his grandparents' house lately. His mom doesn't usually stay away this long and he keeps expecting her to show up. I keep expecting it too, but I'm not ready to call it until she's knocking on his door.

I inch closer to Ethan and with two hands raised high above my head, drop *The Old Man and the Sea* onto his stomach.

He flicks his gaze at me. "Was that supposed to hurt?"

"No," I say. "It was supposed to make you stop reading for two seconds. And don't—" I lean forward and press his open book down against his chest "—start back until you've heard me out."

"Fine. I'm listening."

I draw back and cross my legs. "Remember how I said you could pick what we do today, no questions asked?" I wait for his nod. "Yeah, well that was before I knew you were going to bring us boring old books about boats and sit in your backyard all day."

"It's a good book. There are sharks."

That piques my interest. "When?"

"You have to read it and find out."

I groan and let my head roll back. "I don't want to read it." I glance down at the cover of *The Old Man and the Sea* and notice the corner is ripped. Without even thinking about it, I tear it the rest of the way off.

Ethan reacts as though I set it on fire or something, snatching the book from my hands. "What did you just do?"

"Nothing, it's just the corner," I say, watching him frantically trying to match the torn edge back. "The pages are all fine and it's a super old book anyway."

"So you just rip the cover?" He jerks to his feet.

"I didn't rip it, it was already hanging off."

Ethan grabs his other book, one that looks like it's been reread a million times too and might not survive another. That reality seems to hit Ethan then too because he goes completely still. For a second I think he's gonna cry.

"I'll buy you another copy, okay?" I stand and walk closer to him. "I didn't know it meant that much to you. I thought it was just some old book."

He stands there, nostrils flaring for a solid minute glaring at the books.

I have no idea why he's so upset and he'll never tell me. Sometimes being Ethan's friend is like navigating a minefield with all these emotional detonators hidden everywhere. I never know when I've stepped on one until he blows. "Are they from your mom?"

He snorts.

Okay then. "But somebody?"

He still doesn't answer which suddenly feels irritating. It's not like he was treating them special or anything.

"You maybe shouldn't have thrown it at my head then. How was I supposed to know it was important?" I prop a hand on my hip only to drop it a second later. Ethan's getting more worked up by the second and getting mad back never helps. His mom could show anytime now and the last thing I want is to wake up tomorrow and find him gone before we can make up. This could be our last day together for who knows how long.

"What if we go to my house and get some tape? My mom has all this fancy fabric tape and stuff. I bet we could make it look good as new." Or as good as a tattered old paperback could. "And I'll read the whole thing."

I feel hours of my life slip away at that promise and try not to make a face. Not that it would matter since Ethan isn't even looking at me. In his mind, I feel like he's already gone which means his actually leaving isn't far behind.

"Ethan, come on." I slide around in front of him. "Let me at least try and fix it. And then we can read and I won't even complain the tiniest bit no matter how boring the book is." I mime locking my lips with a key then smile, an expression that feels heavy to hold even for the few seconds it takes for Ethan to look right through it.

He mumbles something like *forget it*, and with an explosion of energy, hurls both books behind him. There's a loud, slapping splash when they hit the pool.

I stare wide-eyed as the books sink and Ethan storms off.

CHAPTER TWENTY-FOUR

NOW

REBECCA

Ethan's been off since the weekend. We had our almost moment in Mathias's studio, but I think he realized right after I did that it wasn't a good idea. Then again, maybe it had only been an almost moment for me. Maybe he didn't even notice. Either way he seemed fine afterward, at least I think he was. This is different. I can't put my finger on it exactly but something has definitely happened.

And he won't tell me what it is.

We're in his room later that week, Ethan absently refreshing his inbox on his laptop while Old Man purrs in my lap. The silence between us is awkward and growing more so with every passing second. The only thing that breaks it is Mrs. Kelly occasionally passing in the hall to check that the door is still open but trying to act like she's not. Ethan said his grandparents didn't comment on his blue hair, but after seeing my matching hue, they've been more watchful, as though dyeing our hair together means we might be doing other kinds of things together. We're not, so the constant checking doesn't bother me, but Ethan is another story.

After about the fifth pass by his grandmother, Ethan's shoulders tense and the second we hear her join Mr. Kelly in the backyard, he gets up and slams the door shut. It's not an earth-shattering slam. None of the pictures fall off the walls, but Old Man starts in my lap and decides he'd rather be outside. The lack of impact seems to bother Ethan. His eyebrows furl tightly as he paces around the small room before stopping at his desk only long enough to give his laptop the same treatment as his door. That one makes me wince. The laptop doesn't look like it can take much more abuse.

"And that's my cue to go." I turn toward the door, ready for a lovely view of Ethan's back on my way out. I've learned long ago that there's no reaching him at this point.

Except…he's not too busy silently raging to notice anything else. He's looking right at me instead of through me.

"What?" Then he follows my gaze to the laptop that definitely snapped one of its hinges. Ethan continues frowning and visibly breathing through his nose for another moment before he's able to get a handle on himself. He rakes his fingers through his blue hair, locking his fingers behind his head. "Oh yeah. Sorry."

"For what?" I say, genuinely shocked by the words that just came out of his mouth.

"Silently slamming things around like a little shit. I'm just—just—" He punctuates that statement by kicking his desk chair across the room, which sounds more violent than it is. The chair has wheels so it just rolls a few feet on the car-

peted floor before toppling over. A short, harsh laugh comes
out of him. "I remember that helping a lot more as a kid."

"Well, I don't," I say, my eyes wide on his. "I remember you
yelling at me over torn books and then throwing them in pools."

His gaze lifts to meet mine. "Guess I'm sorry about that too."

"Wait, wait." I wheel right up to him, faux incredulity
guiding my movements. "Did the hair dye mess with your
brain chemistry or something? Why aren't you storming off
right now and leaving me confused and annoyed?"

He doesn't smile at me; if anything he looks pained.

I drop the act. "Um, that was supposed to be a joke."
Clearly it did not land. More silence threatens to invade the
space between us and I decide maybe he can surprise me
again. "So what's going on with you?"

His gaze travels to his laptop. "It's been days and Bauer
hasn't gotten back to me."

I figured as much, but I hadn't dared ask. Bauer wasn't just
our best lead on his mom, so far, he was our only lead. We
hadn't heard back from anyone else on Ethan's list.

And whatever else I want, Ethan hurting like this will
never be one of them.

I can't force people to reply to messages or return calls,
but maybe I can help distract Ethan, at least for a little while.

"You want to get out of here?"

His answering yes comes almost before I get the question
out.

Ethan watches me intently as I break down my chair after
transferring to the passenger seat of his Impala.

"So I know how to do it in the future," he explains.

I breathe easier when he stows everything in the back seat. The way he was acting in his room earlier, I started to worry that I'd wake up to him gone one day, no word, no nothing, just an empty room. If he's talking about the future here, he's not planning to take off in the middle of the night or anything.

"Where we going?" he asks when his grandparents' home fades from view.

I shrug; already it feels lighter just being away from his room. He does anyway. "Where do you want to go? And don't say California," I add, testing that he really is calmer.

"What, you got something against Disneyland?"

I smile at his profile, not feeling the slightest bit self-conscious that I'm staring. "Sadly, I forgot my Mickey ears."

"Seriously, you own a pair of Mickey ears?"

"Seriously, you don't? Didn't you live near Anaheim for a while?"

He nods. "Sometimes. But we were usually too worried about rent and food to plan any trips to the Magic Kingdom." He doesn't say this with any bitterness, it's just the truth. He glances over at me. "You went with your parents?"

I twist my ring around my finger. "Yeah. A few times."

Ethan laughs a little. "I bet your dad posed for those cheesy Splash Mountain pictures, like pretending he was asleep or on the phone."

"Every time. My mom used to have them all framed on her desk at work."

"Not anymore?"

I press my cheek against my shoulder and hold it there. "I don't know. I haven't been since my dad died."

"What, never?"

I glance over at Ethan and the surprise in his voice. "I'm a bit old for take your daughter to work day."

He falls quiet after that, not moody, angry quiet like in his room, more contemplative. We drive for a few miles, aimlessly turning down streets and staring at the passing homes.

"So you think they are still there?" he asks after a while.

"Hmm?"

"The Disney pictures with your dad?"

My gaze traces over a pair of bicycles left in someone's yard. "I don't know." I'd hate to think she tucked them away in a box like all the others that used to fill our house.

He slows the car and waits for me to look at him. "Let's find out."

I give him a weary smile. "Sure. I'll call her up and ask."

"No, I mean let's go. To her office."

My smile freezes on my face. "And what, break in?" I start to turn back to the window, but Ethan has a look on his face that I know all too well, except I'm usually the one wearing it, not him.

"Come on, aren't you curious?"

"About my mom? No. About your mental state right now? Little bit."

"Thought you were the one who wanted to have fun this summer, the same kind of fun we used to have." He drapes an arm over the steering wheel and leans toward me with a sly smile. "Wouldn't be your first break-in."

I half roll my eyes. "I told you we didn't break into Amelia's house."

"I'm talking about when we were kids."

"Crawling through Mrs. Lowell's cat door to get your football after she confiscated it is not the same thing." My lips twitch at the memory. "You wouldn't even come with me! And don't give me the excuse about needing to play lookout," I add when he immediately opens his mouth. "You were scared."

This time he leans back, inviting my perusal. "Do I look scared now?"

He looks like a lot of things: strong and challenging, wild with his blue hair and teasing grin. He looks like every kind of secret we'd ever had together as kids and a few new ones that send tingles trailing across my skin.

I lean an inch toward him. "She probably changed the door code."

He matches my movement. "Yeah, but I bet you could figure it out."

Another inch. "And there's a few steps."

He shrugs, moving closer. "So I'll pick you up."

I glance at his arms and imagine how easily he could lift me, before returning my eyes to his face and this game that is already way too good. "Security cameras?"

"Ski mask." His grin widens with every one of my so-called objections.

Any closer and we'd get into the same kind of trouble we did at Mathias's studio and I don't want to ruin this. More than that, I do want to know if the pictures are in her office, if she kept them there knowing I'd never see them. I won't take them from her, but to see them again and remember…? Yeah, I want that.

So I lean as close as I dare and grin back. "Let's go."

★ ★ ★

"On the plus side, there's no stairs anymore."

I glance over at Ethan with a flat expression.

My mom's interior design office doesn't have steps anymore. But it also doesn't exist. The little building tucked in between a dentist's office and an accounting firm no longer says Keri James Interiors, it says Chambliss Reality.

"So then she moved?"

"I guess." I gesture at the building. "Obviously."

"Any idea where?"

I shake my head, not ready to share with Ethan how little my mom and I communicate these days, though her missing office space is doing plenty of sharing for me.

"We could still break in," he offers. "Take a selfie, maybe a branded pen."

I have to laugh at that, just a little. "I know you would. That's enough."

We're still sitting in his car—no real point in getting out—and his hand inches across the seat toward mine. "You okay?"

All I would have to do is extend my pinky and we'd be touching. "We'd have gotten caught anyway."

"No, I mean are you okay? I know you wanted to see those pictures with your dad."

He hasn't moved any more, but suddenly he feels too close. I can feel my eyes glossing with the promise of tears and distract myself by reaching out to brush a strand of Ethan's hair. "Even blue, this is really too pretty. You know that, right?" But it isn't too anything. It's kind of perfect.

"You trying to change the subject?"

I let my hand fall back. "Maybe." There's a pause and I

can feel Ethan looking at me even when I turn my face to the window.

"I never said it, but I'm sorry about your dad."

His voice is so gentle that it slips right through my defenses and one tear slides free. It's just a drop, but I'm like a dam with a crack and there's been too much pressure held back for too long.

"He was always really nice to me," Ethan continues when, if my throat hadn't squeezed itself shut, I'd have begged him to stop. "Joking with me even when I was scowling at everything." I can hear the smile in his voice before it drops to almost a whisper and I turn to him, headless of my damp cheeks. "He loved you so much. I used to watch you guys, even when you were in trouble and he was yelling at you. He never let you leave the room without hugging you. And I swear it physically hurt him when he had to ground you. I just—I can't imagine how much it hurt to lose him. And I'm sorry."

My ribs felt like they splintered from the first mention of my dad, but now those sharp edges start to slice. I swipe my cheeks dry. "Why do people say that? Lost him? I didn't misplace my dad. He died. I can take you to the cemetery if you want to see his grave."

Ethan flexes his hand toward me. "Rebecca, I didn't mean to—"

"And you know how he died? He was just so distracted by—how did you put it?" My words turn venomous, spewing from my mouth. "Loving me so much while he yelled himself purple that he didn't see the red light. We got T-boned in an intersection that I still can't force myself to drive through because I know if I do I'll see his body again, crumpled and bleeding and dead." My breath rattles through my lungs when I suck in a breath. "Because of me. Because *I* snuck out." Every *I* is like a knife ripped from my gut. "Because *I* thought my life was so unfair. You know what's unfair? I was the one not wearing my seatbelt. I was the one who got thrown from the car. But I was so drunk that I was like a rag doll. All I broke was my back. My dad had his entire rib cage crushed in on it-self." Air rasps out of me again in words that stab me from the inside but it's not enough. I blink and I see him. Blink again and he's still there. Not moving, not breathing, eyes open. *Blink, blink, blink.*

"Nobody talks to me about him, my mom won't even keep his pictures where I can see them, because she knows it too. It's my fault." That last part leaves my lips like a ghost, words I've never spoken before but that have haunted my every sleeping and waking moment for the past two years. "I'm the one who should have died that night."

There's a fresh kind of horror when I finish my vomit of words and pain that is supposed to stay locked up tight inside me. I can't fling open the car door and run off into the night to find my way home when I'm ready. No, I have to endure Ethan's clumsy apologies, his well-meaning words that can't possibly blot out the ones that came before. I have to sit in his car with my confession trapped between us while he asks me if I want to go home. I don't want to go home; I don't want to go anywhere.

"Yes," I lie. My throat feels raw.

It takes an eternity. And even then I have to get my chair.

Ethan tries to help, so desperately wants to help, and I just want to be done and alone. And I yell at him.

And I hate myself even more than I already do.

CHAPTER TWENTY-FIVE

NOW

ETHAN

"I need to ride to work with you."

My grandfather catches me in my room the next morning as I'm sitting on the corner of my bed and staring at the boots I should already have on. It's like I've been moving through wet cement ever since I dropped Rebecca off last night and not even my grandfather's sudden appearance can make me move faster.

I turn my head in his direction. He's standing outside my open door, his own boots right up to the threshold and not an inch past. "Are you asking me or telling me?"

He sidesteps my question. "Grandma's car is in the shop and I told her she could take mine to the Broadway site."

"I need a few minutes." I reach for my boot and my gaze snags on Rebecca's bag peeking out from under my bed. She must have left it. Ignoring my boot, I grab it instead.

"We'll be late."

I don't answer my grandfather, just stare at her bag.

She thinks she killed her father. She barely looked at me last night after admitting that, even yelling she couldn't meet my eyes. Every time I tried to reach for her, she lashed out, cutting at me with words that sliced deeper than she knew.

I don't know if her mom blames her, but it's enough that Rebecca thinks she does.

Because guilt doesn't fade, it festers.

My grandfather says something else, but I can't look up. He'll see my face and he'll know or he'll guess.

I work to try and sound as normal as possible. "What?"

"Are you sick?" His voice lowers and even though I don't hear the steps he takes, I know he's moving closer.

I force myself to my feet, breaking through that cement that is no longer just thick but hardening, and keep my back half to him as I walk out of the room. "I'm fine. Let's go."

We both end up walking toward the driver's side door, but he yields after only a quick glance from me. We drive in silence for a mile or more, long enough for me to be grateful it's my grandfather I'm riding with and not my grandmother. She would have already asked me a dozen questions by now. My grandfather, when he does finally talk, keeps it work related.

"I need you and Neel to eat lunch at the offices today. We've got some new fertilizer coming in and I want to go over some of the safety rules."

I'm only half listening. Every few seconds I eye my rearview mirror to stare at where I tossed Rebecca's bag in the back seat. Maybe I could use returning it as an excuse to stop by and see her, make sure she's okay, and… "Wait, what? Why?"

"Fertilizer is highly combustible."

I wave a hand at him. "I know, I know, ammonium nitrate." I puff out my cheeks and make an explosion sound. "I'm up to speed, okay? And I've already got plans for lunch."

My grandfather notices when I check the rearview mirror for the millionth time and he cranes his neck around to see what I keep looking at. I can tell immediately that he's seen Rebecca's bag, but he doesn't comment on it.

"And where'd you learn that?"

"I don't know. One of those books in the living room." Maybe I should go see Rebecca before lunch?

"Which one did you read?" His voice is deceptively calm and it makes the hair on the back of my neck stand up.

Am I not supposed to touch the books? Well, it's a little late now. "All of them, give or take." There are only like twenty or so and a lot of them are illustrated.

"Hmmm," is what he says in response. Then, "Are you interested in that kind of stuff?"

Two more mirror checks. "Some, I guess."

"Enough to read an entire bookshelf some?"

I have to read, especially at night, especially since coming here. If I look at a screen too long my mind takes over and I haven't liked the thoughts it's been serving up lately. I wonder if Rebecca's the same way. Maybe that's part of what drew her to jewelry making, a way to drown out her thoughts instead of sinking under them. Had I done exactly that last night by forcing her to dredge up the past?

I mutter "shit" before remembering my grandfather can hear me. "So I read some books. All you guys have in the house are ones on plants and theology, and as interesting as

I'm sure a collection of essays about a guy with an awesome beard named B.B. Warfield is, I decided to start with the plants." Actually, I'll probably read the beard guy book at some point too, but right now I kind of like knowing how to grow a specific kind of flower as well as draw it. Somehow even the chemistry about proper soil PH measurements didn't bore me when connected to creating a landscape; for the first time in my life, it kind of made sense.

Rebecca said I should let my grandfather know I was interested in this kind of stuff; guess I'll find out if she was right.

When we get to Good & Green and I see Eddie and Neel waiting for me by one of the trucks, I look past them to the clock on the wall, calculating how many hours I'll have to wait until lunch and my excuse to see Rebecca.

"Four hours until lunch," my grandfather says. "Come see me on your morning break and if you can answer a few more questions, I'll let you keep your lunch plans. Just say hi to Rebecca for me and your grandmother."

"How'd you know I was going to see her?"

He gives me a look that makes me feel dumber than usual. "There are only two things you've ever really cared about. Not hard to guess which one is on your mind today."

I don't have to wonder what he means. It doesn't matter if I'm away from one or the other, Mom and Rebecca are never far from my thoughts. And yet, for the first time since I left LA, today I only thought about one.

My grandfather turns to head up to the office then stops and looks back at me as though a new idea just occurred to him. "I could bring home some more books for you tonight, good starters on botany, landscaping. If you want."

My thoughts are still torn in two different directions, but I find myself nodding and smiling.

"I'm watching a movie with Rebecca tomorrow," Neel says, when I join him in loading fertilizer bags onto a truck.

I halt, half bent over to pick up a bag. "Oh yeah?"

Neel climbs up into the truck bed and gestures for me to throw him one. "I think I might be making some progress in the whole let's get back together thing."

I maybe throw the next bag harder than I should.

He grunts. "Ease up. You want this to bust open all over me?" He makes the mistake of spreading his arms out wide and I choose that exact moment to throw another bag of fertilizer. It smacks him dead in the chest.

I mutter an apology when he yells at me, but the whole scene just causes Eddie to come over and yell at both of us. It's a good time all around.

"What is going on over here?" Eddie props his hands on his belted cargo shorts. "This is company property, not toys for you to play with."

"It's a sack of sh—" I edit myself midsentence because one lecture at a time feels more my speed this morning "—fertilizer. What kind of toys did your parents make you play with?"

"You break it you buy it. You know how much one bag costs?"

Neel and I share a glance and he shrugs.

"Twenty bucks?" I guess.

Eddie snorts. "Try close to fifty. So watch it." He takes a few steps backward. "Because I'll be watching you."

I sigh and we continue loading the truck. "How did you deal with him before I got here?"

Neel shakes his head. "I just ignore him. You should try it."

I think about that and just barely keep from getting into a staring contest with Eddie. "It's not in my nature to ignore."

Neel makes a show of silently agreeing with me which pulls me up short.

"What does that mean?"

He waves for another bag, but I hold it back until his arms drop to his sides. "Just something Rebecca said. You hang on to things really hard. I think she meant it as a compliment," he adds, seeing my expression. "Like you're loyal, you know?"

I don't know anything, or that's what it feels like as I work the rest of the day—even through lunch. Like does Rebecca need space or comfort, and if it's the latter, does she want it from me or someone else?

Instead of going home after my shift, I drive for a while hoping to clear my head. It doesn't really work until I spot a rare—according to the book I'd read last week—Baja lily growing in somebody's sand-covered yard so I pull over on an impulse and search the car until I find an old takeout napkin and a pen under the seat. I stare at the indigo blooms and start drawing. This will be the first flower I've left for her since coming back and I need it to be a lot of things, a promise, an apology, and a question all at once. I don't just draw the flower this time. I write a few words underneath:

See you tomorrow, so she'll know that I'll never say goodbye that way again.

When I finally get back to my room that night, I find a stack of books on my desk along with a note in my grandfather's bold, scratchy writing that says:

Start with the one by Stern. We can talk about it tomorrow on the way in to work.

CHAPTER TWENTY-SIX

NOW

REBECCA

"You hated it."

I blink, letting the credits come into focus as Neel frowns beside me on the couch.

"It's okay. It's just one of the most famous Hindi movies ever made and I'm only slightly dying inside that you hated it."

"What? No."

His chin drops to his chest. "Don't try and spare my feelings. I'm just going to go walk home in the rain now."

I laugh when he tries to stand and I tug him back down to the couch. "First, you drove to my house, second there's not a cloud in the sky, and third, I didn't hate the movie."

"So you loved it and by extension me?"

I open my mouth. "I—" and let the single syllable word draw out.

"Take your time," he says. "Just know that the entirety of my self-worth hangs in the balance."

"That is not fair. One has nothing to do with the other."

"Aha! So you did hate it." He points a finger really close to my face. I swat it away.

"No, no, I absolutely did not hate it—"

Neel's face brightens to comical levels.

"—but I didn't love it either."

His face crumples with equal theatrics. "You realize you just insulted the Asian Godfather."

I slump a little as he side-eyes me then leaps to the far end of the couch.

"Whoa. Okay whoa. You cannot tell me you don't like *The Godfather*."

I slump farther. "Kind of hard to hate something you've never seen."

Neel pretends to fall dead off the couch. He really commits, face planting and everything. He doesn't even flinch when I throw a pillow at him.

He snaps back to life and knee walks over to me. "Okay, so I just realized that we can never again talk about this because up until now you've been like this perfect girl—"

I cut him off with a pointed look at the pizza sauce I dripped on my shirt earlier.

"—this perfect and occasionally messy girl, and you're coming dangerously close to ruining that image for me."

I nod very seriously. "So you want me to hide anything about myself that threatens to shatter the idealistic picture you have of me even if it's false and/or misleading?"

Neel flops onto the cushion beside me with enough energy to bounce us both together. "That'd be great. Thanks."

I roll my eyes and he offers me the half-empty bowl of popcorn. "Want some?"

"I thought the movie was well done, but it's not the kind of story I generally love."

Neel groans. "You ruined it. We could have had beautiful light brown babies together someday but you just spoke ill of *Gangs of Wasseypur* and that's it. Perfect illusion destroyed."

I grab a handful of popcorn. "And I was so looking forward to hiding away parts of myself for the rest of my life."

He huffs. "Yeah, me too. Well, I mean you, of course. I wouldn't have to hide anything."

I throw a piece of popcorn at his face. "Guess you're through with me now?"

"I'm afraid so."

"If only my movie taste were better."

"If only."

I throw another piece of popcorn, but he moves fast and manages to catch it in his mouth.

"That's impressive," I tell him, aware that his quick move has brought him a lot closer to me. A lot.

"You know," he says, sliding an arm along the back of the couch, "I could be persuaded to overlook that one glaring personality defect."

"Oh yeah?" I eye his continuously sliding arm. "And how's that?"

He moves closer and I'm not really sure if we're still playing our little game. "It'll be super easy, barely an inconvenience. All you have to do is—" his eyes drop to my lips and he's so close I can feel his breath. My heart starts racing. Not a game. "—agree to watch Part 2 with me next time."

I blink at him as a wide grin spreads over his face.

Relief bubbles up inside me that he was just teasing and

not actually about to kiss me. "Part 2? That was only Part 1? I don't think so."

He moves back, but his arm stays across the back of the couch almost touching my shoulders.

"Here's the thing," he says, all confident teasing gone. "I don't actually care if we love the same movies." He cocks his head and pinches up his face. "Let me rephrase, I can get past the fact that we might not love all the same movies, but I kind of need to know if you can…get past my stuff."

"I thought you were perfect." I grin at him but he doesn't fully grin back.

"So perfect I barely watched one of the greatest examples of cinema ever put on film because all I could think about was whether this almost perfect girl would let me kiss her when it was over. I know, I know," he adds when I start to say something. "Longest two and a half hours of my life."

But then neither one of us is smiling. And he's a lot closer and it's a completely involuntary reaction when my gaze slides past him to look at Ethan's window. The lights are off and before I can start to wonder if that means he's home or not, I see Neel's head drop slightly from the corner of my eye.

"Well damn," he says softly.

"Neel…" My brows lift and draw together and I hesitate when I feel the urge to reach out to him.

His head of gloriously glossy black hair moves from side to side. "It's Ethan, isn't it?"

I don't say anything.

"'Cause he can be a real dick sometimes, you know?"

"It's not really him. It's me. I'm not—" I search for the right word "—dateable right now." I mentally wince at the excuse.

Neel comes as close to looking angry as I've ever seen him. "What does that mean?"

"It means I shouldn't be spending time with someone like that when I don't even want to spend time with myself."

He stands. "I'm not going to pretend to understand what that means. And I kind of just wish you'd have said, 'yeah, it's because of Ethan.' Because you never seem to have any trouble spending time with him."

My face goes hot at how accurate that statement is. "I don't know about Ethan, okay? I'm still figuring that out. But I do know about you and me." I reach for his hand. "And we are a million times better as friends. Last time we tried this it didn't work."

"*For you*, it didn't work." Neel looks down at my hand holding onto his loose one and slides it free. "And maybe this time…not for me either."

CHAPTER TWENTY-SEVEN

NOW

REBECCA

The last few days have been awful. First everything with Ethan and then hurting Neel. It's been two days and I still feel sick about it. So sick that I finally tell Amelia what happened while she's driving me home.

"You should have seen his face," I say, remembering the mix of hurt and anger on Neel's features. "It's so much worse that he thinks it's because of Ethan."

"Well, it is, isn't it?"

I scoff at the nonchalance in her tone. "No."

She sighs. "So you really wouldn't have let that beautiful brown boy kiss you the other night if your childhood sweetheart hadn't been right next door?"

"No." Then I frown. "Wait, I don't even know what you mean. Are you saying I would have kissed Neel if Ethan never came back?"

"Are *you* saying that?"

I grit my teeth. "Stop being confusing. I didn't kiss either of them."

"Yes, but which one didn't you kiss because of the other?"

"Neither. Both!"

"So you admit it!"

I wait for her to stop at a light and then start smacking every inch of her I can reach.

She laughs. *"Oh, my life is so hard. All the boys love me."*

"Stop!" I say between smacks. "I'm seriously upset here." Though my own laughter isn't exactly selling that fact.

The light changes and I fall back against my seat. "Neel and I aren't right for each other. He wants a Ginger Rogers to his Fred Astaire and I want—"

"A Clyde to your Bonnie."

I risk giving Amelia a quick hug even though she's driving. Because yes, that's exactly what I want. And I can't have it.

I let her go and sigh. "I haven't even seen Ethan in days."

"Forget where he lives?"

I ignore her joke. "I told him about that night two years ago."

"What, he didn't know about the accident?" She quickly glances over at me before returning her eyes to the road. This is officially the worst time to be driving since it's impossible to position the visor to block the sun beaming from straight ahead and still see enough of the road to, you know, not kill people.

"No, he knows. I've just, never told him everything, from my point of view."

Her mouth opens as though to say, "Ah," but no sound comes out.

I bite down on my lower lip before releasing it along with the truth, the real reason I wish I could take back that conversation with him. "I said more than I meant to."

"Was he weird about it?" she asks in a super controlled voice.

"No, he was…" I trail off and the answer comes to me immediately. He was Ethan. He didn't understand—how could he?—but he wasn't angry or disgusted with me. He listened and then, of course, tried to explain why I was wrong, why my dad dying wasn't my fault. It was though, and I have to live with that fact. But I don't want it to change the way Ethan sees me too. "He wasn't weird at all. I just kinda got caught up in everything and I didn't handle telling him the way I should have."

At that, Amelie snorts, drawing my gaze. "Nothing," she says, when she feels me staring. "I mean it's not nothing. I was just thinking about when I told Mathias about…" With one hand she gestures at her body. "You know I used to cry every time I so much as thought about that day? Couldn't get a word out. Resented my sister for walking away from the car accident without a scratch. Resented everyone. I wasted so much time being angry, and yet, now, looking back at everything that has happened since…" Her hand settles on her belly. "I wonder what I would have missed out on." Then she steals a quick glance at me. "I wouldn't have gone into jewelry design. I was going to be a dancer. Did I ever tell you that? Ballet, become the next Misty Copeland, except for Latina girls. Anyway, God had other plans. Plans that involved opening my shop and meeting you, falling for a hipster artist and apparently bearing two of his children who will be taking ballet lessons whether they want to or not." Her laugh this time is warmer. "It's still hard, you don't need me to tell you that, but hard doesn't mean it can't also be good."

I nod like I understand everything she's saying, but I don't. I still only feel the hard most days. "Aren't hard and good the antithesis of each other?"

She's silent as we reach my neighborhood. I don't think she's going to answer me so I start to reach for my chair in the back seat as she pulls into my driveway, but she stops me with a hand on my arm.

"Hard and good can feel like two incompatible realities, but they aren't. My life is hard in ways I never could have imagined. But it's also amazing because I made a choice. My circumstances weren't going to change, so I had to, in here." She points at her chest and then reaches out to tap mine. "You can't wait until life isn't hard anymore to be happy."

CHAPTER TWENTY-EIGHT

NOW

REBECCA

I'm watching so I see the exact moment Ethan gets home the next day and I'm out the door, crossing the yard, before he can close his car door behind him.

"Hey," I say, but he's already seen me. His movements slow, giving me time to reach him.

"Hi."

I look down at the napkin I found on my window ledge and rub the paper between my fingers. "I didn't see this until today. When did you leave it?"

"Couple nights ago."

"It's beautiful."

He nods before glancing down at his boots and for the first time I notice they aren't solid black. The marks I'd dismissed as scuffs and wear are drawings. More flowers, figures I can't make out, and one that looks exactly like Old Man in an epic battle with a seagull. I want to wheel around and see the other sides but his words stop me. "But you like it?"

"I do." I'd only been half telling him the truth before when I said I hated the ones he left me when we were kids. They were beautiful, less skilled than this one, but even knowing what they signified—him leaving—I couldn't help but love them. "I kind of freaked out when I first saw it before I spotted the words."

"I'll never do that again," he says, staring intently at me. "Leave that way, I mean."

He'll still leave though. That's the part he's not saying out loud, but we both hear like a shout. I'm tempted to let the conversation drift into safe, neutral topics until we can both forget the discomfort that has lingered between us for the past few days, but I've been doing that too much lately and I owe him better than that. I let silence bloom up for only a moment before rooting myself and opening my mouth.

"I'm sorry about the other night," I say and at the same time he blurts, "So you and Neel have been hanging out more."

It's not like in the movies where we both laugh, instantly breaking the tension. Instead, we adopt matching frowns, waiting for the other to continue.

"Wait, you're sorry? For what?"

Embarrassment washes over me like an upended bucket of water. I don't look away though, no matter how much I want to. "For unloading all that stuff on you and then getting upset."

He stares at me for a long, uncomfortable moment. "What part of any of that do you need to apologize for?"

My brows draw more closely together. Why is he making me say this twice? "I just told you."

"Rebecca." He takes a step toward me, then seems to consider the fact that I might appreciate the distance between us in that moment. "I'm glad you said everything you did that night. I wondered—" He shakes his head sharply. "No, I wanted to know what you went through, what you thought and still think about everything. If anything, I'm the one who needs to apologize to you." He doesn't give me time to do more than blink before he rushes on. "I didn't know what you'd be like when I got back, but you were—" he stops here to kind of smile and let that sudden happiness trickle into his words "—kind of amazing with everything, from your jewelry to the way you adapted to swimming and driving and I'm sure a million other things that I haven't seen—can I say that? Is that…?"

I shake my head, dismissing his concern. Maybe from someone else those same words might feel patronizing but they don't from him. "No, it's fine."

"Right. Okay. So, I stopped there. I mean I knew you were probably still dealing with things, but I thought you were mostly okay. You acted like you were and I let myself believe it because it was easier, it was familiar. And then we jumped right into my stuff because that's what we do. Maybe we didn't talk about it as kids, but it was always there, my messed-up mom and messed-up life, filling up the space between us. I never left any room for anything else." He lets out a huff. "I never even thought to try, not really. Neel was the one who pushed me to look and see that maybe you weren't dealing as well as you want everyone to think."

"You talked to Neel about me?" I say it as though that's what I'm upset about and not the way his words are backing me into a corner I don't know how to escape from.

He doesn't let me bait him, and worse, he doesn't retreat.

"Yeah," he says, "And it still took me too damn long to get it. I didn't think about more than I could see in front of me and I should have." He inhales deeply and holds my gaze like a lifeline. "I know better than most people that the real scars, the deep ones, are always on the inside."

His words pierce through me like an arrow, right where I never want anyone to see. I feel my eyes threaten to well up but blinking fast will only betray that fact, so I try to brush his words—his stare—off. "No, it's fine. I'm fine. I just got caught up with things and memories and…" I smile as if to say, *See how fine I am?* "Anyway, let's just forget it, okay?"

"I'm trying to tell you that you don't have to be fine with me." He bends down so slowly that I don't even notice him moving until he's right in front of me. "Give me the hard and the hurt, all the messed-up shit you've been carrying these past few years." He's close enough now for me to see the pulse racing against his throat when he swallows. "The guilt? Nothing is heavier than that."

My hands drift to my push rims, ready to roll back, to reclaim physical distance when emotionally he's drawn way too close. "I had one bad night." My voice wobbles but I keep going. "Don't make it into this huge thing." I've been fighting to blink regularly, but I don't think he's blinked at all, not once, and it's like he's seeing everything, all my worst thoughts laid bare and raw. Almost to myself, I add, "This isn't why I came out here tonight."

He seizes on that. "Then what?" He moves closer, his gaze lighting all around my face before returning to my eyes. "Tell me, Bec, and I'll give it to you."

My breath catches and I'm grateful because otherwise, I'd have shouted out everything, all those quiet longings that I can't give words to.

"Tell me," he urges again, tugging lightly at my chair.

That moment spins out in front of me. All the things I could say without him pushing me away…and the ones that would make him pull me closer. I glance down at the napkin in my hand to see the flower and the words he left. I drag the side of my finger over the surprisingly soft paper, so at odds with the rough scars I feel inside, the ones he wants me to rip open, and I fold it closed again.

"I wanted to ask if you'd heard back from Bauer, or maybe someone else. Because I was thinking, maybe we should…" I trail off when I look up at Ethan and see the way he draws back, shoulders slumped and weary.

"Don't do that."

"What? It's important, right?"

"Yeah, it's important," he says, gaze locked and steady. "But it's not the only important thing. You're important and so is what you said the other night." His eyes soften as his lids lower slightly. "About it being your fault? You know that it wasn't… Rebecca, what happened to you and your dad was a stupid, tragic accident. You're not responsible for any of it."

He reaches for me again, *me*, not my chair, gripping my hands with aching gentleness. His touch may as well be laced with acid for all the comfort it gives me. Needles march along my skin, scratching up my arms and shooting through my veins. "Is that how you feel? About your mom? Will it be okay if something happens to her and you weren't there to stop it? Will you ever be able to believe someone saying it's not your fault?"

The softness in his face hardens, tightening his jaw before relaxing and I think finally I've pushed him too far and he'll leave the way he used to, but he doesn't move. Nothing so much as twitches when his flat, raspy answer comes out. "No, I'll never be able to believe that." When his hand moves toward my face, I almost flinch until he brushes his fingertips along my cheek. "But you'll still say it, won't you? *You* will say it? No matter what happens." His fingers tighten infinitesimally before he drops his hand. "Even if I never find her, and you know that I won't believe it, I'll need somebody who loves me to say it."

CHAPTER TWENTY-NINE

NOW

REBECCA

I wake up to an empty house the next morning and turn on the TV in order to let some morning talk show fill the house, chasing away all the memories of before, the good with the bad, while I contemplate if I have enough time to make an omelet before Amelia picks me up for work. I'm still considering when I notice a piece of mail left for me on the kitchen table.

I recognize it from across the room, a college brochure from Cal State Northridge. Mom must have signed me up for every possible mailer they have because I still get things like this nearly every other weekend.

Information for a college I've already been accepted to, one that's all the way on the coast, a school I don't want to go to because I don't want to go anywhere. I know what I want to do after I graduate and college isn't it.

After the accident I didn't care what my future looked like because most days I didn't care to live it. I was trapped in a broken body with a dead heart and a grave I couldn't bring myself to visit because I was the reason it existed. My existence became a routine of filling hours until I could pretend to sleep, wake up, and do it all over again. Mom made appointments for me, plans for me, and I went along because nothing mattered anymore. When she brought the application for Cal State Northridge, what difference did it make if I felt this way here or there? At least there would be better for her. She wouldn't have to come face-to-face every day with the person responsible for making her a widow. And I wouldn't have to keep hoping for the forgiveness we both knew I didn't deserve.

If she'd left it at that then maybe I'd have never realized that I wanted something different, that I could still want things in this life. But she didn't.

Vocational rehabilitation started out as just one more program she researched, one more thing to fill the hours. I'd met other wheelchair users in the hospital and rehab, they'd even sent a girl my age to visit me when they first transferred me out of the ICU. She was supposed to be encouraging, all smiles and optimism because she'd adapted her goals to her new life instead of abandoning them. But that wasn't what I remembered seeing. I saw a broken, paralyzed girl confined to a wheelchair. I saw a horror I had never imagined for myself and still hadn't reconciled with.

I didn't want to hear how I could be just like her if I wanted to, I wanted to go back. And if I couldn't, why in the hell would anyone think I'd want to go forward?

But when I got paired up with Amelia through voc rehab, she didn't care if I talked to her because she had no problem talking to me whether I answered or not. For weeks, Mom would drop me off at Amelia's shop and I barely said a word to her. I watched her work, listened to her words, saw her flirting with the artist painting her workshop, and I kept my mouth shut.

I did whatever Amelia told me to do, but I didn't ask questions or care if I did a good job. I didn't care period. And I kept on not caring right up until the day a girl only a handful of years older than me came into the shop with her parents. They'd had earrings made for her for graduation and she'd leaped into their arms when she saw them, hugging them so tightly, a perfect little trio of a family. She'd skipped away from them to admire the earrings on in the mirror before twirling back with a smile so radiant that I dropped the metal files I'd been sorting by size.

They clattered and clanged off the concrete floor, rolling in all directions, and before I could even think to go after them, the girl was flitting toward me. She bent this way and that as she came, easily scooping up the tools in seconds and setting them back on the table beside me. She said something nice, I think, something innocent before returning to her parents and leaving with them shortly after.

I didn't mean to cry and I didn't even know what part of it all ultimately sent the tears slipping down my cheeks, but Amelia saw them. Instead of coming over and offering the comfort that would have only made me feel worse, she kept working and let me cry.

When I finally got a hold of myself again, she called me over to her worktable and set down the crucible and blow torch she'd been using. When I reached her, she lifted the medallion necklace I was wearing and flipped it over to reveal the tiny 925 imprinted on the back. "Where'd you get this?"

I glanced down at it and shrugged. "Some antique store."

"So nobody special gave it to you? It's not an heirloom or anything?"

I shook my head then yelped when she yanked on it, breaking the clasp so she could drop it into her crucible. "You'll never learn to love the new life you've been given while you're still trapped in the idea of the old." She spooned something called flux on top of the necklace and then picked up her torch. "That's not your life anymore," she told me and turned the blue-white flame on my necklace, ignoring my protest. I watched the silver melt and liquefy in the bright orange fire and then she shifted and in one quick flick of her wrist, dumped the liquid metal over a bucket of frozen peas.

I had no idea I was watching my first rustic casting but I knew I was mesmerized by the organic-shaped silver item she drew from the peas. She filed down the sharp edges, soldered tiny rings onto each side, and after an acid bath and a dunk in water, added a chain. Then she had me lean forward and fastened it around my neck.

"It's time for you to start discovering that this new life, the only one you have, might still be worth making into something."

The necklace she made didn't look anything like the medallion pendant it had been. It didn't hang the same or catch the light as it once had. It had odd edges and holes, almost like a piece of coral, and the metal even felt different when I ran my fingers over it.

It wasn't the same and never would be again, but there was a beauty to it all its own.

The next day I asked Amelia to teach me how to do what she did. And I didn't just mean with jewelry.

I've made hundreds of pieces since that day, learning new techniques and methods for turning metal and stone into things that people pay me for. Forgiveness still doesn't seem like something I can give myself, but I don't want to view my life as a series of hours that have to be filled anymore. I want a chance to make something new, try or fail, good or remelt and try again, until maybe my life turns out to be worth something after all.

I still have so much to learn, and not just with jewelry, and here I have someone to teach me, someone who's as much a sister as she is a mentor. More than that, my dad is here and all the memories I'll ever make with him. I know what the grass here feels like under my bare feet and the way the Arizona sun warms my legs in the Kellys' pool. I know what it's like to run down these streets and grow up in this city with a boy who even now makes my heart pound.

I lost myself here and I'm only just starting to try and put myself back together.

But I don't see how I'll be able to do that hundreds of miles away in one of these glossy brochures my mom keeps leaving for me.

CHAPTER THIRTY

BEFORE

REBECCA

It's a neat trick trying to climb the ladder to my tree house holding Creamsicle popsicles from the ice cream truck, but Ethan and I manage. I suck in a deep, happy breath once we're up on the balcony. It's just big enough for Ethan and me to sit side by side with our legs dangling over the edge in the twilight.

The definition of perfect in my book.

And then it starts to rain, big, fat drops that plunk down on us. I lift my face up and close my eyes, drawing in that warm almost sweet scent that drifts up from the earth. "Petrichor."

Ethan hasn't drawn away from the rain either and raindrops run like tears down his face even as he smiles. "What?"

"That smell when it rains." I inhale deeply again, silently prompting him to do the same. "When everything is clean and wet and new. It's called petrichor. It's a perfect word for a perfect thing." I open my eyes and he looks all prismatic through the droplets weighing on my eyelashes and suddenly I shiver, a full-body tremor.

"Are you cold?" He draws one knee up, ready to stand and search for something inside the tree house for me.

I catch his hand instead and urge him to stay. His eyebrows pucker the slightest bit gazing at where our hands still touch. I kind of expect him to pull away. It's not that Ethan and I never touch, but it's usually messing around, maybe the occasional brief hug. Not quiet and still in the rain.

He doesn't pull away. And when I tap the back of his hand, he turns it over to curl his fingers around mine.

Petrichor-laced air rushes into my lungs making me feel the good kind of dizzy, the good kind of shivery. I think he knows I'm going to do it even before I do because when I lean toward him, he leans too.

Our lips are shy when they meet and somebody's forehead bumps into the other's but we don't pull back, we—both of us—press forward. He tastes bright and sugary sweet, a Creamsicle kiss that makes me smile against his mouth because I know that's what he's tasting too. I finished my popsicle long before him, so his lips are still chilled compared to mine, and there's sweetness in that too, the warmth and the cold, the rain dripping into our kiss.

That heat all surges to my cheeks when the kiss ends, and Ethan scrambles away from me.

He's moving toward the ladder before I hear it, that too-noisy muffler and the slamming door in his driveway. And then it's more than rain on my cheeks, because even kissing me, Ethan had been listening for her, ready to leave.

CHAPTER THIRTY-ONE

NOW

ETHAN

When I get home from work the next day, I don't even stop off at my room to check on Old Man before heading to the backyard and hoping that she'll already be there. My skin warms from the sight of Rebecca in the pool even before I step out into the fading sunlight.

I linger by the bougainvillea and watch her for a moment. She comes over to swim most days, but after last night I'd felt this uneasy twinge all day that she might want to avoid me. I said some heavy stuff and so did she. I'm not sure where we pick up from there, but she's been filling more and more of my thoughts lately and I'm okay with her filling more.

She spots me then and gives me that smile, the one I caught last night when she was gazing at the flower I drew her, and I have my shirt off before the invitation has fully left her lips.

I surface from my running dive and shake my long hair back, inadvertently spraying her.

"Nice," she says, wiping the stray water droplets from her eyes.

I draw closer, closer than I normally do and she backs up a little to compensate. "Sorry. Long hair problems."

"Try shaking-your-hair-like-a-dog problems."

"You want me to cut it?"

"No," she says too quickly, causing my mouth to quirk up. I know she likes my hair. She's touched it more than a few times and never makes up an excuse like grabbing a stray flower petal or anything. I like that about her. "What's that line from the Bible? A man's hair is his crowning glory?" She flicks a tiny spray of water at me.

"I think that's women's hair." It should be about hers at any rate. Right now she has her curls piled up in a bun on the top of her head with little wet tendrils clinging to her neck. Hers is still blue, but it's faded more than mine so she looks like some kind of water nymph.

"You think? Don't they teach you that in church?"

I lift one shoulder out of the water, still studying the curve of her neck. "For some reason, the pastor is always going on about stuff like the atonement and justification instead of focusing on hair."

She makes a *tsking* sound. "You should really talk to somebody about that."

I drift a little closer and she retreats as much until she bumps into the edge of the pool and uses a hand to hold herself steady without needing to constantly move her arms.

"You know there's a whole lot of pool besides this exact corner I'm in."

Yeah but where else would I want to be?

That thought hits me hard and I come to a stop so suddenly it makes a little wave in the water.

Needing to get back to my mom feels like a tight fist clenching in my chest.

Wanting to be with Rebecca is like that fist letting go.

Not because she needs me, but because I want her.

She'd been smiling at me, but when I don't move away, it falters. "Ethan, what are you doing?"

I have no idea. What am I doing? "Swimming." I can see her breathing pick up in that moment as though she can tell something has irrevocably shifted for me and I swear, *I swear*, her gaze drops to my lips for a fraction of a second before she jerks it away.

"Fine. If this corner is so important to you…" She ducks below the water and swims around me before resurfacing several feet away. "There. Problem solved."

Not for me, not at all.

She glances over at me. "Why do you keep looking at me like that?"

"How am I looking at you?"

She frowns. "Different."

"I've been looking at you this way my whole life." I just didn't realize it until now. I almost kissed her the other day when we dyed our hair. We'd been close and she'd been beautiful, and I remembered how she tasted like Creamsicles. But when she broke the moment, I let myself get distracted. I know the same thing's not gonna happen now. I don't see how it could ever happen again.

I swim a few feet toward her, mindful to still leave plenty of distance between us.

"No," she says, curiosity lifting her voice. "This is something new."

"And?"

"I don't know if it's good or bad."

I grin at her. I can't seem to stop. "Oh, it's definitely good. You should try it."

Her smile is puzzled. "You're acting like you've got a secret."

I cross to the side of the pool where she left her wheelchair and lift myself up until I'm sitting on the edge. I squint at her then shake my head. "Come over here and I'll tell you."

She sighs and the bottom half of her face submerges. When she fully surfaces, her smile is gone, taking mine along with it.

"What's up?" I ask.

"This is nice, swimming with you."

"Yeah…?"

"But I had a not-great day and I'm thinking maybe I should be by myself for a while."

I hesitate because a not-great day could mean so many things. I know there's something going on with her mom. Beyond what Neel implied, finding out her mom apparently moved offices without telling her means there are definitely issues there. Or maybe she's just dealing with all the stuff I keep making her dredge up. "I'll go if you want, or we can just swim and not say a word."

"Or?" she says, because she can tell I'm not done.

"We can try that thing we sucked at as kids?"

She ducks her head to hide a teasing smile before meeting my gaze again. "Kissing, you mean?"

"That's not what I meant." My mouth kicks up into a half

smile. "And since when did our kiss suck? I don't remember hearing any complaints."

Her smile turns sad. "That's 'cause you left right after."

I have no response to that. That was the first time I even mentioned the idea of staying longer to my mom. She hadn't taken it well.

"I'm sorry," she offers. "I don't know why I keep saying stuff like that. I know you had no choice and even if you did, of course you had to go with your mom." Then she lets out a huff of air. "Like I said, I'm not in a good headspace right now. I should probably just go."

"Or," I prompt even though she was clearly done talking, "you could tell me what's bugging you today."

She glances quickly toward her house and sinks a little lower in the water. "I don't think that's a great idea."

"Why, because I'm the only one who's allowed to have problems with their mom?" I take a guess and it turns out to be right, based on the way she starts. "Is it about her moving offices?"

She shakes her head, in response or just not wanting to talk to me about this, I don't know. I could keep pushing and maybe she'd crack like she had before, but I'm not interested in another forced confession so I hold my breath and wait until she decides to lift herself up to sit beside me.

"I'm supposed to go to college." Her gaze darts to me; she tries to hold it but can't. "My mom picked out a school for me all the way in California, as far as she can reasonably send me..." Her voice trails off.

California. That fist tries to tighten around my chest again before releasing. It's a big state and I have no idea what school she's talking about, but there's a chance that we could actually be close to each other, close enough that none of this stuff with my mom would matter. But even as that flicker of happiness hits me, I see how unhappy the thought makes Rebecca. I know how she feels about everything she's building here, the job that she loves... She can't give that all up.

"Can't you—can't you tell your mom you don't want to go?" I know it must not be that simple but I don't understand why. "I mean, not everybody has to go to college."

"I do," she says, her voice soft and heavy.

"But why—"

Rebecca's eyes are shining when she looks at me, silently saying words that can't possibly be true.

"No," I say. "I know you feel like what happened to your dad was your fault, but nobody else does."

"Doesn't she?" When she speaks it's in a voice so hoarse it sounds painful. "She only comes home to sleep and she's gone every morning before I wake up. I had no idea she moved her office and every other week there's something new in the mail from Cal State Northridge. We never even talked about it, but for almost a year now she's been telling everybody I'll be moving there as soon as summer's over."

"Maybe she's got some other reason. I mean, what if—"

"She hasn't hugged me. Not once since he died." Rebecca presses her eyes shut and a fat tear drips down her cheek before she can dash it away. "How can I stay when she wants me gone?"

Rebecca's mom worked a lot when we were younger. I guess her dad did too, but he always seemed around, invested. He was the one who drove us places, showed us how to make giant pillow forts, and helped with school projects. I always thought that was because he was a teacher, but it was more than that. Rebecca's mom is there in a lot of my memories, but almost as a spectator, like someone watching a game they didn't know how to play. I thought she would have changed after the accident, or at least tried. But if her answer to all the tragedy was just to pull away more than Rebecca shouldn't be the one to suffer for it.

"Then move out. Get a place here. She can't force you out of the state." But even before Rebecca shakes her head I know she can. Because Rebecca thinks her mom is right to blame her, right to want her as far away as possible, and no amount of angry, hurried words from me is going to change any of that in one night.

"So yeah," she says. "Not a great day. Hence the swimming." Then she looks over at me. "And hence you too. I don't want to cry anymore, but I needed my friend."

I drop my gaze from hers so she won't see…whatever the hell is going on inside me from her words and must be radiating through my skin. "Well, you have me, you know. Cry or swim or anything."

Her answer is very serious, and almost sad? "You know it's okay if I don't always have you, right? Like right here, right now, no one is forcing you to promise more than that."

I flinch at her words. "What does that mean?"

"It means…" She flounders, searching for the right words. "It means people should want—I," she quickly amends, "—I want good things for you and your future, whether I'm one of those things or not." Her eyes flick back and forth between mine, the setting sun catching the tiny flecks of green in her blue eyes. Every movement hits me harder and harder as her meaning sinks in.

"How could you not be a good thing?" Even hundreds of miles and more days apart than I ever want to put between us again, that's never changed and it's the one thing I know never will. "You're the best thing. Rebecca…you're—"

My gaze drops purposefully, intensely, to her mouth and I hear her soft sudden inhale as I lean in to kiss her.

CHAPTER THIRTY-TWO

NOW

ETHAN

Rebecca's hand finds my chest and she shoves just before my lips touch hers, sending me toppling into the pool.

When I surface all her features are pinched together in shock. Before I take a single stroke back toward her, she's scooting down a foot to where she left her wheelchair and lifting her legs out of the water.

"Wait, you're leaving now? We're not even going to talk about it?"

The glare she shoots at me halts me dead in the water. "Talk? Is that what you did?"

"I thought you wanted me to kiss you!"

She pauses, her knees drawn up to her chest with her arms bent on the lounger behind her, ready to lift herself up. A look of pain flashes across her face before she hardens it again. "You're not staying!"

"Yeah, but—"

She's moving again, up on the lounger in record time and

reaching to throw her towel over her wheelchair. "There's no but, Ethan."

"Okay, I'm sorry, I'm sorry. Just stop for one second." She's moving too fast and I still don't understand what was so wrong about kissing her when she wanted to kiss me as much as I wanted to kiss her…she did, right? I'm wrong about so much all the time but I can't be wrong about her… I can't.

"You think I wouldn't stay if I could? That if I ever had a single choice in my entire life it wouldn't be you?" I scoff, half laughing through the sound. "I don't get to choose anything except right now, with you. Why can't that be enough?"

She hesitates before transferring into her chair, finally giving me a look that doesn't feel like a blow. "See, that's a question you should be asking *before* you try and kiss me."

I scramble out of the pool. "You're right, I shouldn't have tried to kiss you when I don't know what's going to happen tomorrow, but I wasn't thinking about that in the pool just now."

She turns her head and laughs. "That's your answer? You weren't thinking?"

"I may be the high school dropout over here, but yeah. The truth seemed like a good idea to me." My chin hits my chest, and I sigh before I can meet her gaze again. "I don't know what I'm saying except I wanted to kiss you and I thought you wanted that too." Her cheeks flush red and I know that at least part of her wanted exactly what I did. "It's different now, from when we were kids. I couldn't see it at first, but it's the only thing I can see now."

Her voice is like a whisper. "What is?"

It's now or never. "You and me," I say, as her eyes slowly

shutter closed. "And okay, yeah, my timing sucks. I should have said something sooner, but as we've established, I'm not that smart—"

"Stop it," she says, voice still soft, so that's something in my favor. "I hate when you do that. You're not stupid. Not even a little bit."

Then why do I feel so dumb right now?

"It doesn't change anything, you know?" she says. "That part will always be the same, just like when we were kids. You come and it's good, better than good. But every time you leave it hurts so much more. This?" She gestures between us. "Is just going to make it worse. It's not fair to me. It's not fair to you either. Can't you see that?"

My spine stiffens. "So I'm not capable of seeing things like you are?"

She rapid blinks. "No, you're used to giving your whole self up for another person. You don't know how to let go even when it hurts you. I'm not going to let you do that for me." She lowers her gaze to her lap and there's a long, long moment of silence before she says anything.

And it's not what I want her to say.

She doesn't tell me she's been feeling the same way.

She doesn't promise that we'll find a way.

She doesn't ask me to kiss her again.

"Ethan." And just from the way she says my name, I know it's over.

CHAPTER THIRTY-THREE

NOW

REBECCA

I press my palms to my hot cheeks the moment I close my back door and no longer feel Ethan's gaze on me.

He never even stood up after I told him no.

After I told him I didn't feel that way about him, that I couldn't, and that if friendship wasn't enough for him then I didn't think we should continue to be in each other's lives.

My hands slide down to my mouth and I let a finger trace my bottom lip, trying to bring back the memory of his kiss.

What would this one have been like? Nothing like the fumbling earnest moment in my tree house years before. Nothing like the way I've imagined countless times since he came back.

It would have been infinitely more bittersweet.

Sweet because I knew it was coming, that he saw me and wanted me the way I haven't dared to let myself believe he could, and because it would have been perfect. That soft but firm press of his lips, the warmth from his hand on my jaw, that fluttery, fizzy euphoria that sparked from his touch along every nerve ending I had, even the ones I no longer felt...

Bitter because I couldn't let it happen.

Sometimes I feel like Ethan can't see past his own problems. But he's also kind and self-sacrificing and he tries to do the right thing even when he doesn't know what it is. He loves so fiercely it's almost scary, scary because I think he might try to give me what I absolutely refuse to take from him. Something hot and sharp ignites at that thought.

How could he do that, try to kiss me and say all that to me? How could he forget the fact that I'm helping him find his mom so he can leave to rescue her again? He'll go, just like he does every time, only now it'll be his choice. Maybe he'll have sweeter words than he has in the past, a goodbye kiss and an empty promise to return.

Or worse, he'll stay. We'll find her and he'll rip himself apart trying to figure out which of us he has to halt his life for.

I brush the beginning of tears away, digging my fingertips in harder with each pass. It won't be me. I promise that. I'll never—

"Rebecca?"

"Um, yeah, it's me," I call out in answer to my mom.

I wheel farther into the house, then literally skid to a stop in the living room. My mom is there and so is John, in a suit. And about a million red roses. So many.

"What—" But I don't finish asking the question because I see it then. Beyond the formal wear and the petals. The glittering diamond on my mom's ring finger.

She glances away when my shocked gaze lifts to hers, her

right hand twitching as though she wants to cover the left, but then John moves between us.

"I wanted to talk to you about this so many times, but then I realized I wasn't just asking your mom to have me, I was asking you too." He reaches back for my mom's hand, the one newly weighted down with his ring, and brings her back to his side. "I want us to be a family, your mom and me, and you and Layla." His hand slides into the pocket of his slacks and I feel a revulsion slam over me so fast I nearly throw up when he pulls out a black velvet box and hands it to me.

"I'm sure you could make something better, but Amelia said you liked opals—"

"You talked to Amelia about this?"

John nods and I open the box to reveal a pair of raw opal studs that match the ring I'd made.

A tear splashes into the box.

"You like them?" John's grin is clear in his voice and he sighs, gazing at my mom. "I was nervous. Most guys just need one yes, here I am asking for two."

"You said yes, then?" I'm still staring at the earrings, but my mom knows I'm talking to her.

"I did."

All at once I see the future rush up and knock the wind out of me. I'll be gone and John will be here to answer the phone when I call, and sign the birthday cards. Or maybe they'll move, somewhere far away from me and the memories of what I took from her.

"Rebecca?"

I blink up at her.

"John wants to ask you a question." She glances over at her fiancé and I die a little more inside.

"So, what do you say? Will you let me become part of your family?" His smile is so eager, so confident. He can't begin to fathom the way I'm drowning inside. There's no family to join here.

I don't try to stop the tears, and he misunderstands them anyway, dropping to a knee to hug me when I nod, wet swimsuit and all.

But my mom knows. She has to.

"Can I talk to you for just a second? Alone?" I don't wait for my mom's response before turning toward the kitchen. She'll come even if John's the one who makes her.

"I thought you'd be happy for us," she says, walking around to face me. Unlike her fiancé, she knows why I'm really crying.

"Is this what you need? Will he make you happy?"

She blinks at me. "He's different from Dad, but I do love him."

I glance down at the black velvet box. "I like him too."

I'm not looking at her but I can feel a weight lift off her shoulders. "I know. I've never been—" she flounders for a word "—like Dad was, but John has that way to him." She pushes her shoulders back. "And he doesn't mind how I am, doesn't see me as cold. He thinks I'm enough and he doesn't mind filling in the gaps."

"Like filling in the gaps with me?" I say, my voice sounding pained from squeezing it through my tight throat.

"I always try to give you what you need, what's best for you. I don't know how to be that on my own."

She's not expecting me to shake my head.

"What?" She catches herself and lowers her voice, coming closer to me. "What does that mean?"

It means that she never even tried after Dad died. And now with John, she thinks he can be her excuse not to have to.

"It means congratulations, Mom."

CHAPTER THIRTY-FOUR

NOW

ETHAN

I wake up the next morning to a splitting headache from not sleeping and a missed call from Bauer. A week ago, I'd have dived for the phone, frantic for the possibility of news about my mom. But now I just stare down at the screen.

She never called me when she was gone. It was always all or nothing, silence until she showed up. Is that what she's planning to do again this time? Knock on the door one day and tell me to get my stuff? And I'll have to go because I always do. Last night my eyes snapped open every time I tried to shut them because Rebecca was right. Wanting things to be different doesn't change anything. But she's wrong too. I'm not a kid getting bounced back and forth between my mom and grandparents. I'm done letting them do that. Back then all I wanted was to protect my mom, but I want something else now too. Something I'm done walking away from.

So I won't go. When my mom shows up again promising a fresh start, I'll make mine too, and it won't be with her.

The headache almost recedes for as long as it takes to revel in that huge decision for myself, but surges back the second I try to set the phone aside without hearing Bauer's message. My whole life I've lived with fear and worry for her and wanting to stop those feelings from ruling me isn't the same as being able to. I squeeze the phone so tight I expect hairline cracks to slice across the screen when I tap to play the voicemail:

"Hey, kid. Checking in to see if you've heard anything about Joy. I put some more feelers out but nothing yet. Hoping you had better luck. Let me know. Also you reading anything good? I owe you a shit ton of amends and I was thinking I could send you some books or a bike! You said I never sold yours but I feel like I did and—"

I stop the voicemail and toss my phone on the bed before swearing a little too loudly into my hands.

A second later there's a knock at my door. "Ethan?" Concern touches my grandmother's voice. "Everything okay?"

"I'm fine!" I smother a groan before adding that I just have a headache and hope she'll go away.

No such luck. A minute later she knocks again. "I brought you some aspirin."

"I don't like pills," I tell my closed door. "Of any kind."

There's a moment of silence, then, "Could you please open the door?"

My head throbs as I stand. If she'd pounded her fist or given me an order, I'd have kicked my feet up and not even bothered to answer, but I can't ignore that simple request no matter how much I'd like to.

I walk back to the bed after opening the door and sit down without looking to see if she followed. But then the mattress dips beside me and her cool hand brushes the hair back from my forehead. I pull away from the touch leaving her raised hand and pained expression hovering between us.

"You understand there's a difference though." She lowers her hand to the tiny white bottle she's holding. "Taking medicine for a headache isn't the same as…" She trails off and I'm not sure if she's trying to be sensitive for my sake or she'd rather not think of all the ways she could finish that sentence.

"It all starts somewhere," I tell her. I'm sure my mom started with popping painkillers too. I don't know when she stepped up to snorting OxyContin, morphine, and Dilaudid, but I know it all led to her on the floor of our apartment with a needle between her toes because I would notice new track marks on her arms. "I'm choosing not to start at all."

My grandmother's light brown eyes pass over my face before she sighs. "I'm sorry."

"For what?" Her words force me to pull back even more than her touch.

"Making you come here when we did. We should have let you stay a day or two, maybe gotten to visit her."

"That's what you're sorry for?" I say, my jaw hardening. "You took me away my entire life, why should this time be any different?" I glance down at her painkillers. "You know she gave me stuff a lot stronger than that when I got hurt as a kid. One time she even—" I break off when I look up and see my grandmother's face has gone as white as my sheets.

I fall silent. I'd wanted to hurt her, cause her a little of the pain she and my grandfather had caused me, but I didn't think about how it would feel to actually do it.

"It was only a couple of times. And always near her rock

bottom where she realized she needed to bring me to you guys. And I'm fine," I add, when, if anything, more color leaches from her face with every new word I say. "I've never touched anything on my own and I never will."

She starts crying then, soft, pitiful sounds that give way to body-wracking sobs. The aspirin bottle slips from her fingers and rolls across the floor toward the doorway.

My grandfather comes charging into my room then, eyes his crying wife and me sitting block still beside her. I scramble up off the corner of the bed when he swoops forward, but he doesn't spare more than a glance in my direction. She turns into his shoulder, crying harder when he pulls her into his arms.

"Should have… What did we do?" she says through broken sobs. "So wrong…so wrong."

I don't know what to do so I stay pressed against the wall as I move toward the door, grabbing only my phone before hurrying down the hall and outside.

CHAPTER THIRTY-FIVE

NOW

REBECCA

We have to wait a few days after the engagement until it's John's weekend with his daughter before we can all get together and...celebrate.

John made sure to pick a place that had plenty of clearance under the tables because he's never forgotten the restaurant with the pedestals so thick that I couldn't get within a foot of the table.

He's a kind man, sweet to my mom and me both. I should be grinning right alongside Layla as they talk about plans for the wedding and all the ways we're going to blend our two families together.

"It's all happening so fast," I say when my mom mentions the date for the wedding that's barely a month away.

"Well, we've both done this before." John gives my mom a sheepish grin. "And I don't want to wait any longer than I have to before I can start calling your mom my wife. We can get rings, a dress, and a license in that time. Why draw it out?"

I glance over at my mom to make sure she's on board with the timetable John's proposing and she seems fine, nodding along with him.

"Oh, we could do our own version of *House Hunters*," John says. "Narrow down our top three picks with pros and cons. My must-haves are that it be close to Layla's mom's and not too far from my work. What about you, Bug?"

Layla pauses in the act of carefully coloring a picture on her kid's menu to answer him. "Me and Bec want a pool, right?" She beams up at me, her big brown eyes made adorably owlish behind her glasses.

That suffocating feeling I've had since the engagement eases a bit. Layla isn't big on getting wet. Sometimes I can coax her into swimming with me, but for almost everyone else she'll smile and say no thank you. She knows I get to be free in the water in a way I can't be anywhere else and that's reason enough for her to want a pool too.

I pull her into a tight hug just as my mom says, "We don't need a new house or a big wedding. We can have a small backyard ceremony before Rebecca leaves for college and then Layla can have her room."

Layla frowns at my mom for just a second when my arms go stiff around her, but then her face lights up. "Then we can get bunk beds! For when Bec is here. And I'll sleep on the top because she's in a wheelchair and it'll be like having a sleepover all the time. Oh, and we can put star stickers on the ceiling like the constellations." She gets a faraway look on her face as though she's imagining it all. "We'll put star stickers on the underside of my bed for you too," she assures me.

Oh no, we will not. I'd once put stickers on my mom's antique china cabinet and can still remember the absolute horror on her face when she saw them. I'd had to spend hours with oil-soaked cotton pads picking each one off with my fingernails.

But then Layla turns to my mom. "We can get the kind we saw at Michaels that peel off without damaging any surfaces." She says that last part very carefully like she's reciting someone else's words. It only takes me a moment to realize they are my mother's.

"That's a very smart idea." My mom smiles at Layla. "But Rebecca is going to be very busy. She probably won't be able to visit much. What other ideas do you have?"

Layla launches into a million thoughts she has for my room after that and her excitement distracts John from my utter and complete silence through the rest of the meal and the drive home.

"Dinner was nice," Mom says now as she puts our leftover boxes in the fridge. She pauses when she notices the extra weight in mine. "You didn't eat much. Are you not feeling well? Because I can call Dr.—"

"Just a big lunch," I say, watching her move around the kitchen. *Look at me*, is what I don't say but scream inside my head. *Look at me and see, please.* "Mom—"

"Oh, I forgot to mention that John's sister wants to plan an engagement party in a couple of weeks. We're thinking the twenty-third. I'll put it on the calendar so don't make plans, okay?" Her eyes glide right over me when she turns to leave, a quick smile on her face. "Night."

There's a breeze of woodsy perfume as she passes me and a minute later the sound of her shower.

My shoulders hunch in, but I don't make a noise until I'm out the back door, halfway down the path connecting my yard to the Kellys'. I clamp both hands over my mouth to trap the scream that erupts from inside me. I only stop when someone clears their throat from the shadows to my right.

"It's just me." Ethan straightens from beside a bush and pushes his hair back to reveal his face.

"What are you doing?" My voice is only a little raspy, but it's enough to send heat to my cheeks, not just because he's witnessed my private scream fest, but because we haven't seen each other in days.

Ethan shuffles forward a step until he's fully in the moonlight. "Old Man's been savaging a gecko out here—well, trying—and I finally had to break them apart." He nods his chin and I turn to find the cat throwing death glares at Ethan. "Hey, man, if you couldn't kill him in ten minutes," he says, raising and directing his voice to the deeply resentful Old Man, "then, you can't really blame me that he got away, can you?"

I study the cat for a lot longer than necessary. He's a nice distraction while I try to figure out what note I'm supposed to strike here: super casual ignoring the last time we talked, or awkward and uncomfortable because I have no idea where we stand. I settle on a casual response said in an uncomfortable tone. "He looks like he's going to pee on your bed later."

Ethan nods. "Oh, he's for sure going to piss everywhere." His voice rises again. "And then he's gonna be sleeping outside for the week. That's right. And then you can forget about getting any of those little freeze-dried liver treats either. Yeah, think about that," he adds when the cat stalks off.

Ethan turns his attention to me then and I hold my breath when he walks closer. I haven't changed my mind about what I said to him by the pool; he wants too much, but what if, to him, I can't offer enough?

Will he give me an actual goodbye like he promised but take off all the same?

"So what's your excuse?"

I glance up at him. "For being outside or for screaming?"

"Screaming?" He raises his eyebrows. "I thought you were singing. And don't take this the wrong way, but I think you should stick to making jewelry."

My next breath turns shaky because if my mom has her way, I'll soon be hundreds of miles away from the shop I love.

Ethen is suddenly right beside me. "I just said the wrong thing, didn't I?" He swears softly under his breath, then half squats beside me. "I know we haven't talked in a few days and for all I know you might still be mad at me—"

"I wasn't really mad at you."

He rocks his head from side to side and makes kind of an *eeeeee* sound in the back of his throat. "Agree to disagree. But you were always good at knowing when I needed a hug and I feel like you need one right now. So...here's your chance to move away if you don't."

Maybe I was mad, but right now all I feel is sad. So I don't move back when he leans in, wrapping me in his arms.

"It was so much easier when we were kids, wasn't it? Running away from our problems and hiding in my tree house?"

From over Ethan's shoulder, I look up. "It felt like nothing bad could ever happen when it was just the two of us up there."

My hold loosens on Ethan and he eases back, one hand coming up to push a curl of my hair back from my face. It's so sweet it makes my chest hurt. "You know that's not true."

My gaze stays locked on the tree house. "But it felt like that." And it's still there, right there and yet it might as well be a million miles away from me. "There are a lot of things I miss about my life before, but that one—" my gaze roves over every board "—that's one I still dream about."

Ethen pivots on his heel, following my gaze, then returns it to me. "Why just dream?"

I actually don't understand until he starts assessing me. "What?"

"I could toss you over my shoulder, you know, carry you up fireman style. Probably not the most comfortable for you though." Still studying me, he rakes a hand through his hair. "We could piggyback it, but with just your arms around my neck. You might end up strangling me, but—" he cocks his head from side to side "—it could work."

"Ethan, there's no way."

"I just gave you two ways. Oh, oh!" A grin lights up his face in the moonlight. "I could just carry you, like regular, except with one arm under your knees and the other on the plank ladder. You'd have to hold on too, but that should work."

I'm about to object again, but I think he might be right. Again. I think we could do it just like he says. That I could go up to my tree house for the first time since my accident. And I want that, I want it enough to say, "Okay."

"Yeah?" Ethan's smile grows. "Okay then. Where do you—"

But I'm already moving closer to the tree, bumping down off the path and onto the grass until my chair is right up against the trunk. Then I lock my wheels.

Ethan looks a little nervous when he approaches me. "If you're uncomfortable at any moment, promise you'll say something."

"And if you feel like you're going to drop me at any moment, promise *you'll* say something."

That was apparently the key to releasing Ethan's nerves because he laughs. And then he's bending over me, sliding an arm around my back and under my knees, lifting me as easily as breathing. "I will never let you go."

Yeah, I think, *that's exactly why I shouldn't let you hold on to begin with.*

"Ready?"

I nod, securing my arms around his neck and bringing our faces closer than…closer than they've been since we almost kissed.

"Up we go."

CHAPTER THIRTY-SIX

NOW

ETHAN

Okay, so it isn't the easiest thing in the world climbing up a bunch of wooden planks nailed into a tree with a girl in my other arm. I'm able to grab rungs with the hand under her legs, but mostly I'm pulling with my free hand since she's holding on so tight with both of hers. But it is something I'd do a million times over again to see the look on her face once she's sitting up there.

I sit down next to Rebecca and squeeze my legs under the balcony railing to dangle beside hers. "I remember this being bigger."

"Feels exactly the same to me." She takes a deep breath, smiling as she lets it out, and turns to give me a once-over. "You're the one who's gotten bigger."

"Thirteen-year-old me would have had a hard time carrying you up here."

She nods. "Thirteen-year-old me wouldn't have needed you to."

Shit. "Sorry, that was a stupid thing to say."

She shakes her head. "It's okay. I'm just…thank you for doing this for me. It feels really good." She laughs a little. "All I'm missing is the rain."

"And the petrichor?"

She turns a beaming smile my way. "You remember that?"

I duck my head. "Pretty memorable day."

"Hmmm," she says, her smile softening.

"You know that was my first kiss."

She laughs a little. "Um, yeah."

I angle my head at her, my mouth curled up on one side. "That obvious, huh?"

She bobs her head in a slow, exaggerated nod. "Oh yeah."

"Like you'd kissed a ton of guys before me." My smile falters. "Wait, had you? Who? And don't say what's-his-name from up the street, the kid with the faux hawk, because—"

More laughter bubbles up from her, infectious and giddy. "Are you kidding? No. Never. Uh-uh. No way."

"Okay then who?"

Biting the side of her thumbnail, she angles her head at me. "I knew I was your first kiss too."

"You knew it, huh?"

"Well." I shrug. "You did kiss me first."

"Only because if I hadn't you would have left again before we got the chance." The tiniest hint of bitterness creeps into her voice and we both feel it.

"Yeah." I nod. "Probably. Took me a few more years to realize waiting on the things I want isn't a great life choice."

She turns to look out at the night sky and then behind her into the tree house. "We still have one blank wall up here.

You were going to come back with a sketch for us to paint, but you never did."

I don't bother looking back with her. I know every inch of that tree house and have drawn it more times than I'll ever admit. "I tried," I tell her. "I'm still trying."

Rebecca wraps an arm around herself.

"Did I hurt you? Climbing up?"

She shakes her head, and I can see effort behind the motion when she lowers her arm. "I just never thought I'd be up here again."

"Yeah, but you're glad, right? Petrichor and everything?"

Her mouth pulls to the side, but it's not really a smile. Slowly, her arm creeps back up around her middle. "I don't get to be just glad about anything anymore. Am I happy sitting in my tree house again? Yes. Am I also thinking about the fact that I can't swing my legs back and forth or jump up and trace the mural of the moon in the top corner behind me? Or that I can't get rope burn from shimmying down the knot ladder in the back later?"

I glance at her legs, still beside my swaying ones. I hadn't even realized I was moving them.

"It's not just this, now," she adds. "It's all the time. Every new thing I figure out how to do again. It's always chased by the thought that I shouldn't have to adapt to anything, that before, everything was easy. I could just decide and move, do anything." She glances over at me. "Kiss my friend just because I wanted to."

"In case I didn't make it clear the other day by the pool, you can still do that." I was hoping that line would make her smile but it doesn't.

Her hands move up to tangle in her thick curls. "I have to overthink everything, all the time. Like will my wheelchair fit through that door? Is there a step to get into that store? Does that restaurant have an accessible bathroom or do I have to not drink for hours? When was the last time I did a weight shift? Does my head hurt because I have a headache or is it autonomic dysreflexia starting to cause my body to overreact because I can't feel something that's hurting me?" She cuts off only to suck in a breath. "Only I can't ever let myself think too much because this is my life, this wheelchair, this body, forever. And thinking about never moving my legs again, never walking or dancing or feeling or any of it ever again is a spiral, and it's deep and dark and I end up falling forever."

I swallow, unsure of what to say, to do.

"It's just really hard sometimes, even when I want to be happy…" Her voice breaks and something inside me does too. "I don't get to choose anymore." A moment passes and with a sigh, she frees her hands from her hair. "I swear I never say stuff like this out loud."

But she did with me. That has to mean something. "Why not?"

She tries to smile but doesn't quite make it. "Because it makes people feel bad. It makes me feel bad."

I turn that over in my mind. "Wanting things to be easier for someone isn't the same as feeling bad."

"Isn't it?" Her eyes bore into mine. "You can't change my life so how does it help you to know any of this?"

I stare back almost frowning. "It's not about me. Knowing how you feel does help me though." And before she can scoff at that, I shift my foot until it's tucked behind hers so that it's not just my leg swaying anymore, it's ours together.

Her chin quivers just once before she can look away.

"Hey, hey." My voice stays gentle, but she keeps her face hidden from me even as I lean out. "You can always tell me when it's hard and I'll understand." There's another long pause and I hope she hears me, really hears me. "'Cause I know, you know?" I shake my head. "I mean I can't know what it's like, but I know that feeling, not getting to choose? I know that."

She dips her head, not facing me but not fully hiding away anymore either. "I know you do."

I wait until her gaze slowly meets mine. "You were the only happy part of my childhood. Leaving each time? That was awful. I was scared that she'd start using again, scared the wrong guy would end up in our lives, scared that I'd never get to come back here or that if I did, you'd have moved on."

Rebecca's eyes have gone wide. This isn't new information...so why is she looking at me like it is?

"You always acted like you were glad when she came back," she says softly.

"Yeah, I was. 'Cause she always came back clean. But I never wanted to go with her. I wanted her to stay with me." I look away. It feels cowardly but I can't stare at her face when I add, "So I could stay with you."

The air shifts around us, shrinks somehow, and my skin feels like it's constricting too, forcing me to move and twitch. Did she really not know? Hadn't I told her in every way I could?

She doesn't say anything, but I feel her beside me, moving slowly, closer until her head drops onto my shoulder.

"You could, you know. This time you could make your own choice."

I focus on that slight weight, the feel and scent of her. I've been doing that in my mind for days now, imagining finding my mom and telling her that I'm not going back with her. Building a life of my own here and knowing that the next time I kiss Rebecca, neither of us has to let go.

But that fantasy future keeps colliding with the reality I'm still trapped in. Because I already know what happens when I make the wrong choices. I don't even have to call up the memory of finding my mom on the floor, slumped over in a dried-up pile of sick with that needle still stuck in her skin. My mind serves it up on an endless damning loop.

And even if I could choose a different future, or find a way to change it, I'm not the only one who has to choose.

"Will you?" I say, brushing the hair back from her face.

She pulls away then and her gaze trails back to mine before turning soft, almost sad. "I want to." Her lip quivers just once, drawing my gaze and with it the sudden awareness that we're closer than we were in the pool the other day. I can feel her breath, warm and almost sweet on my skin. I'd barely have to move to kiss her. And this time I could wrap my arms around her and pull her against me, feel her chest rise and fall with mine. I could taste her and…

"Would you really choose to stay?"

Her breath catches as I move that fraction of an inch toward her. "Would you?" she asks.

"If I could choose any moment, it would be this one." My fingers slide up her arm and revel in the tiny goose bumps I'm leaving in my wake. If I kiss her now, it has to be different

I have to find a way and she does too. My hand brushes over her bare shoulder to the underside of her jaw and I know I'm lost when she pulls her lower lip into her mouth before lifting her hand to trace my ring. I'm already tasting her in my mind when her words push harder than any shove.

"She came for you once when you weren't here. And I made her leave without you."

CHAPTER THIRTY-SEVEN

BEFORE

REBECCA

I throw the trapdoor to my tree house open and launch myself at the nearest floor pillow, preparing to give myself over to a full, hard cry when a voice stops me.

"Whoever they are, they're not worth it."

I whirl around, wiping at my cheeks to find Ethan's mom sitting on the ice chest.

She offers me a soft smile that's more sardonic than sympathetic. "Then again sometimes a good cry is the only thing we can do, hmm?"

I sit up slowly, staring at her. Alone. In my tree house. "Ethan's not here."

She gives me a look that makes my cheeks heat in embarrassment. Obviously he's not here. "Do you know when he'll be back?"

I open my mouth to answer that Mr. and Mrs. Kelly just took him out to dinner to celebrate his improved progress report, but I stop myself. I need Ethan right now. It's not fair that she gets to show up whenever things are going well for her and rip him away without a care that things might be going well for him here. And it's far too easy to convince myself that I'm doing the wrong thing for the right reasons when I say, "They went camping for the weekend."

"Of course they did," she says, crossing her legs and leaning back against the wall. "My parents and their trees." She eyes me then, thoroughly studying me until I'm nervously tucking my curls behind my ears, sitting up straighter, and generally trying to look as trustworthy as possible. I must pass scrutiny because she sighs. "So why are you up here doing your best My So-Called Life impression?" I frown at her and she waves me off. "Why are you crying?"

When I hesitate, she laughs.

"Sweetie, who am I going to tell?"

It only takes a moment to realize that she'll be gone again soon and, apart from Ethan, there's no one else she could tell. And since I tell him everything anyway...

"My friend's parents are getting divorced so I skipped school to go to Sunsplash to cheer her up. My mom caught me trying to erase the school's robocall message and grounded me without even letting me explain."

She laughs again, deep and from her belly. "Well, no wonder he likes you so much."

I don't really understand what she means, but by then it's too late.

Joy lets me talk the whole thing out, the unfairness, my mom's cold reactions. There are more tears and finally the motherly hug I've been craving for what feels like my whole life. That coupled with praise for the kind of friend I am, makes me lean—physically and emotionally—on her all the more.

"And where does your mom think you are now?"

I sniff as the remnants of my tears finally fade. "In my room."

"Won't she come check on you?"

I shake my head. "She'll wait till my dad comes back from fishing tomorrow and make him deal with me."

Her smile stretches wide and she draws a flat metal bottle from her purse. "Well, then I have just the thing for you. Just a sip," Joy adds when I hesitate. "A little is fine. I give it to Ethan sometimes when he's sick or can't sleep."

My gaze shifts from the bottle to her face, apprehension creeping in and cooling the easy, warm feelings that had sprung up between us. Ethan told me about the times he "got sick" like his mom and I know he had to have been talking about something like this. "What if I throw up?"

"That's only if you drink a whole lot of it. And I won't let that happen." She urges the bottle to my lips. "Go on. I promise it'll make you feel better."

I take the bottle, not because I believe her, but because I believe Ethan. He said it made him sick, but also that afterward his mom cried and brought him to his grandparents. I don't want to throw up, but I don't want Ethan to have to leave this time. And if I drink it with her, she won't be able to give it to him.

So I drink way more than a sip. The drink burns, sending liquid fire igniting down my throat and blazing in my stomach. I cough and new tears stream from my eyes.

Joy laughs and takes a healthy swig for herself without so

much as batting an eye. "That warmth curling in your belly? Hard to feel sad when you've got the sun inside you."

I don't feel sad anymore, just determined. The faster I drink the faster she'll leave. I drink more while Joy talks. Then more. I still sputter and cough, but less so. "It's like drinking fire," I say when I get control of my voice back.

"Mmmm," she murmurs around her own pull. "Wait till your whole body feels like that." She sets the bottle down and runs her fingers up and down the insides of her forearms. "All tingly and buzzing, like you're floating and flying at the same time."

I am feeling kind of loose and buzzy, not sick at all. But I still need Joy to go before Ethan gets back so I reach for another drink with an arm that feels weirdly heavy and uncoordinated, but she moves it away.

"You think that maybe that's the way you were meant to feel, and everything else starts to feel empty, blank, like you're asleep all the time." She curls the bottle in her lap, gazing at the liquid that sloshes inside. "All you want is to be awake, but it's not as easy as it used to be. And then later, you look back and realize you'd give anything to be able to sleep again."

Her gaze isn't focused on me until I reach for the bottle again and somehow fall over.

"Shit," she whispers, then again and again, the words soft and yet somehow harsh.

It all seems very funny to me and I laugh before slapping a hand over my mouth.

Suddenly she's right in my face, taking me by the shoulders and shaking me hard enough for my head to snap back and forth. "Let her yell at you, do you hear me? Let them ground

you and lock you in your room and tell you who to stay away
from. Let them be unfair and hate them if you have to, but let
them do it. Otherwise, you might end up so awake that you
can't even see what's wrong with giving alcohol to a child."
She settles back to sit on her heels and a laugh that turns wa-
tery slips free. "In a damn tree house full of pictures your kid
painted." And then she's not laughing at all.

Her hands run through her hair, clutching together when
they meet at the back the same way Ethan sometimes does.

"You'll go now?" My tongue feels sluggish and I laugh
again at the slurred sound of my own voice. "And leave
Ethan?"

She looks around everywhere but at me. "Look, just stay
up here for a while, okay?" She tugs a sleeping bag over to
me and almost roughly pushes me down onto it. "You sleep
up here sometimes, right? Sure you do. That's fine." Her
voice is getting faster. "Just stay here and don't—" She breaks
off. The tree house falls silent except for the cicadas buzzing outside and the mourning doves calling to each other.
She grabs her purse and the nearly empty bottle. "Don't tell
Ethan I was here."

CHAPTER THIRTY-EIGHT

NOW

ETHAN

Rebecca calls my name when I stand but falls silent as I stumble from the balcony into the tree house that isn't tall enough or big enough or anything enough for what I'm feeling.

Right here. My mom was right here and Rebecca never said a word. They split a bottle of who-knows-what and then she left.

I stare down at the unfinished wood. This exact spot.

I remember that day. Rebecca had wanted me to ditch with her, but I was finally doing not horrible in school and I didn't trust myself to miss a day and be able to catch up. It was one of the rare times I said no to her and I could tell it stung, enough that she did something so stupid afterward that I still get angry thinking about it now—I jerk my head up at her as the pieces all click together.

"Ethan," Rebecca says again. The emotion in her voice is different now. She's not worried I'm going to take off and leave her up here—I would never do that under any circumstances—but she's still afraid that she's damaged something between us.

There isn't enough room to let me think.

"You should have told me," I tell her. I hear a shift and I know without looking that Rebecca has brought her legs up and swung them around so she's facing me. "All of it."

"I didn't want you to go away."

I whirl on her. "That wasn't your choice to make."

She bites her lip then nods. "I know. I knew it then, but I still did it."

"Damn it, Rebecca," I whisper. "You're not supposed to lie to me. Everybody else does, but not you." I slump down to the floor.

It doesn't matter that my mom came back a couple months later and took me away for good. It doesn't matter that she stayed clean for longer than she ever had or even that the extra time here gave me the memories I've lived on for the past four years…

All this time I thought that it was for me. I thought my mom could see what was happening to me and it was finally enough for her to do what she hadn't really tried to do my entire life. I even said it to her once; I thanked her.

Acid scalds up my throat and burns all the way back down.

It hadn't been about me at all. It took messing up somebody else's kid for her to make a go at staying clean, actually trying, and not just pausing.

But she's not here and beneath the flare of hurt there's mostly resignation. The deeper cut is the one I never thought to defend against.

Rebecca lied to me.

I never thought she'd do that, ever.

"I thought I was helping you," she says, and it's only the small note of panic in her voice that breaks through the pain slicing into each and every one of those clung-to memories.

"By lying when you of all people knew what that meant to me?" My face twists as I shake my head and new implications hit me.

My mom got her drunk. At twelve years old. And then she just left her alone.

I don't have to ask if that was the first time Rebecca ever drank. And I know the last time was exactly two years ago.

And my mom was the beginning.

I glance up at her, meeting her gaze. She's staring so intently at me, waiting to see what fate I decide for us.

She doesn't seem to get the fact that she should be mad at me too.

I feel guilty and ashamed, but she lied to me about the most important thing in my life. I don't know how to reconcile those feelings.

So I don't. We sit there in silence, staring at each other from across the tree house we practically lived in growing up, wrestling with our own thoughts.

"I'm sorry."

I flinch at her apology. I'm nowhere near ready to hear it. Or accept it. "So now my mom not only screwed up my life, but she gets to be the reason you ruined yours too. You get that, right?"

Her knuckles turn white around her ring. "I'm not doing this."

I know I should back down, but I don't, even as the blood drains from my face. "Just say it. I know you're thinking it."

She shakes her head, sending her curls flying. "Was it

messed up that she got me drunk as a kid? Yeah, but I know she did worse to you, that's why I did it!" Her eyes are flashing then and she's breathing heavy from emotions held in too long. "That was the first time I ever drank anything, and yeah, it wasn't the last. So what do you want me to say? It's your mom's fault that years later I got drunk at a party and got my dad killed? Does that make you feel better, give you one more thing to feel guilty for?"

"Shit," I yell, ripping at my own hair. "Shit, shit, shit!" The word gets louder each time until I'm screaming it.

Her face is twisted and as angry as I've ever seen it. "You don't get to feel guilty for something I did or for something your mom did."

"Then what do I get?" That volcanic anger that used to rise up inside me is ready to erupt. I come so close to launching myself up and kicking the balcony railing down. The muscles in my thighs coil to the point of pain.

"Be mad at me!" Her face turns red as she yells back. "We keep avoiding things between us because we don't want to waste our time being angry, but we are angry, and burying it doesn't make it go away."

"I don't want to be mad at you!" My words start off like fire but when they're out all I'm left with is ash. "Why'd you tell me this, huh?" My fingers curl remembering the warmth from her skin and the softness I touched only minutes before. "So I wouldn't kiss you? Wouldn't want to stay with you?" I don't even blink when my voice cracks. "Was that all so much worse than this?"

Heat still flushes her cheeks, but her lips tremble too. "I couldn't keep lying to you."

I lean toward her, the tendons in my neck straining against the control I force into my words. "That's bullshit." She knows it too because she can't hold my gaze for more than a heartbeat.

It's worse when I lift her in my arms again to carry her down from the tree house. She holds me so close that I can feel her heart pounding. Mine struggles to beat at all.

"Please don't leave like this," is what she says once she's in her wheelchair and I turn away. "Stay and yell, but don't just leave."

I still, my back half to her. "I'm not leaving Arizona until I find her."

"I'm not talking about her. I'm talking about me, about—"

"I can't talk about *you* right now!" My voice punches that word. "You lied, *you*. And I can't let go of that or any of the rest of it just because you want me to." I suck in a breath. "I need some time."

"How mu—"

"I don't know, but I don't need you to help me look for her anymore."

Rebecca's chin clenches, trying to suppress a quiver.

"Bauer came up with some more names and I've talked to a couple of them. I'll keep at it. There's not much more you could do anyway." I can't keep looking at her after that and when I drop my gaze to my boots I hear Rebecca draw in a breath.

"For what it's worth, I want her to be okay," she says, in a voice that isn't nearly as composed as her words. "I won't lie and say I want that for her sake, but I want it for you. I've always wanted that."

I nod, still unable to look up. "I know." It hurts just to give her that small response, but when I try for more, my throat closes tight.

I wait a minute hoping the feeling will ease but it doesn't.

There's nothing more to say as I leave her there at the foot of our tree house.

CHAPTER THIRTY-NINE

BEFORE

REBECCA

There's a creak of wood below Ethan and me that tells me someone is climbing up the tree house ladder. I expect it to be my dad wanting me to empty the dishwasher or maybe Mrs. Kelly calling Ethan for lunch, but then I see the blond head appear through the trapdoor and suck in a breath as Joy looks around.

She spots me first and there's a moment of hesitation when our gazes lock, both of us remembering the last time she was here. My hand moves to curl around my arm, touching skin that still feels too sensitive from the cast I just got off. As if pulled by magnets, our gazes shift to Ethan.

He lowers the book he was reading and for the first time ever, doesn't immediately smile and go to her.

He looks at me.

It's quick, barely a glance, but my heart beats that much faster knowing he thought of me in that moment.

Joy sees it too and I feel the weight of her gaze settle on me, kicking up my pulse for a difference reason.

"Hey, baby," she says, starting her words meant for Ethan while still looking at me. Then she turns to him. "Aren't you going to give me a hug?"

There's a stiffness when he walks to her, but she ignores it and pulls him in tight. "My big boy. Who told you to keep growing while I was gone, hmm?"

I press myself against the wall at my back, trying to stay small and silent as they share a moment that is only meant for the two of them. But then her gaze lifts to me and she has a smile for me too.

"And look at you. Not such a little girl anymore either. No wonder he's always wanting to come back here."

"Mom." Ethan draws her attention back to him. "You promised to call this time, so I could be ready." He glances at me again, his meaning clear.

Her smile drops like a weight she was holding. "So you'd rather stay with your girlfriend than go with your mom, is that what you're saying?"

A muscle jumps in Ethan's neck. "No, that's not—and she's not—"

Her head whips back to me. "What have you been telling him, huh? Are you making up stories?"

Fear trickles ice down my spine and I mutely shake my head.

"Mom!" Ethan steps in front of me. "What are you talking about?"

She blinks at him then glances quickly to me and my wide

eyes as I continue shaking my head, silently willing her to hear me: *I didn't say anything. He doesn't know.*

And then she laughs making Ethan and me jump. "I'm kidding. I just thought it would be funny to mess with you." She looks around and moves to sit on the closed cooler. "Maybe don't take everything so seriously next time." Then she tosses out a hand in my direction. "Rebecca gets it."

Ethan turns to search my face, giving me only an instant to force my features into some semblance of a smile. I must not do a very good job though because his frown only intensifies.

"I knew she was kidding," I say. "It's just my arm is kind of aching again."

Joy looks at where I'm holding my forearm. "What's the matter, honey? Drawing too many unicorns lately?"

Ethan's frown lessens only slightly when he answers for me. "She fell off the tree house balcony and broke it a couple of months ago. The cast only came off yesterday." Then to me, "Should I get your mom?"

"No," Joy and I answer together, and then she laughs. "If her mom thinks her arm hurts then she won't let Rebecca come with us to get ice cream before we leave. You said you weren't ready to go yet," she adds. "So we'll get something cold and sweet first."

"Oh, um," Ethan says as his neck flushes red.

"I'm grounded," I say. "I'm not allowed to leave the yard for another month."

"Another month?" She snickers. "And just what could you have done to get grounded for so long?"

Ethan and I fall silent, remembering. Well, I remember,

Ethan only thinks he does. Because I lied, about him and to him, and I only feel bad about one of those.

"I stole a bottle from our liquor cabinet to drink up here by myself," I say, with more force than I've shown since she showed up. "Ethan's the one who found me crying after I fell and took me home."

CHAPTER FORTY

NOW

REBECCA

Ethan is there outside the shop when Amelia and I come out
to leave a few days later. I must make some kind of sound in
my throat because she halts midway down the ramp to crane
her neck and look at me.

"What? What's wrong?"

But I can't look away from Ethan and when she follows the
line of my sight, she sighs and releases the death grip she has
on her push rims and glides the rest of the way down.

"Hey," he says, when I follow behind her.

"Hey."

"Hey to all of us," Amelia says. "And what brings you
here, Ethan?"

He tears his gaze from me, flicking it to her then back to
me as though the answer should be obvious.

"Ah, to be seventeen and not need a reason for anything."
She pushes toward her car.

When she's far enough away that I don't think she'll hear

us, I tell Ethan the thought that has been plaguing me since the tree house. "I wasn't sure I'd see you again."

Ethan steps closer to me. "You saw me yesterday."

I shake my head, dismissing his accurate but also totally inaccurate response. "Leaving on your way to work."

"I told you I wouldn't just leave."

"I know, but…"

"I wouldn't lie to you."

Ah, but I would. "Is that why you're here? To make me feel bad? 'Cause I was doing fine all on my own."

"No." He shoves his hands into the pockets of his jeans. "I've just been thinking about some things." Not looking at me, he asks, "Why'd you do it?"

"Lie about—?"

"No." His gaze lifts to mine and I can see how bloodshot his eyes are. He looks like he hasn't slept in days. "Why did you drink with her? You never liked her, and as far as I can tell you wouldn't have wanted to be around her any longer than you had to. So then why spend, what, an hour or more with her?"

Surprise hits me and I respond without thinking. "How did you know it was that long?"

"Because I've been there with her. She likes to talk when she drinks."

Oh.

He presses when I don't respond. "You're not gonna tell me?"

I don't want to. He was so upset before and I don't want him to feel worse, about me or any of it. Ethan and guilt go together like…well, like me and guilt. I don't want to give him an excuse to bury himself in that feeling any deeper than he already has.

But then he goes on, answering for me. "I was really mad when I figured it out. So mad I even had my bags and Old Man in the car."

I wince, imagining how absolutely gutted I would have felt to find him gone like that. "Why didn't you go?"

"I told you I wouldn't—"

"Lie to me," I finish for him, unable to keep the tremble from my voice. "That's why? Is this your goodbye then?"

"No." He looks down, his head shaking slowly. "I didn't leave because I don't want to anymore. And you don't have to say it. I know you drank with her so I wouldn't have to."

I bite my lips when my eyes flood. "I'm sorry. I know it was wrong to make those decisions for you, but I couldn't help it. I remembered you talking about getting sick like her and I didn't want you to have to go through that again, but I don't know that's what would have happened. Maybe..." My voice trails off when the saddest smile I've ever seen lifts Ethan's face.

"She brought it with her, Bec. Told you it would make you feel better, didn't she? Like floating and flying at the same time?"

I don't have to nod, and it breaks my heart how he knows exactly what she said. "How old were you?"

"Does it matter?"

And it doesn't matter that he's not leaving. I'm gutted anyway. "Alcohol?"

"Do you really want to know?"

No. Not at all. "If you want to tell me."

He steps closer, tipping his head so his hair falls forward to hide his face. The blue has almost completely washed out. "I still need to work through a lot of that for myself. I don't think I'm ready to go there yet. I just—"

"It's okay." I don't need him to justify his reasons, especially not when I woke up this morning thinking I might not ever be this close to him again. "We don't have to go there, but I'll always be here, you know?"

"I know. That was the part of this I couldn't reconcile until, well, until I did." He brushes his hair back and his gaze stills on mine. "I know you thought you were protecting me back then, but I'm not okay with you lying to me. You can't—" he clears his throat "—not again, okay?"

I swallow. "I won't." He's not the only one who hasn't slept well in days. There's only so much of that situation I can blame on being a kid, especially since it took me every one of these last few days to understand what I'd set in motion. I'd told him not to feel guilty for my actions or for his mom's, but I'd given him an impossible task. Of course he would blame himself, more so now that he's forgiving me. It's so much easier to hide in anger and he's letting that go.

For me.

And all he's asking for in return is honesty.

I allow my head to dip down for barely a second before urging it back up and facing him. "You were right to call bullshit in the tree house. I thought about those lies all the time until it felt like that wall wedged between us, but I could have told you the truth at any point before then. I waited until I needed it, until it was the only thing I had left to keep you away." I suppress that need skittering through me now when he draws closer and sits on the low railing beside me. "Because I couldn't have pushed you any other way."

"You don't need to though."

He wants it to be simple, but he knows it isn't. Even if he finds a way to stay, I don't know how I can.

"But we can take it one day at a time and maybe…" But he trails off because neither of us knows what maybe looks like.

"Maybe," I say, trying out the word and finding it a lot less scary than I thought. Maybe isn't now or nothing. It isn't never.

Ethan shakes his head, half smiling at me. "You were right too, about us avoiding fights when they came up. I don't think we should do that anymore."

That's what I have to let go of. Throughout our childhood, I learned to bite my tongue and hold things back, anything to keep from ruining what little time we had together with angry words and bruised feelings. Those weren't the memories I wanted him to take when he abruptly left.

"So if we fight…?"

He gives me a look that forces my mouth to quirk.

"Okay, when we fight…?"

He catches the frame of my chair and angles it so we're knee to knee. "We'll come back like this and we'll find a way through."

I don't know if he realizes how much he's asking from me. I have to trust him not to leave, to still be there in the aftermath, however long it takes to get there. Does he understand?

His hand flexes around the frame of my chair, as though he's fighting not to draw me closer.

My chest rises and falls with a breath. And I nod.

Ethan's full smile is magic when it comes. It starts with his eyes, the light brown melting into amber. Then his lips twitch as though he's reluctant to let his mouth lift up but knows it's a lost cause. There's the tiniest flash of teeth before he gives in and a grin overtakes his entire face.

Even little girls dream about smiles like that.

"You want to get out of here?"

"More than you will ever know."

He laughs when I beam up at him. "Good, 'cause I don't know what I would've done if you had plans."

"Oh wait," I say, scrunching up my face. "I'm supposed to have dinner at Amelia's." I glance over my shoulder and she takes that as her cue to join us.

"Any chance you'd bail on her?"

"Hey. We have *Call of Duty* and long, pensive stares at my house too," Amelia says, then laughs at her own joke. "Or you, know, I could always ask Mathias to throw another steak on. You're a meat eater, right, Ethan?"

"Yes, ma'am," he says with all the enthusiasm of a starving cowboy.

Amelia pretends to shudder, talking to herself as she opens her car door. "I'm a ma'am now? I'm officially ma'am age?"

I duck my head to hide a smile, then ask Ethan, "So?"

"Yes." He points a finger at Amelia's car. "That."

CHAPTER FORTY-ONE

NOW

ETHAN

"So," Rebecca asks, once we're in my car on our way home after dinner. "What'd you think of Amelia and Mathias?"

I can tell she's nervous about my response because she hasn't stopped running her hands over her knees. These are people who are important in her life and it feels good to know that I am too. "I liked them."

"Did you really?"

I have to bite back a laugh because she notices how fast she's rubbing her palm on her thigh and jerks it away. "Really. I mean Amelia talked about you the whole time and Mathias talked about painting. What's not to like?"

A hint of a smile touches Rebecca's face. "She didn't only talk about me."

She kind of did. Some were embarrassing stories but mostly I could tell how proud she was of Rebecca. "She thinks a lot of you."

Still smiling, Rebecca glances down at her lap. "I think a lot of her too."

I hear a ding and Rebecca pulls her phone out of her bag, reads something on the screen and laughs before turning it to show me. "Looks like you were a hit with them too. Amelia said Mathias wants to have you over for a play date this week."

"A what?"

Rebecca taps out a response. "He's gonna text you tomorrow about coming by his studio next time you're free. Apparently, he's very excited to show off his paint brushes."

"Really?" I say, my voice pitching higher than I mean it too. "Oh yeah, that'd be great." I hadn't gotten to look around as much as I would have wanted when Rebecca and I dyed our hair and I hadn't wanted to disappear on Rebecca tonight when Matthias offered to give me a better look after dinner. "He started telling me about how he painted the hangar and giving me some tips about larger scale murals. It'd be good to, you know, hear some more."

There's something soft about the smile Rebecca gives me. I feel it deep in my chest and have to fight not to look away.

Before I can stop her, Rebecca leans over in the car and hugs me, doubling that warm pressure in my chest and enveloping me in the scent of the chocolate cake we had for dessert. I can't stop myself from wondering if she'll taste—

"Ethan, it'd be great." Rebecca's smile rivals the sun when she beams at me. "Oh, I'm so happy right now."

She sits back, regrettably breaking that last physical link. The space between us does clear my head though and allow me to focus on her words.

I don't know what will come from hanging out with Mathias, but I'm more than okay with how it makes her smile at me. For now it's enough.

"Maybe you can show him some of your sketches?"

I make a noncommittal gesture, not wanting to admit the only other person who even knows they exist is her.

"I didn't even hear you guys talking about all that."

"It was while you and Amelia were in the kitchen." And with one single comment, I turn off the sun. "You were kind of quiet after that."

She shifts in her seat but there isn't anywhere to go, so finally she looks over at me. "I haven't told her about my mom wanting me to go away for college, but she knows I'm keeping something from her."

"You should tell her." I don't know Amelia all that well, but I know enough to trust that she would encourage Rebecca to talk to her mom.

Her head leans from side to side in half acknowledgment. "Amelia likes to push me, which is good, I know, but sometimes she pushes so hard." She fiddles with her ring, sliding it almost off before pushing it back on. "I know what she'd say, but it's not as simple as you make it sound."

I don't remember ever thinking it was simple much less saying it. "Has your mom ever been to the shop and actually watched you?" I've only been a few times, but it's like watching something grow and bloom before my eyes. No one could see her there and doubt that she was made for it.

"Not really." She tries to smile but it's weak and I'm not about to let this go.

"Then show her. I mean if there was a chance that she'd see and understand, why not take that?"

She doesn't look at me when she answers. "Because there's a chance she won't see at all. Or she will and it won't change anything. She'll still want me gone."

The defeat in her voice stabs right through my heart. "What about what you want?"

Rebecca lifts one shoulder like she's talking about something small when in reality it couldn't be bigger. "I want her to want me to stay. To forgive me."

I ease to a stop at a light and close my eyes. I know that kind of want, that all-consuming desire for another person to set you free, but I don't know how to give it to her any more than I know how to get it for myself.

"It's coming up, you know, the anniversary." She winces slightly at that word; it so often means something to celebrate when in this case...not at all. "Some people like me call it a life day. Like it's the anniversary of the day we survived something that should have killed us. They have parties and everything."

I don't need to ask to know that's not something she wants. That day will always be more than the day she survived.

"I'd give anything to go back and be here with you," I say, surprising us both with my words.

She stares at me a long time until I feel her gaze like a brand before saying, "You can be here for this one." It's almost hesitant the way she says it, like she's not sure she really means it.

"Yeah?"

She nods, then nods again with more conviction. "I don't, um, it's a hard day. My mom, she kind of deals with it in her own way, so it's just been me, you know?" Her words trip out, stumbling in places, but she keeps going. "But if you were here, maybe—"

"Yeah. I mean yeah." I agree readily even though I know I don't fully understand what I'm committing to. Except that it's her.

"Okay then. Good." She gives me a smile that is hard fought and I can feel her struggling to keep all the pieces of herself together. So I don't even think before reaching out for her hand and wrapping it tight in mine.

She squeezes back.

CHAPTER FORTY-TWO

NOW

ETHAN

I'm the one whistling at work the next week. I'm not dancing around the place, but there's no denying the lightness in my step, which makes the contrast between me and Neel that day all the more apparent.

We're stuck digging tree holes around a mammoth backyard and instead of crooning to the plants and spinning his shovel through the air...he's just working.

"Okay, what gives?" I ask when Eddie yells at us for no reason and Neel doesn't say anything in response. "Are you feeling alright?" I offer to cover for him if he needs a drink in the shade for a few, but he just shrugs me off with a mumbled, "I'm fine."

I step in front of him when he starts to move. "You're actually not fine. Clearly." He looks miserable and I don't know what I'm supposed to do about it. Besides Rebecca, I've never really gotten close to anyone. There was no point with everything always going on with my mom. The whole friend thing is new to me. Still, I feel like I have to try. "Hey, tell me some more about that musical guy you like, the German one who wrote all the songs."

His eyes narrow. "German guy? You mean Irving Berlin?"

"Yeah!" I grin, relieved that I've gotten him talking.

"His last name isn't where he's from. He was Russian." He looks at me like I'm unbelievably stupid and I feel my neck flush.

"Russian. Fine. Sorry. Wherever he's from, what's his best song?"

That you're-an-idiot-look doesn't leave his face. "What do you care? It's not like you listened to the playlist I sent you."

I did actually. It wasn't my thing, but I'd promised to check it out so I had. A couple of the songs got inadvertently stuck in my head and I really enjoy his dumbfounded expression when I start to sing one.

"Blue skies, nothing but blue skies," I point up, "do I see." And then I improvise because I can't remember the rest of the lyrics. "And a pissed-off guy, yelling at me."

He doesn't even crack a smile.

"You know what, fine. Be a dick." I start to turn away but Neel lets his shovel drop to the ground with a thud.

"She doesn't want me—she wants you. And it sucks. There, are you happy?"

I'm happy he's talking to me, but it turns out that seeing your friend get his heart broken does, in fact, suck. "Sorry, man." Then I step closer to him as the rest of what he said hits me. "Wait, did she actually tell you she wants me—"

Neel shoves me. I wasn't expecting it at all and I end up tripping backward over my own shovel.

There's a moment of shock on both our faces. And then instinct kicks in and I scramble to my feet and charge him.

He goes down hard but surprises me with an immediate swing at my head that I narrowly avoid. We roll, each trying to get the upper hand.

And then the water hits us.

"Get up! Get up!" Eddie is yelling as he hoses us and for once it's warranted.

We break apart, panting and glaring, both at each other and at Eddie who sprays us both one last time in the face before turning off the water.

"Acting like animals. What does this say, huh? Right here?" He jabs me in the chest and then Neel. "Good & Green not Bad & Muddy!"

I hear a snort from my left and glance over at Neel. Seeing him struggle not to laugh is more effective than any hose at cooling my temper. My shoulders start to bounce and Neel covers his mouth with his hand. Eddie is so caught up in his lecture that he doesn't even notice until the laughter erupts from both of us. And we can't stop. Eddie is threatening to fire both of us on the spot or at least call my grandparents. That last part doubles me over and has Neel hooting.

Eddie brandishes his phone at us before storming off, very loudly saying my grandfather's name so there's no doubt who he's talking to.

"He's gonna get us both fired," Neel says, laughter still making his words come out choppy.

"No," I say, grinning. "Just me. I'll tell them I started it."

Neel sobers. "I'm the one who pushed you."

I shrug. "I'm not going to let you get fired because I tripped and got angry."

"Because I got angry first and pushed you."

"You were upset. I get it."

Neel shakes his head. "No, I was being a dick. I'm sorry. Rebecca is allowed to like whoever she wants and after that—" he gestures at the dirt we were just rolling around in "—I'm getting why that wouldn't be me."

I pluck at my stained shirt. "Not exactly Good & Green over here."

That makes him smile, but only for a moment. "We haven't seen each other in forever. Did she tell you?" He waits for me to shake my head. "We've been texting a bit but it's not the same. All she ends up talking about is you." There's no hiding the hint of accusation in his voice. "When we were together before, it just kind of happened and then it stopped happening. I always just figured it would happen again, you know?" He gathers up the hem of his shirt and wrings the water out. "And now I'm finally getting that it won't."

I don't say anything. He thinks I am the reason they won't happen again or at least part of the reason. And I'm not gonna pretend I don't want that to be true.

"What do you wanna do about it?"

"Well as fun as fighting was, I think I'm over that."

"That wasn't fighting," I tell him. "You knocked me down. I knocked you down." I shrug.

"No, no, don't tell me that. The closest I've come to a fight before this is when my older sisters would pin me down and take turns tickling me. This has to count."

I muffle a laugh. "Okay then. It was a fight."

"That I won."

I cock my head at him. "I'm pretty sure the hose beat both of us."

The hose in question is still in Eddie's hand and based on the way he's gesticulating while on the phone, he's definitely making our non-fight sound much worse than it was.

"I'm not gonna let you take the blame for this," Neel says, watching Eddie too before turning to me. "And just so you know, I don't think you're a dick. I even get why she likes you."

I kick a clump of wet dirt off my boot so I don't have to look at him. "Yeah, well, we have a lot of history."

"You know it's more than that." Unlike me, Neel has no problem getting right at the issue. "I care about Rebecca, and I know you do too. Just…don't make her wait around while you're figuring out what you want."

I let his words linger in my mind all the way back to the warehouse where my grandfather is waiting outside to also yell at us. Much to Eddie's disappointment though, we get to keep our jobs, though Neel's and mine are about to become much less pleasant for a few weeks as punishment. I'm not looking forward to that.

But Neel and I are good. And according to him at least, Rebecca wants me.

Figuring out what I want isn't the problem. It's been the same for me since she was that scrawny kid in the rain banging on my window. I tried to pretend it wasn't there when I first came back, but I want her more now than I ever did.

I want Rebecca. Just thinking that thought makes me feel lighter, like I've had this huge burden I've been carrying my whole life, and all this time she was there carrying it with me. And now that I see her, I don't even notice the weight anymore.

She does that for me.

She makes me believe her when she says I have something worthwhile in my head. That I'm worth more than…the mistakes I've made and the life I've been living.

I can't offer her anything close to that. She already knows about the possibilities for her future, but I can keep telling her that her past doesn't keep her from deserving one.

I sat in my room last night thinking about Rebecca, staring at my wall, and reading the last few texts from Bauer. We found an old friend who claimed to have seen my mom with one of her ex's a week ago, but that lead had turned into nothing. Bauer is still looking, but he has a job and a family, and despite him insisting that helping me is just one of the many amends he owes me, I can't expect him to search indefinitely.

But no matter what I want, I know I can't build any kind of a new life while the pieces of my old one are still so broken.

CHAPTER FORTY-THREE

NOW

REBECCA

"Rebecca! I was wondering where you've been lately." Mrs. Kelly opens the front door and smiles when I knock the next day. "Did you want to come in or do you need the pool gate unlocked…?" She glances at the periwinkle summer dress I'm wearing instead of the swimsuit she almost always sees me in.

"I'm actually not here to borrow your pool for once. I was looking for Ethan?"

She pulls the door closer to herself giving me room to pop my casters over the threshold and muscle the rest of the way inside. "Oh, that's good. He's been so isolated this week and then he and Neel got into a fight—"

"They did?" I turn once I'm inside to face her. "About what?"

She sighs. "I have no idea. He doesn't talk to me. Maybe a word here and there, but he wasn't very happy that we made him come here."

I glance at my lap, unsure of how much to say here but, remembering my own recent fallout with Ethan, I can't say nothing. "It's more than just bringing him here. You know that."

Her brows pinch together. "We've done everything we ever could for him."

"Yeah." I nod. "And maybe one day he'll be able to see all the good stuff, but it's not gonna happen when you keep treating him like he's still a kid. He had a right to know when his mom left rehab—like, the second you found out, he should have found out. Keeping that from him was a betrayal that you can't undo with a car and cookies." I soften my voice when it starts to rise. "I know you think you're protecting him, but believe me, he needs to be able to trust you more than he needs anything else."

"Rebecca." Mrs. Kelly draws back in shock. I don't think I've ever so much as frowned at her. I never had a reason to before, but the way she and Mr. Kelly have treated Ethan is wrong.

"I know you love him and he—" I inhale because I know how complicated Ethan's emotions toward his grandparents are "—he loves you too, but you've been making these big decisions for him his whole life and you never talked to him about any of them. Do you know how messed up that is? You want him to trust you, then start trusting him. He's not a child and he hasn't been one for a very long time."

Something dims in her expression letting me know she understands that last statement all too well. It's frustrating to watch her remain silent though. Ethan's starting to look at things with his mom differently and I think he's going to need his grandparents now more than ever.

"He's so angry," she whispers, glancing down the hall toward Ethan's closed bedroom door. "I didn't realize how much until recently."

There's a stretch of silence after that before she adds, "I'll think about what you said." Then she steps back and lets me pass.

"Grandma, I told you I'm not—"

"It's me," I call through Ethan's closed door. A second later he opens it enough to poke his head out.

"Hi. I thought you were babysitting Layla today?"

"She ended up going to a friend's house." And then, because he still hasn't opened the door more than a few inches, I add, "Is it okay that I came over?" He hesitates, glancing over his shoulder, and my stomach drops. "I should have texted." I thought after last night we were okay again. Is he having second thoughts?

"No, it's not that. I'm glad you're here. It's just..." He sucks in a breath then opens the door all the way.

"Oh," I say, in a voice that suddenly feels rough as sandpaper. "Oh, wow."

His hand rubs at the back of his neck as though seeing the scene through my eyes.

"You've gone full *True Detective* in here." I stare unblinking at the back wall behind his bed which he's turned into one giant conspiracy board with papers and maps and all kinds of notes tacked up everywhere with a picture of his mom in the center. "All you're missing is the red string."

"It's what I've been doing these past few days." He rubs his neck some more. "And nights."

I can't bring myself to look at any one thing too closely. I don't want to know how close he is to finding his mom, not when it was only last night that I started feeling like I really had him back.

"We don't have to stay in here. My grandparents just left for Bible study so the living room is free."

I nod, registering that I heard the front door open and shut a minute ago. "Okay." Then let him lead us down the hall.

Once we're both sitting on the couch, I know I have to ask. "Anything?"

Ethan doesn't need more than that one word. "Nothing."

I feel guilty at the relief his answer gives me. At his request, I'm not actively helping Ethan look for his mom anymore, but I still think about it constantly. There was a lot more on that wall than I helped him find. He may not know exactly where she is yet, but he's got more than nothing.

He gets to his feet then and hurries out of the room returning with a plate of cookies before I can do more than mildly panic over that one tiny question about his mom. "She made them about an hour ago, so they're fresh."

He bites his cookie though I'm not sure he's even tasting it, which is saying something because Mrs. Kelly makes Martha Stewart look like a hack. That thought leads me to a hopefully distracting question. "Hey, so what happened with you and Neel? Your grandmother mentioned something about a fight?"

Ethan stops chewing his cookie. "When were you talking to my grandmother about me?"

"Not about you," I say. When I realize I'm about to do the very thing I just told her to stop doing, I shake my head. "Actually we were. Just now when she let me in." I watch his muscles tense up and guilt sloshes around in my stomach as I keep talking. "I guess you guys haven't really been talking and she's worried about you." He must be doing a good job of keeping her out of his room because if she saw his wall, she'd be miles past worried. "Do they know that you're looking for your mom?"

"No." That's all I get, that one clipped-word answer.

"I'm trying here," I tell him. "But you have to try too."

His fists unclench first, then his shoulders, and finally his jaw. "I know. Sorry. No, they don't know. I don't think they'd be real supportive."

"Maybe you should tell them."

A flicker of anger flashes in his eyes before he banishes it too. "What good would that do?"

"They could help," I offer, remembering the way Mrs. Kelly had looked at the door. "They love you, you know?"

He doesn't respond to that, but he stays relaxed beside me. And then he shifts his hand until the backs of our fingers brush together. "You know. That's all I need."

I should draw away. There's an entire wall not twenty feet away from me full of reasons to not let us touch even this tiny bit.

A hint of a smile plays at Ethan's lips when I don't.

"You never told me what you and Neel fought about."

His smile quirks higher on one side. "Actually, it was kind of about you."

CHAPTER FORTY-FOUR

NOW

REBECCA

I can't help but smile when I look out my window the next night and see a familiar tall, dark shape coming out of the Kellys' house with a squirming cat in his arms.

I try not to look like I'm hurrying as I hurry down the hall and out the front door. Ethan hadn't responded to my text earlier, but I know Eddie gets on his case if he's on his phone at work. Besides, seeing him in person is so much better.

I breeze down the ramp, letting the momentum carry me across the walkway and onto the driveway so my hands are free to gather my curls up into a loose ponytail. That smile stays on my face until I see…

Neel.

He stops, seeing me too. "This isn't what it looks like."

I squint one eye at him. "So you're not stealing Ethan's cat?"

"No. I'm—" But Old Man's yowl drowns out whatever else

he was going to say. The cat twists himself like a pretzel to break free from Neel's grasp and darts off into the darkness.

"Looks like your nefarious cat-stealing plan's been foiled… by the cat itself!" I dramatically bring the back of my hand to my mouth and gasp. It's either that or laugh. There was zero chance he was ever getting Old Man anywhere he didn't want to go.

"I wasn't stealing anything."

I drop my hand. This is the first time I've seen Neel since the movie night at my house. Normally we see each other at least a few times a week. Even if it's just dropping off orders or picking them up, we find a way to turn them into more. Except for these last two weeks he hasn't once asked me to hang out and I haven't felt like I could ask him.

Lately, whenever we've texted, we've ended up talking about anything other than the friendship I hope we both still want to salvage. With a mental grimace, I realize just how often we've been defaulting to the topic of Ethan. It's not like I've been asking for updates while they are at work or anything, but Ethan is the biggest part of our lives that overlaps right now, so it's just felt easier to talk about him. Although in hindsight, maybe it was just easier for me.

"Look I'm—" I start to say just as he begins, "Hey, so about the other night—"

We both kind of laugh, but even that feels strained.

"I never wanted to hurt you, ever," I say, finally feeling brave enough to bring this up now that we're face-to-face.

He nods. "I know." And he says it so kindly that a sigh of relief leaves me.

"Then can we just go back? Forget that it was awkward or weird and just be friends again? 'Cause I've really missed you."

Neel's expression twists, just slightly and just for a moment, but I recognize pain when I see it. "I'm gonna need another minute, some space, you know?" My stomach bottoms out and he must see the reaction in my face because he's quick to add, "Not forever. I could never do that, but," his voice slows and he pauses before saying almost too softly to hear, "I need it not to hurt and right now it still does."

He could've hit me and it would've hurt less. There's nothing I can do but nod and blink too fast.

A bush ruffles to my side and I catch a glimpse of Old Man, grateful that he's once again providing a distraction from an uncomfortable situation. "Um, I know you and Ethan got into a fight, but really? His cat?"

Neel hears the bush too and whirls, apparently trying to develop the superpower of night vision as he squints underneath. "No, we're good. I was being stupid and kind of took it out on him, but we talked and decided we're better at fighting Eddie than each other."

I fold my arms. "Then what? And how did you get Mr. and Mrs. Kelly to let you walk out of the house with Ethan's cat in the first place?" My arms tighten as I ask the question and a half-formed answer tries to take shape in my brain.

"I was just supposed to feed him. That's all."

My fingers dig into my sides. "What are you talking about?"

Neel squat-walks over to the nearest bush to look beneath it. "Ethan got some text when we were leaving the site. I don't know who it was from or what it said, all I know is one second he's standing there looking like the world is ending and the next thing he's running to his car, flat-out running, and yelling at me to take care of his cat while he's gone. Do you have any idea—" Neel halts when he turns to look at me, at the utterly still and unmoving thing I've become. "He didn't tell you?"

My head moves left to right, once.

Neel stands, any search for the cat abandoned. "Well, maybe he's coming right back. Maybe…" Neel's voice trails off because he can't even convince himself. There'd be no need for Ethan to ask Neel to feed Old Man if he was only planning on a quick trip.

"It's his mom," I say, staring off at the bush beyond Neel. "She must have texted him, needed him." My voice goes cold as another possibility occurs to me, one that makes any thought for myself and Ethan leaving me like this again completely vanish. "Or something happened to her and a hospital or some other authority contacted him." My gaze shoots to the Kelly house then to Neel. "What did they say? Are they packing?" If something is wrong, like drop-everything-and-don't-even-come-home-first-wrong, then they have to be going too. I start pushing my chair toward their house, but Neel moves to block my way.

"No, I don't—" He twists to look at the quiet, mostly dark house behind him. "They were on the phone with him when I got there. It didn't sound like…you know."

I dig for my phone with hands so urgent that I almost drop it.

No missed calls. No texts. The one I sent him earlier is still unread.

"Anything?"

"No." I go back to being that unmoving thing. Except for my eyes which blink up at Neel.

"His grandfather just kept saying, come home and they can talk...so, um, I don't think anything is wrong, not like you were thinking." He's having trouble holding my gaze. "And then it sounded like the call got dropped, so maybe his phone died or something...but I'm sure he'll reach out when he can," Neel says. "Once he gets wherever—"

"California," I say, as my vision goes blurry. "That's where he's going. That's where he always goes."

Neel shifts on his feet, his discomfort heavy and thick in the air around him. "His mom has got some issues?"

"His whole life," I say.

"He, um never really talked about her."

"He did to me. I've been helping him look for her." I shake my head. "Or I was until he asked me to stop." I glance at the Kelly house and imagine Ethan's room the last time I saw it with his search wall. "Just last night he told me he hadn't found her, but I guess something turned up today."

His mom turned up, somewhere, somehow, and she needed him. That's all it took for him to become that little boy again, the one who dropped every good thing in his life to try and safeguard hers. A knot forms in the pit of my belly.

His grandparents could have been a good thing. His job at Good & Green could have been a good thing. His friendship with Neel and possibly Mathias could have been so good. And me. I was trying to be good. I was trying to be his maybe and trying so hard to find a way past maybe. I shift my head down as that knot reveals edges, sharp and serrated, when those thoughts slice into me.

One.

By.

One.

Ethan could have started a life here with dreams and a future full of people who could have loved him so much if he'd just stayed.

But he's never been able to think that way, to look at his mom and feel anything but responsible.

For not making it better.

For not keeping her safe.

For not saving her life.

"You okay?" Neel's face shifts in front of my own, sweet and concerned.

I silently shake my head. I don't know what I am, but I know what I want to be.

"I'm trying to be mad at him, you know?" I wrap my hands around my phone, squeezing to feel something besides the pain stabbing inside. "To take off like that and I'm the last to know. He thought of his cat before he thought of me. I'm only finding out now because I saw you through my window and thought you were him."

Neel's face falls a little hearing that, but even though I'm the one hurting him I can't find enough energy to feel sorry for him as well as myself.

"Why can't I be mad at him instead?" I don't mean for my voice to crack, but it does and then Neel pretends not to hear it. "He promised he'd never leave like this again, that he'd talk to me and say goodbye. He promised he'd be here to-morrow." The anniversary of the worst day of my life.

But he won't.

CHAPTER FORTY-FIVE

NOW

ETHAN

I didn't stop to think once I read the text from Bauer.

> **Bauer:**
> I found the ex-boyfriend she's
> been staying with. Planning to go
> to his place tonight. Feel like this
> is it.

Adrenaline spiked through my bloodstream making my hand jumpy as I texted him back.

> **Me:**
> I can be there in six hours.
> Where do I meet you?

I know the place he tells me to go to, a restaurant off Fay Avenue that we could never afford to eat at. And then I just drive. All I can think to do is get there, find her, and make sure she's okay.

Images of the way I found her on the floor and the taste of vomit on my lips as the 9-1-1 operator talked me through giving her CPR pound through my head, weighing my foot down heavier and heavier on the gas pedal.

When my phone rings, I answer without even registering the name.

"Bauer?"

"Ethan," my grandfather says. "What is going on? Neel showed up and said you took off?" His voice is tight, bracing himself for the news he's been dreading for decades.

I swerve around a car that's going too slow and don't answer fast enough.

"Ethan—"

"It's okay. She's not— I found her. I'm heading to meet somebody who knows where she is. I can be there in—" I pull my phone from my ear long enough to glance at the time "—six and a half hours." I speed up. "Less maybe." Then I notice the low battery icon and the nearly nonexistent sliver of red that's left.

"Just come home and we'll figure out a plan."

Multiple blaring horns yank my eyes back to the road and the red light I'm blazing through as cars on either side of me slam their brakes.

Shit. I inch my foot off the gas and tighten the one hand I have on the wheel, barely hearing the increasingly agitated words coming through the phone.

"—not a good idea."

I didn't even see that light. I could have been hit or slammed right into—

Rebecca.

My foot eases all the way off the gas just as my phone dies and my grandfather's words cut off.

Cars blur around me, some honking, others staring.

I didn't call Rebecca; I didn't even think about anything else when I got Bauer's text except getting to my mom.

My car rolls to a stop, right in the middle of the lane.

I chuck my worthless phone on the floor and yell.

And then I accelerate because I've never been able to do anything else.

I rewatch my mom's overdose in my mind for 372 miles until I reach Bauer's restaurant and practically throw myself from the car to escape the memory the second I see him. He's scanning the parking lot for the skinny little twelve-year-old kid I was the last time he saw me so his gaze travels right past me before jerking back.

"Holy shit, kid, look at you." He laughs. "You're as tall as I am."

Taller from my vantage point. "Where are we meeting the ex-boyfriend? Does he know we're coming?"

Bauer holds up two meaty hands. "Whoa, whoa. Gimme a sec. I haven't laid eyes on you in over five years."

I want to protest, but I'm noticing things about him too. I may have gotten taller, but he got wider. Not much, but considering he used to be whip lean, it's noticeable. So's the hairline that's slightly receding at the temples. Gone are the twitchy movements too. Now he's got his feet planted staring at me steadily.

He pulls a pack of cigarettes from his pocket and taps one out. "You know I didn't think you'd drive right out here like this." The cigarette bobs between his lips while he talks. "I could have gotten off work, put on something that isn't smeared with steak sauce." He gestures at the white apron he's wearing, and then, as an afterthought, snatches the hairnet from his head.

His brown hair is a few shades darker than my own and once it falls free, you can't really see that it's receding anymore. He fusses with it for a moment. "Better?"

I nod. I don't remember him being vain before. "My mom?"

"You're like a dog with a bone, aren't you?" He shakes his head. "No *how are you* or *it's good but weird to see you*. 'Cause it's feeling all kinds of weird to me. Kylan—that's my sponsor—said to keep it simple when I saw you so I'll try." He takes a deep drag drawing my gaze to the glowing red tip of his cigarette illuminating his pale skin before offering me one.

"I thought you were a dad now." I eye the pack of cigarettes he's holding out to me.

"Oh, right. Shit." He repockets the pack. "Okay, so Jensen, the ex, all I knew about him is that he lived in a van and always had a hard on for his camera. But then I remembered he had this sister who used to hook us all up with the sweetest—"

"Bauer," I grind out.

"Right, right." He taps his forehead with the hand holding the lit cigarette, sending little sparks of ash dangerously close to his hair. "Twenty years of frying your brain and it can be a little hard to stay on point. Where was I?"

I inhale through my nose before answering. "Jensen's sister."

"Exactly, so she was a lot easier to find and it turns out she still talks to her brother on the regular. Wanna guess what he told her last time they talked?"

"He's with my mom." I'm suddenly so lightheaded I nearly bend over to brace my hands on my knees. She's okay. She's with Jensen. He wasn't ever that bad of a guy. He never let her do any of the really bad stuff when she was with him. Couldn't have cared less about me, but the feeling had been mutual. Still of all the people she could have taken up with, Jensen was one of the better options.

"So let's go. Where are they?"

"You didn't get my messages? I've been calling you for hours."

"My phone died and I didn't bring a charger or...anything."

"Like *anything* anything?" He squints past me to look through the window of my car. "Your grandmother let you come out here without at least a toothbrush and clean underwear?"

When I don't answer, his gaze settles back on me. "You didn't tell them, did you?" He takes a drag on his cigarette, holding it until he hits the filter. "Ah, kid, you can't be doing that." He starts patting down his pockets. "Call them on my phone and let them know you're okay." Then he stops and turns to glance back at the restaurant. "I left it in my locker. Wait here."

I catch him by the arm when he starts to leave. "Who cares

about my grandparents right now?" But even as I say it, I remember my grandfather's voice earlier. After he stopped yelling, he'd just sounded worried.

"Don't be like that. I didn't raise you to be any better, but you have to be anyway."

"*You* didn't raise me at all."

He sighs, hands on his hips. "You think I don't know that? Before I got clean I didn't have relationships, I took prisoners and held hostages. So, yeah, that's what I've earned, but did they?" He shakes his head. "Can't say that, can you?"

I flex my jaw staring at him.

"So I'm gonna go get my phone for you."

This time I stop him with just my words. "I don't know the number, okay? So unless you've got a charger in there, I'm not calling anybody."

He mutters something about kids and technology, but then he's moving again, not toward the restaurant, but toward the passenger side of my car. "Then I guess you're coming home with me."

I've got my hands in my hair, pulling it back from my face and trying not to jump out of my skin from impatience. "The only place I'm going is to find my mom. So just give me the address."

Bauer's gaze immediately darts away and a sinking feeling pulls at my limbs.

"What?"

"I drove by the place earlier just to check it out, you know, make sure there wasn't anything you, uh, wouldn't want to see." He drops his cigarette and puts it out with his shoe, not looking up at me even when it's just a smear on the asphalt.

"They weren't there. But," he adds quickly, "I paid one of the neighbors to call when they come back. Might be a day or two…less than a week, for sure."

I try telling myself I can wait that long. What's a few days after all the time I've already waited? But my hands only tighten in my hair. And then his hand is patting me on the shoulder. I look from it to Bauer.

"Well, I don't know." He snatches his hand away. "Am I supposed to hug you or something?"

No, I don't want anything else from him except finding my mom. And if I can't do that tonight and one of his amends is offering me a bed and a phone charger, then what other choice do I have?

"Just get in the car, Bauer."

CHAPTER FORTY-SIX

NOW

REBECCA

I'm still awake when the clock ticks over to midnight. As if on cue my chest cinches tight and the pressure behind my eyes spikes until it spills over.

Today is the anniversary of my accident.

Today is the anniversary of my dad's death.

I dig my teeth hard into my lower lip, rolling my eyes up to stare at the ceiling and pleading with my body to stop, to let this feeling be added to all the other parts of me that don't feel anymore.

Sometimes I don't know what's worse, mourning the past or the future I'll never get to have.

I woke up the other day and forgot how it feels to run.

Two years.

730 days since I took my last step, since I saw my dad's face, heard his voice.

Two years since I fell down drunk in some stranger's house and he had to come to rescue me.

My tears turn hot.

I'd been crying that night too, angry that I was being yelled at, controlled. Upset over the loss of freedom I knew was coming for me.

My hands reach up to press over my mouth, to smother the increasingly loud sounds escaping from my lips.

Mom heard me last year. She even got up and I heard the floor creaking outside my door. I cried harder thinking she'd come in and that we'd pool our grief together, sink under it but still find our way back to the surface afterward because we'd be together.

But she hadn't.

The floor creaked again and she was gone, back in her half-empty bedroom, left to cry alone because of what I took from her.

My hands press harder, my lips squeezing together to the point of pain.

I hear her when she gets up the next morning and I rub the sandy-feeling grit from my eyes. I'm in my chair in less than a minute, out of the room and down the hall, catching her by surprise as she pours her morning coffee.

"Rebecca!" She presses a hand to her chest. "You startled me."

"Yeah, I'm sorry, sorry."

She goes back to pouring her coffee and I finally notice that, unlike me, she's dressed, and in a skirt and blouse.

"You're going to work? Today?"

The hand pouring the coffee wobbles, sending a small splash onto the counter.

"I'll get it!" I practically charge her, bending dangerously far to the left to grab the paper towel roll as I pass it. But she moves just as I reach her, and instead of stopping beside her, I run into her leg.

She cries out first from my impact and then from the hot coffee that splatters all over her chest. "Rebecca!"

"Sorry, sorry! Mom, I'm so sorry. Here." I start shoving pieces of paper towel at her, tearing them off and trying to pat her dry myself.

"Stop it!" Her bark makes me freeze. She takes the paper towel roll from me and sops up her blouse as best she can before squatting down to clean up the dribbles that splashed on the floor.

"Mom, I can—"

"It's easier if I do it."

Fresh tears spring to eyes already swollen from the night before. I know she's right, but I need to help, to do something. I reach for her mug, intending to rinse off the outside so she can pour a new cup.

"Just leave it," she says in a voice that hints at a night as sleepless as my own. When she stands, I glimpse red-rimmed eyes and know I'm right.

For some reason the thought is soothing. I know she misses Dad but she doesn't show it in obvious ways all the time. I've never come home to find her choked up over her wedding rings or misty-eyed while wrapped up in one of his old shirts, and she's never cried in front of me, not even in the hospital.

I've never even caught her going through old photo albums. We never had many framed family pictures around—Mom used to frequently stage and photograph different rooms in our house when she was trying to build up her portfolio, and personal items were strictly forbidden—and the few with Dad were all gone when I came home from the hospital. I'd hoped she'd taken them to her office with the Disneyland photos Ethan and I tried to get, but now that I know she moved, they could be anywhere.

That briefly soothing thought fades. She may have been crying over him last night, same as me, but right now she's planning to leave me alone for an office building she's never even mentioned.

I can't find actual anger inside me for that, just heavier sadness. It's further proof of how much distance there is between us, and if there was ever a day for us to start turning to each other, this is it.

She takes her mug to the sink and turns on the faucet.

"Mom?"

"It's fine, Rebecca. Why don't you go get dressed?"

"No, that's not—" I swallow my suddenly parched throat. "I was hoping you wouldn't go to work today." She doesn't immediately cut me off so I continue. "Maybe you could stay home, with me?" My eyes threaten to fill with tears. "It's just that today is hard, for both of us, and I think maybe it could be less hard if we didn't have to spend it alone."

My heart starts slamming in my chest as soon as I finish, and I watch the back of her silk-clad shoulders, looking for signs that she's trembling as much as I am.

"I don't know that that's a good idea." Her voice is thin, choked. "But I still have that therapist's number if you want me to call and make you an appointment."

"No, I don't want— Mom, no one loved him like we did.

We should be together." I blink away fresh tears. "I miss talking about him. Don't you?"

Her hand has wrapped around the edge of the counter and she's staring down at the sink. "Please don't ask me to do that. This day is hard enough without—"

She doesn't say *you* but the unspoken word ricochets like a bullet inside my skull.

She finally turns to face me. "I think it's best if we stay busy like we normally do. I'm going to work and you should too." She tugs at the wet spot on her blouse. "I—uh, I'll probably be late tonight so don't wait up." Then she's striding past me, hesitating for the briefest moment when she reaches me. "We just have to get through it. Tomorrow will be better." Her hand twitches at her side and I think maybe she's going to touch me but she doesn't.

My arms steal around myself when she's gone, trying to hold the breath that will shudder out of me.

I haven't tried with her in so long, and never actually asked her to grieve with me over Dad. My fingers dig into my arms thinking about how I'd all but begged her to stay with me and she couldn't do it.

I need—

I need something—

Somebody—

I can't be alone in this house today.

I can't—

I'm unsteady as I push my wheels to get back to my room, weaving too close to each wall as I shove. Everything I have is holding back that breath, keeping it locked inside.

My phone is on my nightstand and I grab for it, thumbing

frantically for Amelia's name only to see an unread message already waiting for me.

Amelia:
I'm here if you want to talk about
anything. Say the word if you want
to come by later and I'll pick you
up. Just know I love you lots and
I'm thanking God for you and the
amazingly beautiful life you have
ahead of you.

My face crumbles as I read the first lie she's ever told me. And I can't look at it.

Ethan's name is right below hers in my messages and I tap without even thinking.

And the breath tears free.

Ethan:
…

CHAPTER FORTY-SEVEN

BEFORE

REBECCA

"Oh no," Dad says, pushing open my bedroom door with the basket of folded laundry. "I thought we were done with this."

From my bed, I peel my puffy eyelids open to look at him then close them again.

A rolled-up pair of socks hits me in the head.

"Dad!"

"Honest mistake." He holds up the palms of both hands. "I was aiming for your face."

I grunt and turn away from him.

Another pair of socks hits my head. I don't react this time. He'll eventually run out of ammo. I can outlast him.

"Hey, Rebecca, come on." The corner of my mattress dips as he sits beside me and then his hand is resting on my head. "You gotta snap out of this."

"He should have been back by now." My voice is muffled because most of my face is buried in my pillow. "It's been so long."

Dad's big hand strokes my hair. "I'm sorry."

But that doesn't help, I want to say. *It doesn't change anything.* Ethan's still gone. Instead I roll over and into Dad's waiting arms. "He's my best friend."

"I know." I feel a light kiss on the top of my head. "I know."

Ethan has been gone five months this time, five months! That's longer than he got to stay.

I hadn't said it out loud, but this last time I was starting to think, to hope, that maybe his mom wouldn't come back. That he'd get to stay.

And I'd get to keep him.

"I hate her," I say.

"No, no." His hands on my shoulders pull me back so I can see his face, and his round blue eyes under thick bushy brows focus intently on mine. "Don't say that. You don't ever want to have hate in your heart for another person."

I can feel my chin quiver under his stern words. Ethan's been in and out of my life for years and every time he goes away it hurts more than the last time. And he's always different in little ways when he comes back, like pieces of him have been chipped away. He won't laugh at our inside jokes the same way or the sight of something innocuous will send him into a silence so deep it takes me days to draw him out again.

Once he came back with only one set of clothes that he refused to change out of for a week. I finally pushed him the pool. In January. He stopped swearing at me only when I jumped in too.

Another time he came back with half his head shaved and bruises on his arms that he only ever showed me. I offered to partially shave my head too but my dad caught us with the clippers and eventually persuaded Ethan to let him even out Ethan's hair instead.

And whenever I asked him about what happened when he was in California, he got so angry, like bash-his-skateboard-through-his-grandfather's-windshield angry. I'd been so afraid he'd get into real trouble for that that I'd come up with this elaborate story about a freak haboob dust storm that made him crash into the car. I don't know if the Kellys believed my lie, but the truth hadn't been something either of them wanted to consider either.

He's been gone for months and every time I look out my window to his empty bedroom I want to cry all over again.

"You can't stay in bed again today." Dad's voice is softer now. "Mom and I are starting to get worried—"

Yeah, right, they're both worried. That's why mom is here with him right now instead of her office again.

"—about the smell."

When I don't even crack a smile, Dad hugs me again. "Can you call him or write him?"

I shake my head. "We don't do that."

"What can I do?"

I let him hold me. "Just don't ever leave me."

His arms tighten. "Easiest promise I'll ever make."

CHAPTER FORTY-EIGHT

NOW

ETHAN

I wake up to an earthquake until I open my eyes and see it's just a little boy in Spiderman footie pajamas jumping on my bed.

"Hi, Ethan."

"Hi—" I yawn "—Os." Because this has to be Bauer's son. They'd all been asleep when we got in last night. I'd only stayed awake long enough to plug in my phone using the charger he leant me.

"I'm supposed to check and see if you're awake and if you are do you want pancakes."

Considering I haven't eaten anything since lunch yesterday, pancakes sound real good right about now. "I could eat."

Os leap-spins off the bed in a move worthy of Peter Parker himself, and sprints down the hall yelling, "He's awake and he wants pancakes!"

The second the door shuts, I grab my phone.

No messages from Rebecca but there are a ton from Neel.

Neel:
You didn't talk to Rebecca?

Neel:
I know I called you a dick
before, but seriously?

Neel:
DICK.

Neel:
Also I wasn't trying to steal
your cat.

Neel:
Who incidentally is also a dick.

I swipe over to my texts with Rebecca, my thumbs hovering over the keyboard.

She knows I'm gone by now and Neel or my grandparents will have told her enough to understand why.

She won't know my phone died so she'll think I just didn't care enough to tell her, that I took off without saying goodbye. Again.

She'll think I didn't care about hurting her.

Shit.

What do I say to her? I've never left and then reached out after. I always severed that part of my life when my mom took me away and then, when I came back, Rebecca and I just got to be happy and forget all about the hurt.

I drop my phone on the bed and cradle my head.

I don't think happy is gonna happen like it used to, if it ever really did, and I can't even blame anyone else for causing it this time.

Leaving yesterday was my choice. I can only try and hide from that fact for so long. I chose to keep going. I chose not to say goodbye. I chose to break that promise.

I pick up my phone again and start typing.

> **Me:**
> I messed up. I got word about my mom and I panicked and made a whole bunch of decisions without thinking about anything else and then my phone died. I'm with Bauer and we know where she is, or where she's gonna be in a day or two. After that I'm coming back.

> **Me:**
> I'm not gone, okay? I'll text you more when I can.

I send it then wait, and when there's no response right away, I tell myself she must still be asleep.

"Ethan!" a little voice yells. "Mom said to tell you breakfast is ready!"

"I said go tell him, not to yell through the house like a wild animal," a woman's quieter voice says.

I look at the phone again then force myself to set it down

and walk into the kitchen where I find Bauer's very pregnant wife, Tara, at the griddle.

"Um, hi. Morning."

Tara, a petite woman with short dark curls and a light olive complexion, smiles at me from over her shoulder and wipes her hands on a towel then comes over to hug me before I can even think to back up. "It's so great to meet you. Bauer hasn't stopped talking about you since you two reconnected. He's so glad you're here."

"Oh yeah. Where is Bauer?"

"Walking the dog." She moves back to the stove. "I know, you're probably thinking he's a line cook so he's the one who should be flipping pancakes." One golden brown circle gets added to a fluffy stack beside her. "But Bauer's the dinner guy. I do breakfast most mornings," she continues, before directing me to sit at a tiled table. "Plus, I figured you might want a few minutes before he attacked you again." She smiles. "I love him but he's a lot."

Understatement.

She sets the pancakes in front of me along with a warmed bottle of syrup. "Juice—" she points to the fridge "—coffee—" she points to the counter. "Help yourself."

"Thanks." My stomach growls audibly, pushing all other thought from my brain. I'm about to start shoveling food into my mouth when I reflexively think of my grandmother and force myself to wait until both Os and Tara are sitting too. Then I start shoveling.

"Bauer's said you always ate a lot," Tara says, though not really to me, more like an observation.

The bite of pancake in my mouth turns hard as I try to

swallow it down. What exactly had Bauer told her about me? About how he knew me? How do you persuade your wife to let an old girlfriend's kid stay in your house?

Bauer comes in then leading a massive dog that looks part horse but wags its tail like a puppy. I lose what's left of my appetite as I'm forced to watch him greet his family with kisses and questions about their plans for the day. A far cry from my faded memories of him with my mom. They mostly argued about money and the fact that there was never any food in the house. He usually only had one thing on his mind even when he could pretend otherwise.

I get more of a reserved greeting when he looks to me. "Ethan. Mattress okay for you?"

"Fine. Good." I didn't notice one way or another. All I want to do now is ask about my mom and if Jensen's sister has called yet. But I'm not sure I can do that in front of Tara.

Os announces he has to poop and tears out of the room as Bauer sits and starts forking a plate of pancakes for himself. "I didn't get to introduce you last night but this is my Tara."

"Oh, we've already been chatting," Tara tells him before looking over at me. "You know you really should call your grandparents. I'm sure they are as worried about Joy as they are about you."

Bauer catches the shocked look on my face and between bites says, "Oh, she knows everything." He stabs his fork in my direction. "Don't keep secrets from your partner. Fastest way to ruin a relationship."

Rebecca's face flits through my mind.

When I think about what might happen after we get the

phone call and find my mom, the pancakes in my stomach threaten to come back up.

So I'm not. Thinking beyond the call. Beyond finding out where my mom is and making sure she's okay.

Everything else has to come after.

He smiles at Tara and she smiles back until he adds, "Hard to believe she used to be a cokehead, huh?"

Tara hangs her head in her hands. "You did not just say that."

"What?" Bauer says. "He's known plenty of cokeheads."

Just then there's a yell from Os. "Mom! Can you help me wipe my butt?"

Tara pushes back from the table. "Maybe talk about the embarrassing and regrettable parts of *your* past while I'm gone, hmm?"

Os yells again and Tara calls in a singsong voice that she's coming.

"To be clear," Bauer says, "she's not a cokehead anymore."

I nod. "I gathered."

Bauer inhales two more pancakes before he notices that I'm not eating with him and sets his fork down. "Listen kid. There's some stuff I've been meaning to talk to you about. Amends and everything. I could have done a lot better by you." He glances down the hall. "I look at Os and he's not my blood, but he's my heart, you understand?"

"Bauer, you don't have to—"

"No, no." He holds a hand out. "You wouldn't let me send you books and you said no to getting you a bike, which I get since maybe you don't like riding bikes anymore, but hell, you barely let me give you a place to stay last night. Please let me do this."

I sigh because I know he's not gonna give up. "But not here, okay?" He may be comfortable with his wife knowing everything about him but I'm not. "Let's go for a drive."

CHAPTER FORTY-NINE

NOW

REBECCA

Luis repeatedly slams a wooden piece against his puzzle when it doesn't fit, then cries when his hand hurts. I bring his tiny fist to my mouth and shower it with kisses until he's giggling and brush his silky, fine hair back from his face with a sigh.

"So easy when you're a baby, isn't it?" Amelia sits on the couch and smiles at her son. "Ready to burn down the world one minute and the next..." She laughs when Luis starts gumming the piece then holds it out to me with a long, glistening string of drool still connecting it to his mouth.

"Hmm." After that noncommittal response, I take the puzzle piece and trade it for a fabric book with crinkly pages that he loves. Once he's engrossed in his book, I scoot back on the floor until I can lean back against the side of my empty wheelchair to watch him read.

"You're not gonna tell me how today went, are you?"

I glance over at her. "There's not much to tell." Such a lie and the flat expression on her face tells me she knows it.

She lowers her non-crinkly page book to her lap. "You know I didn't just invite you over so you could play with my kid and give me a break from doing floor transfers while dealing with morning sickness. I mean, I love that and please don't ever leave, but also you can talk to me. Sometimes I say things that are almost helpful."

"You say a lot of helpful things," I tell her as I clean the puzzle piece with a wipe and reach to pop it into its opening. "But I just want to forget about it." If the fatigue in my voice doesn't communicate that sentiment strongly enough, I let my eyes fall closed.

There's maybe a second or two of silence from Amelia before she says, "Okay, but—"

I groan. "No, but." Luis is very aware of tones so even though I'm feeling irritated, I keep my voice soft and even. "I'm not ready to celebrate my life. It doesn't feel like a good thing right now and I'm not really looking for you to tell me all the ways that disabled lives can be great."

Matching my gentle tone, Amelia says, "It's okay to accept your disability and still mourn too, especially on life days. I can look at my husband and son and be so happy, but also have to go lock myself in the bathroom sometimes and cry. It's a complicated thing, and your feelings about it will change and grow alongside you. *But*—" and she emphasizes the word so much that Luis looks up at her "—if you keep trying to convince yourself that your feelings don't matter and that if you ignore them long enough that they'll go away, they build until eventually—" She makes an impressive explosion sound that causes Luis to laugh and crawl over to the couch, pulling himself up to his feet so she can lift him onto her lap. "So maybe just explode with me because you know I can deal with the carnage."

"That was a really good explosion sound," I tell her, because it was and because I'm not ready to respond to what she actually said yet.

"I've been working on it. Mathias can do all kinds of explosion sounds and laser guns and everything and I am not going to be the lame parent who can only go 'pew, pew pew.'" She snuggles her son and takes on more of a baby voice. "No, Mama is going to be just as good because I still have a crippling need to prove that I can be as capable as my able-bodied husband even when it comes to ridiculous things like making battle sound effects for a baby." She sighs and turns to me. "See what I mean about complicated?"

She plays with Luis for a while after that and I watch her. Nothing today went like I wanted it to and I get what Amelia means about talking about it instead of keeping everything bottled up, but at the same time I don't see the point. Ethan isn't here and my mom wouldn't stay. How does saying any of that out loud make me feel better? Right now I just feel numb and I don't want to risk losing that.

"You know," she says after setting Luis back down to crawl over to me. "Things are going to be really different when the new baby comes. We'll keep a bassinet in our room for the first year probably and the addition we're planning will be done before then. I never use the office in the guest house, so we're just going to turn it back into a bedroom. It's pretty big too and it's just going to be empty..."

I freeze in the act of helping Luis balance to walk, that

numbness beginning to seep away. "Why are you telling me this?"

"Because I'm not stupid and you seem to think I am. Also because Neel talks a lot." She gives me a reproachful look. "College in California, really?"

I lower Luis until he's sitting and squeeze my arms into my sides. I understand what she meant about emotions building until they explode. It's almost as if my heart has started beating a countdown. "I was going to tell you."

"But why? Unless you're a phenomenal liar, you love working in the shop as much as I do. And okay, fine, maybe you'll want to start something of your own eventually, but there is still a lot I can teach you right here. Why would you want to give that up for an expensive degree I don't even think you want?"

Tick.

"I can't."

"Yes, you can. That's what I'm oh so subtly trying to tell you. If you just need to move out of your mom's house then you can move in with me and Mathias. We already talked about it. You'd have the whole guest house to yourself and unlike a college dorm, there's plenty of privacy. Plus we were already planning to remodel the bathroom and make it accessible."

Tick. Tick.

"I know there's a lot with you and your mom and maybe you feel like college is your way out, but it's not the only way. Maybe it's not even the best way. Just think about it, okay?"

Tick. Tick. Tick.

"I'm not going to push you, but I'm serious. Mathias and

I would love it. Luis and this new little one too. Promise me you'll give it some thought."

"I will." But I won't. I can't. I'm scrambling for that numbness to come back but it's not there.

CHAPTER FIFTY

NOW

ETHAN

The first thing Bauer does when we get in the car is call his wife and assure her we'll be home in time to make dinner.

The strangeness of that word, *home*, throws me off so visibly that Bauer doesn't try to talk to me for miles.

I don't think I've ever had a real home, not the kind I just left with noisy breakfast tables and pancakes with warm syrup. Mom and I moved around a lot and while she made sure we had something over our heads each night—even if sometimes it was only the roof of a car—it was always just a place to sleep and nothing more.

I suppose I came close when I stayed with my grandparents but no matter how many home-cooked meals they served or stuffed animals they filled my room with, can a place really be a home when you know that every night spent there might be your last?

I used to tell myself I didn't need a home, that four walls

and a roof meant nothing when my true home was a person, the one person who loved me and always came back for me no matter how long she'd been away.

That kind of thing was easier to believe when I was a kid and I knew where my mom was even when she had to leave me.

Had to leave me.

That's how she always said it. *Ethan, I have to leave you for a little while.* Had to like it was against her will, as though some kind of outside force was driving us apart when she wanted nothing more than to be with me. *I'm not good for you right now. But I'll get better and this won't happen again.*

"You ready to let me start now?" Bauer asks, pulling me out of my memories. "Dinner's gonna come a lot sooner than you think."

I really don't think I am. Those things that my mom said wouldn't happen again? Messed-up choices she made or let happen when she was high? Bauer was around for more than a few.

"I'm sorry, Ethan. Not for me, but for you. You were just a kid and I—" He shakes his head. "I was human shit. Pure and simple. It was wrong what happened to you, what I let happen. I should have been better." His eyes are red and wet when he lifts them to my face. "And I shouldn't have left you."

I start to scoff, but he's staring at me like I'm supposed to be hearing more than he's saying.

"You don't remember me from when you were little, do you? I used to think that was better for you. I told myself that for years after I left." He sniffs and drags the heels of his palms over his eyes. "But then I got clean, met Tara and Os. I started to understand what it means to be a father, that I'd been one long before Tara got pregnant."

I eye Bauer and the increasingly agitated way he's moving. Something is wrong. All my muscles tense in agreement. "Look, I get that this is part of your program and everything, but I'm really not asking you for anything more than a place to sleep till that call comes in, so whatever—" I gesture between us "—void you think you have to fill for me, don't."

"That's what I'm trying to say to you. It's only a void because of me." He slams a hand against his chest and then lets all his air out. "She never said, but I knew from the first time I held you. You look just like my dad." He pulls his hair back from his head. "And I hate to tell you this, kid, but this hairline is hereditary." He drops his hand. "Well, you gonna say something?"

I've been moving away from him as he speaks, pushing my back against the window until there's nowhere else to go. "You're lying," is my brilliant response. I remembered guys before Bauer, lots of them.

"We weren't together long that first time. She was serious about staying clean for you and I wasn't serious about anything. So she took you and left. I did send money whenever I had any. And then years later we fell in again together." He squeezes his eyes shut, maybe remembering how he was then with me and comparing that to how he is now with Os.

My chest starts rising and falling, pumping my blood faster and faster. "Are you shitting me with this right now?"

"No." He holds my gaze. "I'm not."

"So what now? Do I get to move in? Get matching PJs with Os for the family Christmas card? Hey, maybe I can even get Tara to adopt me. You know, make it all official before I change my last name to whatever the hell yours is!" My voice tears out of me, loud and harsh. "I mean that's why you're telling me this, right, *Dad*?" I laugh under my breath. "'Cause you're my dad now and not some asshole who used to put that shit in my cereal and laugh while I staggered around the kitchen until I fell and sliced my arm open." I raise it to show him the scar I still have. "Or how about that time when I was, what, four and you guys left me alone without anything to eat or drink for days and I had to live off ketchup packets and water from the toilet. Or when you left after introducing her to the guy who used to lock me in a closet whenever he came over."

He looks away long before I finish, wincing with each new memory I hurl at him. I wasn't sure he even remembered all that stuff but I can tell he does.

"You want me to keep going, Bauer? 'Cause I can. You know I can." He looks like he's gonna throw up, but it's nothing to how I feel. "Accidents," I say. "Mistakes. That's what she called them. Because she's my mom and she would never hurt me when she wasn't sick. And since you're my dad now, I guess that's what I have to tell myself about you too."

"No, I don't need any pretty lies," he says, and he's crying though his features haven't moved. "And I don't need you to forgive me. I need you to know I'm sorry." He looks half his size when he stops talking. "I—"

"Hey Bauer?"

He glances up at me, all hopeful. "Yeah?"

"All I came out here for was to find my mom. She's not here, so I'm leaving and you can get out of my car."

CHAPTER FIFTY-ONE

NOW

REBECCA

I'm not surprised to see Ethan in the parking lot when I leave the shop the next day, exactly one day after I needed him. He'd texted me that he was on his way home late last night and again this morning, hoping to see me before I left for work. I hadn't responded.

He's sitting on the hood of his car as I let the door close behind me and when he looks up, I wonder if he's half expecting me to smile like I always did as a kid when he came back, ready to forget how much he'd hurt me.

But he's stoic as he jumps down and walks toward me.

"You didn't answer my texts." I can't tell if there's an accusation in his voice.

"Did you find her?" Even as I ask I know he didn't. If he had, a text was all I would have gotten from him.

"No."

"I'm sorry." I don't reach out to touch him though. My hands have remained clamped around the push rims of my wheels since that first heart-stopping sight of him. I'm afraid that the only thing they'll do if I let go is ball into fists.

"I really needed to talk to you, stuff about my mom, yeah, but it turned into so much more. There were things I needed to tell you."

"I'm right where you left me," I say, so lightly that it's possible he doesn't hear me. I'm not smiling though and he thinks he knows why.

"I get that you're mad for the way I left, and I was mad at me too. I shouldn't have taken off like I did. I just got Bauer's text and it was like all my other thoughts, *bam*!" He slaps the side of his head. "You know?"

No, I don't know. My brain is a swirling mess of thoughts and the important ones, the vital ones are always drowning out the others. The thing is, Ethan had made me believe I was one of his important thoughts, one that he couldn't hide from even if he wanted to. I could never hide from him. Even now, questions about him crowd forward.

"Is Bauer still helping you look for her?"

As I'm sitting there trying to keep myself held as tightly as I can, he kind of explodes, spinning around to jump down from the ramp railing onto the ground several feet below. He kicks a deep spray of gravel from the edge of the otherwise smooth parking lot and the cords in his neck tense right before he lets out a yell. He kicks again after that, smaller and less focused.

"See this is why I needed to talk to you. So I'm there, meeting his new family—'cause he's clean now, has been for years—and then yesterday he tells me all this stuff that I can't deal with, so I leave, go to the address where she was supposed to be and I'm just wasting this whole day waiting for the phone to ring…"

I hear it, the ringing. It floods my ears drowning out the rest of his words about pancakes and little kids in Spiderman pajamas, about huge dogs and nice houses, about driving.

All I'm hearing is that he could have called me, asked about me, been there for me in even that small way when he had to know I needed him, when one single tiny thought about me should have been enough to get through to him yesterday, and it wasn't.

Part of me expected that to be the first words out of his mouth, not just the generic sorry, but the specific one, the only one that really matters. I thought he had remembered and that shame and regret had been what kept him from calling. I think I could have dealt with that, not understood but gotten through the hurt of it.

But now? Hearing this? I'm right back to yesterday, alone when I didn't have to be, by myself when he was supposed to be with me.

He can't understand. I know that and I'm trying to understand that from his point of view. Because he will feel bad when he remembers. He'll be sorry and apologize and maybe make new promises for next year. But yesterday still has such a hold on me and he won't be able to take it back when the broken promise of his company made it all so much worse.

Because I'd let myself want him, count on him. Not just his presence, but his promises.

And he wasn't there for me. He didn't even think of me.

"He told me he's my dad," Ethan says out of nowhere.

Yesterday gives me a minuscule amount of slack. "But I thought…?"

"I just always assumed the first time he was with us was what I remembered as a kid, but he said they were together before that," he says. "He could be wrong, and I mean what would it change either way?"

It would change a lot knowing who his father is. He'd told me a bit about Bauer. Enough to know that while it hadn't all been good, he'd cared about Bauer. And if the guy was really clean and, from what it sounded like, interested in having a relationship with Ethan…yeah, it could change a lot.

"He paid somebody at the apartment to tell us when my mom came back, but I checked it out and it doesn't look like anybody's been there in days. Which means she could be anywhere." The muscle flexes in his cheek. "She could be dead."

"Don't say that." My voice comes out fast and harsh, startling him from his train of thought.

He meets my hard gaze and then nods a little. "I know, I know, but I don't know—" his hands are free to make the fists I can't let mine make "—anything! I'm tired of it. The worry and that sick feeling." He drives one of those fists into his gut. "It's always there, even when I was a kid and she was supposed to be the one taking care of me, I felt it. And it just gets bigger, you know? Not me. It." His hand falls away. "I wish I could just be mad at her. I get close sometimes, but I can't ever let myself get there, and then I've got all this anger and nowhere to put it." His voice had gone soft but it strengthens again looking at me. "If you'd just answered my texts. Why can't that be enough for you sometimes? Why is it always all or nothing? I needed you yesterday."

My chin trembles, the only part to move as that final part of me breaks.

CHAPTER FIFTY-TWO

NOW

ETHAN

I swallow, taking in Rebecca's rigid posture for the first time. "I had all these thoughts in my head about dealing with everything when I came back, telling you everything. But then Bauer said what he said and I didn't find my mom and you wouldn't talk to me."

She glances away while she smooths her face. "I didn't know what you were going through."

"Yeah but that's my point. You didn't know just like I didn't know everything you were dealing with after your accident. I couldn't be physically here so you wouldn't let me be here at all. We still could have talked and heard each other's voices all these years. I could have been *there* for you every day, and you should have been there for me."

I see the way my words hurt her, the way her chin trembles that tiny bit more.

"I'm not saying this to make you feel bad, I'm saying it so you can stop. We both messed up, so maybe, just this one time more we can pretend we didn't. 'Cause I don't like feeling let down by you."

A sound slips from Rebecca, sharp and broken. It takes all the strength out of my words.

"This time wasn't the same as me leaving you a flower without a word when we were kids. I had to go when I got Bauer's text. I couldn't think of anything else, not even the cars around me. It took mindlessly racing through a red light for another thought to get through to me and by then my phone was dead. But you were what got through." Nothing else could have slowed me down even for a second, and yet for her, I completely stopped. "I know I broke my promise but I was only gone a day, and I wish now more than anything that I just stayed here with you yesterday so we could—"

My head snaps to her, still right outside the door at the top of the ramp, tracing the white-knuckled grip she's had on her rims from the moment she came outside. Not letting herself move, barely letting herself talk.

Not because she's angry, or not only.

I take two strides, leap up to grab the railing and swing over it until I'm right there, right beside her where I should have been yesterday, where I promised to be.

"Bec—"

She knows what I've realized and there's so much misery weighing down her features when she tries to smile. "It's okay."

But it's not. How could it be? I took off without a thought in the world except for what turned out to be nothing, what part of me always knew would be nothing, and I left her on the hardest day of her life.

I didn't even call her.

"Don't say that." My eyes are the ones that are shiny as I wrap my hands around the frame of her chair, a poor substitute for holding her. "Don't let me off the hook when I messed up this bad."

"I know you didn't mean to," she says, which isn't the same as *I'm okay* or *it didn't hurt to be forgotten and abandoned.* That's what I did.

For the first time since coming out here months ago, the sick knot in my stomach isn't because of my mom.

"And I missed being here for you for what? The chance to chase down someone who's made it clear she doesn't want to be found?"

"Not someone," Rebecca says softly. "Your mom."

A phrase grows inside me, harsh and angry, ready to erupt out of my throat. Seventeen years' worth of rage, but I swallow it down.

This moment isn't about anyone else but Rebecca and me. It's not about my anger, it's about hers. Or it should be.

"You should be yelling at me."

She shakes her head. "I'm not angry at you."

That's so much worse. "Was it—are you okay? Did you—"

She drops her head to stare down at her lap, drawing a quick audible breath that's as effective as a scream in cutting me off. "Can we not?"

"I just need you to know—" I reach for her hand, but she draws it away, the rejection involuntary but clear.

"I do. I know." She retreats back behind that smile, which hurts more than anything.

"Why couldn't you be mad before, huh? If you'd just texted

me back, I still could have been here with you." I want to jerk
her chair, angry at both of us. "Why do we keep doing this?
If I'd called you first and told you what I was doing, you'd
have come with me, wouldn't you?"

Her silence is answer enough and I hear my jaw crack from
how tightly I clench it.

"What if I don't go back?"

She shakes her head so slightly it's barely a movement. "You
literally just left."

I do shift her chair this time, just enough to lock her gaze
to mine. "But I don't want to. I don't want any of that anymore. I want you." I scoot closer. "Do you hear me? I'm done
leaving."

Gently, she pries my fingers from her chair. They fall without her having to do more than nudge and she moves back.
"And I'm done asking you to stay."

CHAPTER FIFTY-THREE

NOW

REBECCA

I hate my dress. The skirt is too narrow so it keeps riding up, meaning that all night I've been in a fight to keep from flashing my soon-to-be stepfather's family.

The venue for Mom and John's engagement party, Antonio's Restaurant, is beautiful but it's been a nightmare for me since we got here.

The doors all weigh a ton and feel like they are vacuum sealed on the inside. I've nearly pulled myself out of my chair twice just trying to open them.

I can't remotely get under the tables because of the pedestal bases so I have to eat my dinner with my plate in my lap, which is as fun as it sounds.

This is where they had their first date so when John's sister wanted to reserve the pre-ADA-built venue as a surprise, what could I say but sure?

I just have to keep smiling at every concerned look or word from anyone and say I'm fine, point out some nice bit of inaccessible architecture, and hope to distract them long enough to get away.

I don't blame the restaurant. I knew from a single glance that it wouldn't be wheelchair friendly; most older places aren't. I get it. Short of tearing it down and starting again from scratch, there's not much they can do. Amelia would say there's something they can do, and she'd do more than say it, but I'd prefer to appreciate its old-world charm from the outside than deal with all the inaccessibility from the inside.

And I would have if John's sister hadn't told my mom right in front of all their friends that I didn't mind the party's surprise venue at all.

Not in the slightest.

So when the wineglass in front of me is filled along with all the others, the protest on my lips dies. The deep red color swirls invitingly and it's far easier than I ever thought it would be to pick it up.

Catching my reflection in the arched mirror to my side stills my hand as my gaze traces every curve of my wheelchair and the memories of how I got there. They go further back too, to parties and beers, and tree houses and flasks.

I've never tasted wine though.

I see one other thing in that mirror: Mom and John as they ascend a few steps out to a balcony, heads bent together in intimate conversation.

I haven't had anything to drink since the accident and it turns out I'm still a lightweight. They bring wine bottles out for our entire table and no one seems to notice when I help myself again, and again, and again. It's not like I'm staggering around or anything.

Can't stagger in a wheelchair. Sway slightly, maybe.

The wine helps a lot.

Who cares if somebody bumps my wheelchair and causes my chicken parm to slide off my plate and onto my lap? So what if I scrape the skin off the knuckles of both hands squeezing through the stone arched doorway of our private dining room? And who even really notices when the waitress stands right beside me and asks the woman to my right—a former client of my mom's—what I would like to order instead of asking me herself?

Not me.

And more wine for me.

More wine when the happy couple is toasted.

More wine when Layla wriggles her way over to her dad's lap and pictures start snapping along with calls for me to join them. I graciously decline because even three glasses in I can see there's no chance I'm fitting through the mess of people and chairs to reach the other side of the table, not without literally making every other person move.

More wine for me.

And even more when everyone makes their way out onto the balcony after dinner to enjoy the stars. Those five uneven stone steps leading out onto the balcony? Why should anyone give those a second thought at my mother's engagement dinner?

No thank you to the two guys I've never met before—John's cousin's I think—who offer to carry me up. We'd never fit anyway and then I'd just be trapped out there, waiting on the benevolence of even more strangers to have to carry me back down

The wine bottles are empty now too, and even though I glimpse champagne flutes on the cocktail tables outside—perfect nose height for me—it's not worth it. I just want to go home. But that's one more thing added to this list that I can't do on my own tonight. I rode with my mom and John who look to be having a grand old time.

Yeah, I'm done.

My hands fumble pulling my phone from my purse, sending it tumbling to the cobblestone floor and skidding under a nearby side table with flowers on top. My head spins a little when I reach down to try to grab it, but it's not happening. Frustrated tears threaten behind my eyes and the wine is turning sour in my belly. I'm remembering this feeling, the sloppy coordination and my memories becoming angry crayon strokes scribbling through my brain. Broken glass and flashing lights.

Sticky and red.

I shake my head, wanting the images gone, but they don't leave, just slosh around.

The private dining room is all but empty now save for a much older woman shuffling toward the balcony with a hand hanging on the arm of a younger male relative.

A waiter will have to come soon, just to check on things. That or someone will come in off the balcony in search of the bathroom that has an accessible stall but a door I can't open. I'll ask for help with my phone then.

I can wait. No problem. It's fine.

So fine.

But my eyes are stinging and—

"Rebecca? Why are you still in here?" Mom appears in

the doorway, her cheeks flushed and a smile fading from her face as she looks at me. "John's nephews offered to carry you up. Everyone's waiting." The disapproval in her voice is what breaks the damn inside me, not for tears, but for something equally unrestrained.

"Oh, are they? Everyone's so concerned for me?" I surge forward with an unsteady push of my chair. "Is that why we're in this restaurant with all its WE HATE WHEELCHAIRS signs everywhere?"

She rears back. "What are you talking about? There aren't any signs—"

"Yeah, Mom, there are." My voice comes out in a slight staccato as I push forward again, bumping over the cobblestones. "Sign." I deliberately shift course to the table and make it all of two inches underneath it before slamming into a thick pedestal. "Sign." I point at the narrow door leading into this room and the even narrower one to the balcony. "Sign, sign." With another jabbing point at the five ascending steps, I say, "Sign, sign, sign, sign, and sign. Want me to go on?"

Her lips pull tight. Could that actually be shame on her face? "Joanna said you were fine with this restaurant. I made sure she knew to run everything past you. Why didn't you tell her it was a problem?"

"Because I couldn't!" I yell, but the crowd outside is so loud that only my mom and possibly a passing waiter in the hallway outside hear me. "Not with her going on and on about how romantic it is here." I imitate her voice. "You don't mind, do you, Rebecca? I'm sure you don't." I move to set my empty glass on the table but misjudge the distance, and it shatters on the stone floor.

My mom jumps back, her gaze snapping from the glass to me. "Are you—?" Even in the dim meant-to-mimic-candlelight glow I see more color flush her cheeks. "Rebecca, have you been drinking?"

My face twists up like I might cry, but I force it into scowl. I try to spin toward her but my footplate gets caught on a wooden grapevine carving spiraling up the length of the table pedestal and knocks my foot off. The table is so low on my thighs that I can't reach beneath it to fix my foot. I can't back up straight either because there's a chair behind me wedging me in.

"Let me—" Mom starts toward me, but I shoot a dagger glare at her.

"Don't."

She halts midstride, staring wide-eyed at me.

I bang forward then back, again and again with increasing force each time, fully aware that I could inadvertently smash my foot and break something, but I'd rather that than my mom helping me.

Finally, the chair behind me topples sideways with a bang, freeing me to back up and reposition my foot. There's no helping the angry tears that have left tracks down my face.

"You should think about this stuff." I make a sweeping arc through the air with one arm, taking in the restaurant as a whole and not caring if she can hear the slight slur in my voice. "I'm your daughter and you should think about me. Just a little. Don't make me do this." I gesture at the tears I am powerless to stop. "And for what? A nice party out there with your friends? Did you even notice the stairs or think for even a moment about this, right now, everyone out there toasting you and your new life, knowing I couldn't be part of it?"

She ducks her head, fast, but not fast enough. I see the tear slip free.

"Or do you just not care at all anymore?" My accusation is as sharp as it is quiet. I don't want anyone else hearing this. I don't even what to hear it, to make it feel truer than it already does.

Her head shoots up. "You know I do. I always think about you first."

But the thing is, I don't.

A cheer rolls in from out on the balcony.

"You better go," I tell her, brushing my cheeks dry. "John's probably missing you."

A busboy comes in to gather up plates and stops short. "Um, I can come back." He turns to go but I ask him to pick up my phone first. I hug it tightly to me when it's safe in my hands again.

"We'll fix this. I can get everyone to come back inside," she says.

"Don't bother." I'm already pushing Send on the text I just typed and moving toward the door. "Someone's picking me up. Have a great night, Mom. I won't wait up."

CHAPTER FIFTY-FOUR

NOW

ETHAN

Rebecca:
Can you come pick me up?

We haven't talked since the night outside the shop, and as far as I know Rebecca hasn't been over to swim in that time either. It had felt like the end, like she was done with me, so when I get her text and the pin she drops for me, I don't stop to think what might have changed or might be going on. In truth, I don't care. I grab the keys to my grandmother's car—mine has been temporarily confiscated after my impromptu and unannounced trip to LA—and am out the door in less than a minute. If my grandparents hear me leaving, that's another thing I don't much care about. They can ground me for longer later. In that moment, all that matters is Rebecca and the chance to fix things between us.

I pull up and see her out front with her arms wrapped around herself despite the heavy, humid air promising rain

later. I stop to suck in a breath, not just because I've been aching with missing her, but because she's stunning.

Her curls are pulled up and pinned with little clip things
that sparkle under the light as she moves to meet me. She's
got on a nice dress too, silk or satin, in a pale yellow color
that makes her skin look more golden than any metal she
could forge. But that just-soothed ache comes back with a
vengeance as I walk toward her.

The shimmer above her eyes can't hide how red they are
or distract from the mascara smudges under them. There's a
big red smear of marinara sauce on her dress and her knuckles are—

"Bec, what did you do to your hands?" I drop to a knee
and reach for them, turning her hands to better see the angry
scrapes in the dim moonlight.

"What's that old movie with Brad Pitt?" She snaps her fingers a few times trying to recall it. *Fight Club!*"

"You hit somebody?" There's no keeping the horror from
my voice.

"No, but doesn't that sound better than narrow stone doorways?"

"Narrow stone doorways?" I frown until she pulls her other
hand from mine and mimes pushing her chair, her gashed-up
knuckles sticking out on the side.

I point at the restaurant. "In there?" I'm standing again
and moving toward the entrance, ready to do I-don't-know-
what when I realize something else that turns my aching
chest ice cold.

"You've been drinking."

Her grin doesn't come close to touching her eyes. "See? I

told you you weren't stupid." Her voice grows thin, hard as she brushes a light finger over her scraped knuckles. "Me, on the other hand. So dumb." She glances back at the restaurant that looks like it was built back in the forties or something. "I know better than to try to go to a place like this and anybody who loved me should have known that too."

"Rebecca!"

Her mom is pushing out a heavy-looking door with John right behind her. She catches sight of me and hesitates. I figure she's about to order Rebecca to go with them, but she only looks at her daughter for a moment before directing her words to me.

"She can't transfer by herself if she's unsteady." There's another quick glance at Rebecca. "And then when you get her home, she'll need—"

"Stop!" Rebecca says, staring at her mom like she's never seen her before. "What are you doing?"

Her mother blinks. "Making sure you get home safely without falling or hurting yourself."

"That's what you care about right now? Not that I've been drinking for the first time since I broke my back and Dad—" She clamps her jaw shut and sucks in a breath through her nose. "Not why? How do you not care about that?"

Her gaze flicks to me and then John. "We'll have to talk about that later."

Rebecca laughs and the sound raises the hair on my neck. "Right, 'cause we talk so much and you never shut me down when I try. No, you're right, Mom. Great plan. So go on, tell Ethan what to do, or tell John. Or maybe you can go get another waiter, anybody but you."

She doesn't wait for a response so she doesn't see the way her mom clutches for John's hand to keep herself upright. Rebecca ignores everyone and wheels over to the car door, banging it against her chair a few times before she moves clear enough to open it all the way.

I meet her mom's gaze as I move to Rebecca's side, unsure what I'm looking for there, but knowing that it's not just Rebecca I'm talking to when I say, "Let me help you."

She shoves me away at first, but even that move lacks coordination. "I'm fine!"

"Are you?"

"No." Her response is almost snotty so it takes me a second to hear the actual word. "But I don't want any help right now. I just—" She looks up at me and we're close enough for me to see that she's…barely holding it together. "Can we go?" she whispers. "Please?"

I nod and she doesn't protest when I scoop her into my arms and lift her into the car, but she doesn't look at me either when we drive away.

I don't head home and she doesn't tell me to, she doesn't tell me anything, not even when I turn off down some residential street and pull over, shifting into Park and then immediately pulling her easily into my arms.

Beside me, Rebecca makes a sound, soft, like she's trying to hold it in but can't. "I told her tonight. That I see it, this whole new life she's making without me. She said it's not true but it is." She starts nodding. "It is."

"Then she's a fool," I say into her hair. "Anybody would have to be not to want you."

Rebecca pulls back just enough to search my face with her tearstained one.

And then she kisses me.

It's soft, unsure, like for once I might be the one to push her away.

My arms slide up her back and pull her close, swallowing the little gasping sound she makes before her hands rise up to twine into my hair.

She tugs just enough to send my head spinning. A feeling no artificial high could ever give sparks in my chest, pulses through my limbs as I drink her in, almost crushing her to my body, deepening the kiss until I can feel her heartbeat hammering against my own. Until I can taste the wine on her tongue and the salty tears slipping from her lips to mine, until—

I pull away, panting, wanting to hold her to me again with a need that's almost painful, that *is* painful when I see her glassy eyes spilling over.

"What?" She searches my face, her hands still in my hair, but loose now.

I shake my head at her. "Bec…"

She goes stiff, her arms jerking away from me. I can almost see the thoughts assaulting her as those same arms that held me moments ago, encircle her now like a vice. "You're leaving again."

"What? No. I told you before that I would stay, but you were drinking tonight." I let her see in my eyes what that means to me, and she knows better than anyone what that means to me. "After everything and now you're kissing me…? I'm not okay with that and I know you aren't either."

She flinches back with every word, so I reach for her hand to flatten against my chest so she can feel the way my heart is still pounding because of her, because of that one moment when everything I ever wanted was mine.

But her eyes don't soften, they narrow.

CHAPTER FIFTY-FIVE

NOW

REBECCA

I pull my hand back as soon as he smooths it over his chest. I don't want to feel him anymore. I don't want to feel anything anymore. If I could I would draw my paralysis up the rest of my body until nothing could touch me ever again.

I jerk farther away, using my hands to brace against the seat, and shift closer to the window so our legs no longer touch. One of his hands falls to my thigh, resting there until I wrench that part of me away too.

I can't feel it anyway.

I dig my teeth into my lips as another tear comes dangerously close to falling.

You were drinking…

I squeeze my eyes shut at the memory of his words and the look in his eyes, that mix of pain and guilt and…hurt.

"You gotta talk to me," he says, the fingers of his right hand inching closer to my bare leg, and I start viciously tugging the ridiculous dress back down again.

I don't want to see my skin, to see the parts of me that haven't felt like mine in years. They feel dead, my legs. And they are. They don't move or register touch, and the parts that I can feel are wrong, miswired. None of it's right and I don't want it anymore. I pull with all my strength on my skirt.

My dress rips, right along the seam, and something inside me tears too.

"Why? Why did he have to die and I have to break?" I'm gone then, my body shaking with sobs I can't control. "And she doesn't want me. *You* don't want me, never enough to stay." I whimper and pull into myself when he tries to reach for me. "No. I'm done. Do you hear me? I'm done. I can't do it anymore."

He hesitates then moves his hand forward, deliberately trailing over the newly exposed part of my leg, the same part that I had him trace that very first day we found each other again out by the pool.

Sensation sparks to life, not quite like it used to before the accident, but I feel his skin on my skin, warm and alive, and my chin quivers. And then I cry harder when, just as deliberately, he moves his hand to the side and that feeling fades until it's only pressure, only the slight weight that I register. He's trying to make me understand that to him, there's nothing broken about me.

"Then tell me. Yell if you want at whoever you want. I know I deserve it." His other hand rises to cup my face, angle me toward him when I turn away. "But trying to hide from what you feel like this?" He shakes his head. "One drink is too many and a thousand is not enough."

I brush his hands away, both of them. I don't want his hands on me, the one I feel on my face and the one I don't on my leg. I don't want any of it because all of it hurts. "You don't know anything about what I feel."

A thread of anger weaves its way into his voice. "I know what it's like to be around somebody who wants to feel anything other than what's going on inside."

"'Cause I'm your mom now? Is that what you're saying?" I sneer at him to hide the sharp sting from his words.

"You know I'm not."

"But that's what you want, isn't it? Another broken person for you to throw your life away for?" He has to know that's what I am, that's what he's trying to make me. And I forgot for a minute, because I was sad and a little drunk, but I'm not the stupid one here.

"Rebecca. Stop." The muscle in his jaw clenches. "You drank too much and you're mad at me for reasons you won't be when you sober up enough to think clearly."

"Oh, really? So I'll wake up tomorrow and magically I won't care that you left and forgot me on the anniversary of my accident and my dad's death? Hey, maybe I'll even laugh about my mom not caring about me yet again." That stinging pain inside me grows and collides with the deep cut from his rejection and crashes into the festering wound of my mother's apathy.

"But I disappointed *you*, right? That's what you said outside my shop when you lectured me about unanswered texts." I lean into his face when he tries to drop his gaze. "No, you don't get to do that, look the other way and pretend that everything is fine when you leave. I'm not letting you do that anymore." Another sob tries to claw its way from my throat.

"I break again every year on that day and the only time you cared was when you had to face me afterward."

His eyes are fierce when they snap to mine. "That's not true. You don't know—"

"Stop! I'm sick of that excuse. What don't I know? What's gonna make this all better?"

But he doesn't say anything because nothing will.

"You're so smart, Ethan. Always one step ahead of everybody. Am I thinking clearly enough for you yet? Is that what your mom did? Realize she loved you enough to get sober without rehab? Call you right away because you were her first thought when she got out and not her next fix?"

His face goes hard, unmoving, and I know I've gone too far, that I should take his suggestion and stop, but I can't because inside it still hurts too much.

"At least you got to save one of us tonight, huh? Does it make you feel good? Being the hero?"

"I was never the hero," he says, staring straight ahead when he restarts the car. "And none of this feels good."

CHAPTER FIFTY-SIX

NOW

ETHAN

I tear through the house when I get home, pulling out drawers in every room I pass, yanking open cabinets, searching for...

The light in the kitchen is on and my grandfather comes barreling out, my grandmother right on his heels looking like she's already been through the war he's ready to start.

"Where have you been?"

I don't look at him, just move to the other side of the desk in the study and pull open another drawer. "I'm not doing this with you right now. I've had a shit night and I'm not interested in adding anything else to it."

"Look at me when I'm talking to you. You took your grandmother's car. Where were you?"

I grit my teeth. *Stubborn old man.* "I had to go do a thing."

He shakes his head. "No, you don't get to take off without telling us where. Not again." He comes right at me, stopping mere inches from my face and I have no chill, none whatsoever with his flaring nostrils that close. I scramble back.

"You knew I was in LA last week. You called me—"

"You said all of ten words on the phone. We didn't know when you'd becoming back—if you'd be coming back." He stops then, noticing all the drawers I've opened. "What are you doing?"

I try to shove past him. "Looking for my keys."

"You don't have keys, and you won't be getting them back for another month, or did you forget our conversation from last week?"

Oh, I remember the ass-chewing he's referring to, and I'm not about to sit through another. I dart a quick glance at my grandmother, remembering the relief in her face when I'd come back…it's gone now, replaced by tight-lipped worry.

"Ethan, we need to know where you are. I know you understand that."

"No," I say calmly even as a long-denied part of me starts to smoke and spark inside. "You don't need to know, you *want* to know, which means I don't have to tell you shit. That's the rule, right?" I glance back and forth between them, one face hard, bordering on furious, and the other close to tears.

"What are you—"

My grandmother cuts my grandfather off with a hand on his arm, never taking her eyes off me. "No, it's not the rule. We were afraid you'd try to leave and find her, and we didn't want to lose you both."

"That's not up to you," I say, my jaw hardening. "You kept everything from me."

"We thought we were keeping you safe," my grandmother says, headless of the flames threatening to lash out and burn her, "That's all we ever tried to do. You were so young."

The sparks leap onto the fuel of her words, blazing up in an instant. They were the ones who didn't know. I was there, living the life they didn't want to think about.

"But we should have told you this time." Her face softens even as her eyes well up. "I'm sorry. She'll always be my little girl, but I knew she wasn't going to stay in rehab no matter what she promised us. You're seventeen, Ethan. Next time we wouldn't have been able to keep you with us."

"Yeah, well, it's a little late for sorry." I turn my attention back to the desk and finally spot the keys. "And as soon as I get my keys, I'm—"

My grandfather slams the drawer shut, barely giving me time to snatch the keys and my hand back first. "You have a job and responsibilities here, people who care about you. You don't even have a car and you're not going anywhere else in your grandmother's."

I whirl on him. "You can't keep me here." But his expression tells me that's exactly what he'll try to do.

"This life already took one person I love from me and I won't watch it take another."

The fire inside engulfs my last bit of restraint and explodes out of me. I shove him back. "Won't watch it?" The words scorch my throat. "Is that how you pretended it wasn't happening? Just closed your eyes and imagined that she was fine all these years?" I feel the wetness on my cheeks, but the fire inside won't stop, not anymore. "I didn't get to look away or pretend. I saw everything, lived everything, only I wasn't big enough to stop it." I shove him again and he lets me.

"What could we have done? We tried everything to help her get clean, everything, but she wouldn't—"

"You shouldn't have let her take me!" Their faces turn ashen as soon as I scream it. "This life you gave me here, food and clothes and somewhere safe to sleep…" I glance at the wall as though I can see through it to Rebecca's house across the yard "…somebody who loved me without asking for anything in return. And then you let her rip me away from all of that over and over again just to watch her fall harder every time."

My grandmother's tears are streaming silently down her face, but she isn't moving, neither of them are.

"You were her parents. You should have done more to protect me and save her." I wipe at my face and draw my shoulders back. "But I'm big enough now."

I ignore my grandmother's tears, shouldering out the door and moving faster than even my grandfather can grab for me.

"What do you think you're doing?"

I see more than his red face and flaring nostrils. I see my grandmother's faintly trembling chin and too-shiny eyes, all of it together makes my hands shake as I scoop up Old Man from the hall on my way to the garage. "Making sure you don't have to watch."

CHAPTER FIFTY-SEVEN

NOW

REBECCA

Tap, tap, tap.

I look up from the computer in Amelia's office where I've been responding to custom order requests all morning to see her in the doorway.

"You've got a guest," she says.

I must do some kind of full-body jerk because Amelia's expression turns soft and she shakes her head.

"No, sweetie, it's not Ethan."

She knew, of course she did, that I was hoping it would be him. Well, mostly hoping, and maybe just slightly dreading. It's only been two days, but it feels like a lifetime since we last spoke and he left again.

At least I got a text this time.

Ethan:
I got into a fight with my grandparents so I'm going to go stay

with friends while I figure things
out. I don't know if you want to talk
to me or not but I need some time.

Waking up to his message had been the perfect chaser to my hangover, one that ensured I suffered emotionally as well as physically the whole next day. Mom's complete vanishing act since the engagement dinner disaster has just been the icing on the cake. I haven't seen her once, but I know she's been coming home because of the new table in the kitchen, with four skinny legs in the corners and extra clearance under the top. It looks nice too, not like the inexpensive, wobbly one she'd first gotten after the accident. There's also a new ramp at the front door, solid and blending in with the design of the house instead of clashing against it. Every time I get home from work I notice other new changes. The house looks more in keeping with her design aesthetic, but why bother spending money to improve the accessibility when she knows I'll be leaving for college soon? According to her, I'll be much too busy to visit often so why not just wait a little longer and get rid of it all?

That last part of me that can still feel hurt by her wonders if it's all just a show for John and Layla, but I don't want to go there.

At least I know she's not my guest. Hope blooms inside me again when I consider that it might be Neel, ready to be done with his space from me. When I raise my eyebrows at Amelia, silently asking who's here, she just backs up, inviting me to go see for myself.

When I wheel out into the shop it's to find John waiting for me. "Oh, hi." My greeting is somewhat awkward because I haven't seen him since the engagement dinner either.

John's smile is dim for him, still plenty of teeth but not the full-watted grin he usually offers me. "Hey, sorry for showing up like this. Amelia said you might have a few minutes?"

I push over to him, trying to act like I'm not nervous over what brought him here. "Sure, what's up?" *Don't say Mom, don't say Mom…*

"It's about your mom."

I make an instant course correction, using only one hand on my next push so I turn to the side instead of continuing toward him. "That's not really something I want to talk about with you." Or anyone, but since he's the only one asking…

The truth is I've thought a lot about my mom in these last forty-eight hours, and while my face flames hot when I remember—vaguely—some of the things I said and did that night, I can't wholly regret them. I haven't been able to tell her how I've been feeling since—forever. I don't like that I messed up the engagement dinner or upset John, but at least she knows now, at least I got to tell her.

Some of it anyway.

"Hey now," he says, in that soothing deep timber of his. "We're family, or we're going to be in a few days. We got to be able to talk to each other."

I stop and glance over at him. "There's a lot between my mom and me."

"I know, and I'm not asking to know all of it or anything

---

you don't want to tell me." He hesitates then points at the wheelie stool beside me, asking permission.

I nod even though I really, really don't want to have this conversation with him. Unlike my mom, John isn't the type to let a situation resolve itself or hide from something he may have done wrong. If I don't hear him out now, he'll just keep coming back.

The stool is too small for him, most things are, but he doesn't comment as the metal creaks under his weight. We both hold our breath for a moment waiting to see if it will hold. Finally, John lets out a low laugh.

"Well, that was close."

"I'll make sure we get a better stool in here for you."

"Oh, it's no problem."

"No," I say more firmly. "You should have a place to sit when you come here. We're kind of big on making sure everybody is accommodated here."

He looks at me, then nods. "You're right. That's important. Thank you."

"You're welcome."

He sighs then rubs his hands over his thighs. "I guess that's as good a transition as any for me saying I'm sorry. The restaurant the other night was…well, I should have said something as soon as we got there even when you didn't. Joanna was only thinking about me and Keri and how we'd had our first date at Antonio's, not about how challenging it would be for you. I forget sometimes that you're still just a teenager, and you shouldn't have to advocate for yourself alone all the time, especially not with somebody like my sister. Can you forgive me?"

Short, to the point, and sincere. I hadn't thought I needed an apology from John, but hearing it from him, I realize I do, that part of me was hurt that he'd let it happen. It paled in comparison to how I felt about my mom's role, but John is my friend and he should have done better by me.

"Yes," I say. "Thank you." It's a little stiff as far as accepting apologies go, but it's what I can give right now. Plus, I know he's here for more than that, and when he finally gets to it, I kind of wish I'd stayed hidden in the office.

"Good," he adds with a pat on my hand that is equal parts nerdy and sweet. "Because I have a favor to ask you and it's a big one. I want you to make your mom's wedding band."

I slip my hand free with more than a little effort. "I don't think that's a good idea."

"Why not?"

I gawk at him. "Really? How about because we barely talk? Or she's counting down the days until I'm out of her house?" Those big hands reach for mine again, but I pull them back. "No, it's okay. I'm not saying any of this for pity, just so you'll understand why you shouldn't ask me to make her ring."

John doesn't really understand how things are between my mom and me. He thinks he does, but we only ever show him our best behavior. We hide the ugly truth from him as best we can because we both care about him even if we can't care about each other. My chest goes impossibly tight. "She won't want it if it comes from me."

"You know that's not true—come on now." He shakes his

head. "You and your mom are very different people and that means you love in different ways too. Your mom has never once let me hold her hand in public, but she brings me lunch every Tuesday from Julio's even though they moved forty-five minutes away. Last year, she spent months helping me track down this antique dollhouse for Layla's birthday and somehow found one that looked almost exactly like the one my grandmother had. Layla still randomly hugs her for that and she's getting so much better at letting her."

"And that's great for you and Layla," I say, trying to hide the bitterness in my voice. "But it's not like that with me. I don't need lunches or dollhouses and she wouldn't try to give them to me anyway, not anymore."

John's face turns soft. "I won't pretend to know what these last couple years have been like for you both, but from what I see, you both want the same thing, and I think this wedding ring could be a way for you to reach her."

I suck in a shaking break. "Reach *her*? I've tried so many times. Why isn't she reaching for *me*?"

"Are you so sure she isn't?"

I try to laugh, but it comes out more like a cry. "I'm sure." The engagement party erased any doubt I had left.

"She's not like us, not like how I understand your dad was. This—" he scoops up my hand again before I know he's going to "—is easy for us. To tell people we love them, to show them. To let them in when we hurt or we've hurt others."

"It hasn't felt easy for me," I whisper.

"I know, but you keep trying." He squeezes my hand. "You've got that from your dad and it's not going anywhere."

The stool creaks when he stands, forcing me to crane my neck way back to look up at him. "I love a lot of things about you, but that one's right at the top."

"It won't matter. A ring isn't going to make her talk to me. And I'm not the only one who can try."

"That's true." He kisses the top of my head. "That's very true. But we're about to start something big with this wedding and I think it could be a fresh start for all of us, especially you and your mom. Might be worth everyone trying one more time, hmm?"

Amelia gives me plenty of space once John's gone, leaving me alone with thoughts that refuse to dissipate until I pull out a piece of paper and start sketching. The ring design doesn't come easy which is why, when my phone rings, I answer it even though I don't recognize the number.

"Hello?"

"Oh, hey, yeah, I wasn't expecting you to pick up. Nobody answers phones anymore. Is this Rebecca?"

I don't know the man's voice. "Who's this?"

"Bauer. I'm Ethan's…well, it's kind of complicated. I don't know if he's told you about me, but I'm—"

"You're his dad."

I hear a big, relieved sigh from Bauer. "He told you. I wasn't sure, but I figured if he'd talk to anybody it'd be you. He's still upset about it, huh?"

I glance over to make sure Amelia is busy and hopefully not listening. "Um, he's…actually, he's not really a fan of people talking about him."

Bauer laughs. "Yeah, I noticed. Touchy little dude some-times. Not that he's little anymore. I don't know where he's getting the height from 'cause nobody's dunking on my side, you know? Hey, you don't know if anybody's tall on Joy's side, do you?"

"I— His grandfather, I guess." I frown. "And how did you get my number?"

"Ethan wrote it down on a piece of paper he left at my house. See, his phone died last time he was here and he couldn't remember anybody's number, and I know he would always want to be able to call you if that happened again. Oh, and he didn't have a charger. Did I say that part?"

"I'm sorry, but is there a reason you're calling me?"

Another laugh. "Oh yeah, I was just wanting to check in on him. Make sure he got back and everything's okay. I keep calling but he never answers."

It doesn't feel like talking about him to let Bauer know this little bit. "He made it back fine, but he left again a couple nights ago. Said he was staying with friends."

"Friends? Where, in Arizona?"

A pit starts to form in my stomach. Ever since getting his text I'd been slamming the brakes on my thoughts whenever they tried to stray toward Ethan. He'd said goodbye and that he needed some time. Since I did too, I'd been more than happy to give it to him. But I hadn't thought about where he was, not really, or what friends he might be staying with. "Hold on, let me check with somebody." I put Bauer on speaker and text Neel

> **Me:**
> sorry for texting. I promise I'll give
> you all the space you need I just
> need to know if Ethan is with you.

Neel responds right away.

Neel:
Haven't seen him in a few days.
Everything OK?

> **Me:**
> Can you check with Eddie?

Neel:
There's no way he's with Eddie.

> **Me:**
> Check anyway.

"Hello?"
"I'm still here," I tell Bauer. "Texting a couple of his friends."
"Anything?"

Neel:
That's a big no from Eddie. What's
going on? Is Ethan in trouble?

> **Me:**
> No, it's fine. Thanks for checking.

Neel:
When I said I needed space
I never meant silence. I'm here
if you really need me.

                            Me:
              All good. Thanks. And me too
                        if you need me.

"Nothing," I tell Bauer, keeping my messages open but thumbing to my last conversation with Ethan. "Who would he stay with in LA?" That pit grows larger when I realize how little I know about Ethan's life away from here. He must have some friends, but is he close enough to any of them that they'd let him crash for a while?

Bauer makes a sound like he's blowing all the air from his lungs. "You're the only person he ever talked about besides his mom. Can't you call him? Or text him? It's not like he'll ignore you, right?"

I reread Ethan's message and his request for time. I hadn't responded even though I know he wanted me to, even just with an okay. It would have been a sign, a gesture that this time apart wasn't final. And I hadn't given it to him. Once I finally let myself be mad at him, it was harder than I thought to stop, even when I wanted to. Even when I knew I'd hurt him too.

"He, um, might not answer me either."

"Ah, so you guys are on the outs too?" Bauer says after a moment. "You know it's probably my fault. He left my place like a bull in a china shop, ready to charge anything that got in front of him. I'm guessing that was you."

I stare at my phone. "It wasn't your fault. It was us, and a lot of things that we'd been trying to hide from for years." From the very beginning, if I'm being honest. I made that choice to smile the first time he came back instead of telling him it hurt that he just left without saying goodbye. All these years, those missed goodbyes built up until this last one brought them all crashing down.

It's all such a mess now, anger tangled with regret and sadness. But I don't know how to forgive him for breaking his promise this last time when it still hurts so much. Even though I'm breaking a promise too. I wasn't coming back after our fight and finding a way through. I wasn't even returning a text. Was that my way of hurting him back?

When all he had to do was say goodbye?

And all I had to do was say hello?

My thumbs hover over the screen, but I bite my lip, hesitating. That anger, that hurt, it's still there right at the surface, ready to spill out again from the slightest cut. But it isn't the only thing there.

Me:
Still need time?

I wait, holding my breath. But unlike Neel, there's no immediate response.

"Nothing, huh? Could be his phone died. Kid never has a charger."

I don't think that's why though, so I stay silent. And

angry. And other things that dig that pit inside me deeper and deeper...

I take Bauer off speaker. "It doesn't matter anyway. I know where he is, but you're the only one with the address."

CHAPTER FIFTY-EIGHT

NOW

ETHAN

Old Man drops a dead mouse onto my lap when he jumps back through the car window and I guess that's my sign it's time to eat again. I check the take-out bags from the day before but come up empty.

"How about we go get burgers instead?" I pet my cat and hide his "gift" in the bag then start my car—only to slam the brakes a second later when another car pulls up, blocking me.

I swear when Bauer gets out, his heavy brow looking heavier than usual.

He slaps my trunk as he approaches the passenger side door then bends down to frown directly at me until I unlock it for him. Once inside, he grabs my phone off the dash and holds out the glowing screen to me. "Look at that, it does work."

I sigh and roll my head toward the window. "I didn't feel like calling you back."

He tosses the phone at me. "So now you get me in person. Worked out for you." He shifts, then reaches underneath him to pull out the fast-food bag that I've been using as a mouse coffin. He swears when he looks inside and then throws it outside, leaving Old Man no choice but to growl at him and leap out after it.

"That your cat?"

"Yep."

"He gonna bring that bag back in here?"

"Yep."

Bauer rolls the window up.

Old Man gives him a death glare and stalks off to a nearby tree, waiting.

"How'd you even know I was here?"

"I didn't. Rebecca figured it out."

My head snaps to him. "You talked to her? What'd she say?"

"About you? She was pretty tight-lipped on that topic, protective even. Said you got back but left again to stay with friends." He nudges the fast-food bags I've been piling up by his feet. "Guess they haven't been feeding you."

Between the trash and the obvious fact that I haven't showered in a couple of days, he knows the only "friend" I've been with is the cat currently plotting to kill him.

He sighs. "Ethan, what are you doing?" When I raise my eyebrows at him and glance purposefully out the window, he sighs again. "I know what you're doing here." He points out the window then motions to the car. "I mean what are you doing *here*?"

I glance away, staring at the apartment building I've been watching for days. "She's gotta come back sometime."

"Maybe, but maybe she doesn't need to see you living in

your car and stinking of dead mice when she does, you ever think about that when you were making this plan?"

I resist sniffing my shirt. "I didn't have a plan, okay? I was in Arizona and I got into—"

"A fight with your girl? Yeah, I figured that part out." When I stiffen, he adds, "Not that she told me but when she texted you and you didn't respond, well, I do have a few unfried brain cells left."

I glance down at the phone he tossed at me and turn it over. It immediately lights up telling me that along with a million missed calls from Bauer and my grandparents, I have an unread text from her.

I put the phone back down and hear a sound I'm getting pretty tired of when Bauer sighs yet again. "What? You got some brilliant fatherly wisdom for me?"

Bauer backs himself into the window. "Hell no. I'm just glad the only things you're hiding in these bags are rodents." Then he eyes the bags again. "That's not a thing kids are snorting these days, is it?"

I sigh in a way that sounds eerily like him.

He raises his hands. "Okay, okay. But there are kids out there eating laundry detergent, so snorting crushed rat bones or whatever isn't too much further. And—and this isn't fatherly anything—you've done dumber things lately."

I scowl at him. "Did you just say that to me?"

"Did you take off on that girl again? Yeah," he adds, when my scowl turns inward. "Sounds pretty dumb to me."

My words quiet. "You don't know anything about it. Or me."

"Maybe, maybe not. I know she's the only thing you talk

about with anything close to happiness in your voice. I know you talk to her even when you won't talk to anybody else." His voice softens. "I know you hurt her, and maybe she hurt you some too."

I turn away to stare out the window only this time the only thing I see is my own reflection. In my mind I see Rebecca when I came back from Bauer's this last time, the pain she tried to hide when I realized I'd broken more than one promise. And then I see her again and again, younger with that same expression better hidden behind a smile, but there all the same. I see her beside me in the car when she couldn't hide anymore because this time I hurt her too deeply.

I didn't mean to, but then again I never did.

She meant to hurt me this last time though, and she knew just what to say to cut deep.

It hurts every time I think about it, but I still lift my phone again and swipe to read her text.

Rebecca:
Still need time?

I do, but I text her back anyway.

Me:
Bauer found me. I don't know if I
should thank you for that or not.

When those three little dots appear by her name, I almost can't believe my heart starts beating like it does every time I'm near her.

Rebecca:
You're okay?

                                                            Me:
                                                    Yeah. You?

Rebecca:
I'm okay.

I don't know what more to say right now, or if I'm ready
to say it. But I couldn't put my phone down right now if I
tried, so I send her one last text.

                                                            Me:
                              If I call you later, will you answer?

She makes me wait this time, almost a full minute.

Rebecca:
I'll answer.

Air passes through my lips, emptying my lungs, but I'm
the opposite of deflated.

"Now that wasn't dumb," Bauer says. He can't see my
phone but I guess he didn't need to. Then he joins me in staring out the window. "You know that neighbor is gonna call
me. You don't have to do *this*."

But I did. And he knows why.

This time I stop him before he can sigh. "I don't have a
dad. I never did."

"I know that. I'm never gonna pretend otherwise. Telling you—" he struggles to find the words and settles on something vague enough not to raise my walls even higher "—what we are, that's not about erasing the past or trying to make it something it wasn't. It was shit. *I* was shit. And if you tell me to get out of your car again, I will." I'm seriously considering doing just that when he adds, "But I hope you don't."

I glance over at him to see he's staring at me with a kind of intensity that halts anything I would have said.

"Because you've got a family in me and Tara and Os, and a flesh and blood little sister on the way. I don't want you to miss out on them or them you, just because once upon a time I would have snorted rat bones if I got it in my head they'd get me high."

The corner of my mouth lifts, just a little.

"And if that's too much right now, hey, fine, just come home with me, sleep somewhere that isn't your car, and eat something your cat didn't literally drag in here."

He waits then, trying to be still but only half managing it.

A bed would be nice, actual food too. Somewhere to call Rebecca from. I glance out the window again. "You sure that neighbor's gonna call?"

"If they want my money—and they do—they're gonna call."

I nod. "Alright then."

CHAPTER FIFTY-NINE

NOW

REBECCA

I gnaw my lip as the phone rings, drawing dangerously close to biting through it with each passing tone. I have to answer. I told him I would but now that he's actually calling…

"Hello?"

"Hey." Ethan's voice fills my ear, not soothing my nerves but shifting them. "You answered."

"I almost didn't," I tell him, because it feels like we're finally done hiding.

"Yeah," he says, in a way that makes me realize that calling wasn't easy for him either. "Bauer said you were the one who figured out where I was."

"He called me," I tell him quickly. "You said you needed time but I thought maybe…" I lower the phone for a second wondering why I ever thought this was a good idea. "I just… I wanted to make sure you were okay."

There's such a long pause that I check the phone again to make sure he didn't hang up on me.

Nope. Still connected.

"I'm not mad," he doesn't add *about that*, but I can hear the unspoken words as though he did. "I'm actually with him now. At his house."

"That's good?"

"Yeah. I mean he said the guest room is mine for as long as I want it."

"But...?" I know there is one, I can hear it in his voice.

"It's just different, you know?" I hear a sound like he's shifting on a bed. "I mean he cooks dinner now and washes dishes. Earlier I overheard him making a dentist appointment for his kid."

"Okay?" The tone of his voice implies that I'm supposed to be scandalized by this in some way, but I'm not sure why.

"My memories are of him getting high with my mom and laughing at the cockroaches that ran across our kitchen floor."

"I guess that would be weird. But he's trying right?" There's a pause, a long one. "Ethan?"

He laughs but there's no humor in the sound. "I just realized that you've already made this conversation entirely about me and I let you. I always let you. Next you'll ask me about my mom and my grandparents and I won't even realize what happened until it's too late and you're gone."

"I don't always do that." I tug at the hem of my sleep shirt, wishing I was wearing a lot more even though he can't even see me. "And you have a lot going on. Huge things."

"And you don't?"

I don't have an answer for that.

"Are you okay? With your mom? The wedding is...?"

I twist the opal ring around my finger. "It's in a couple days."

I picture his face going tight in the silence that follows. Neither of us mention where he will be in two days.

"Are you going to talk to her before?"

I hesitate and the smile I force doesn't reach my words. "We're not talking at all right now. She's been busy with wedding details, I guess, but it all feels like another excuse to keep us on pause. She'll marry John, I'll leave, and we won't have to deal with anything. I won't have to tell her what I want and she won't have to tell me she can't give it to me."

Ethan's silent. For like a really long time. I'm about to say his name again when he says, "Do you really want to live your life that way, on pause? You know what you want, so tell her. Maybe she'll surprise you, but even if she doesn't, you've got to stop blaming yourself for what happened and acting like you don't deserve anything good because of that one night." He softens his voice. "You were a kid who got drunk at a party. That's what you did. That's all you did. You weren't driving the other car. You didn't run that light. Bec, you didn't kill your dad."

He can't see the tears I blink back, but he can hear the hitch in my breath.

"But if your mom can't say that, don't spend your whole life trying to make her give you what she can't." He takes a deep breath that seems to steal the air from my own lungs. "Don't be like me, okay?"

"Don't be like you?" I almost laugh but hold it back because I'm not sure it wouldn't come out like a sob. "You always do what you want. Look where you are!"

His voice matches my intensity. "Yeah, look! You think I want this? That I ever wanted this? This made you hate me, and don't say it didn't," he adds, with a ferocity that's almost scary. "Because I saw your face when I came back and I finally understand how you must have felt every time I went away."

I can't hide the tremor in my voice. "It was never hate. Don't you dare say that."

"It wasn't far from it."

"Yes, Ethan, it was. It was so far from hate that it broke me. You hurt me, and you only did that because what I felt for you was never hate." That tremor gets worse. "I know I said some horrible things to you the last time we talked—"

"Because I left you alone on the worst day of your life without even a second thought! Are you seriously about to say I didn't deserve it?"

His harsh truth knocks the wind out of me and my voice is hoarse when I hurl my own truth back. "No, but I don't get to repay hurt for hurt and expect to feel better. It doesn't work that way. Even now when I'm mad, I still miss you." That last part comes out like a confession. "I'm mad that you forgot me and most of all I'm mad that you didn't have a choice when we were younger and even if you did, I know you'll always pick your mom even when it hurts you."

His voice is soft when he finally responds, tired and pained, but not angry. Broken is the closest thing I can compare it to. "But we're not kids anymore."

A tear slips down my cheek. "No, we're not."

"So, what? We grow up now? You talk to your mom and I leave mine?" His voice gets louder like he's pressing the phone closer to his face. "Does that fix everything?" He doesn't give me time to answer and I wouldn't have known what to say anyway. "'Cause it didn't work out so well the last time I tried. I was just a couple of floors away in the laundry room the

EVERY TIME YOU GO AWAY   353

day she OD'd. I stayed long after the clothes were dry reading a shitty book that I don't even remember and watching half the apartment building come in and out. I left her alone knowing exactly what she would do, what I was too tired of fighting." His laugh is bitter. "See, all this time you've been blaming yourself for an accident, but I've been blaming myself for something I actually did."

My heart crashes into my lungs, breaking and shattering like our car that night. "No, you're not responsible for something she chose. You couldn't have known what would happen."

"But you could?"

There's no bite in his words, but I still want to recoil from them.

I hear a voice on his side of the phone, high like a child's. "You—uh, have to go?"

"No, I—" But we can both hear the noises from his end getting louder. And this call is a poor substitution for what we really need.

"It's fine. I should go too."

"Wait." His voice is suddenly urgent. Then he sighs. "I don't know about what's gonna happen tomorrow or after, but I just need you to know, me too, okay?"

The noise, the child is right next to him now, talking to him so that I almost can't hear Ethan. "What?"

"I miss you too."

CHAPTER SIXTY

NOW

ETHAN

It's early when I slip down the hall and out the front door, early but not early enough. Bauer is sitting on the porch step with a mug of coffee in one hand and a second steaming one beside him. He doesn't even look back when I open the door.

"You never could sleep in, even as a kid."

I hesitate then sit, setting down the actual cat carrier Tara got for me with Old Man grumbling inside, and pick up the other mug. "Don't all kids wake up early?"

"Tara's had to spritz Os in the face with a water bottle to get him up before."

I laugh into my mug.

"So you saw the message?"

"You're not the only one who can pay neighbors." I'd gotten it late last night after my call with Rebecca. I thought about leaving then, but for whatever reason, maybe this reason, I waited

"And you were just gonna take off? No goodbye for your old man?"

I take a sip of coffee. "It's how you left." He can't deny that though I don't feel any better for having brought it up.

His gaze snags at the bag by my feet. "Not coming back, huh?"

It's obvious that I'm not. "Come on, Bauer, what do you want from me?"

"Hell if I know. Something? Anything? I'm not exactly going by a book here."

And I am? Bauer was never my dad. Just 'cause he's clean now doesn't mean all the neglected parts of his old life suddenly fit together with his new one, no matter how hard he tries to make them.

"For what it's worth coming from me, you're a good kid. Not because of anything I did, and don't take offense here—" he holds his hands out palm out "—not 'cause of anything your mom did either. You're gonna be a good man too." He taps his temple. "I can see these things now that I'm not tripping balls 24/7."

I let out a short laugh. But then it's not funny anymore. And I have to ask him, even if I can't look at him when I do. "How'd you do it?"

"You mean where's my magic pill and can I give you one for Joy?" He sips his coffee. "All I can tell you is one day I woke up and I wanted to stop more than I wanted to use. There was maybe this much difference between the two." He holds up his thumb and index finger so there's only the slightest sliver of sunlight peeking through. "It didn't completely stick from that day on, but I started fighting again, started getting help, the hard kind I said I never needed." He lowers his coffee and gazes down at his reflection in the liquid. "And I looked at myself in the mirror and stopped saying that I was fine."

I glance down at my own coffee and the image of myself.

"It's not easy," he adds, "and it's not a battle anyone else can fight for you. It also never ends, but I think maybe that's enough reality for this morning."

Especially this morning. I set my coffee down. "Say bye to Os and Tara for me?"

He nods and watches me stand. "You gonna let me come with you?"

"Not this time." It's gonna be hard enough by myself.

He grabs on to that, rising to stand too. "But sometime? You and me again, there'll be a sometime?"

I honestly don't know if I want that from him and I'm not going to lie. "Maybe. I don't know."

He takes a step toward me, almost like he's gonna… I tense and move back. He nods a little, dropping one arm and extending the other.

Shaking hands with my father. It's as much of a trip as I ever want to experience. "Take care, Bauer."

"Hey," he says, just as I reach the last step. "Is it okay if I call you sometime? On the phone, you know? Not like—" he gestures to himself and the way he's raising his voice. "We could talk about books or something, or anything that's going on in your life. You're working with plants and stuff now, right? Maybe you could help me with the backyard."

I glance past him, imagining the largely blank space behind his house and without even meaning to I start mentally overlaying circles all around, a bubble chart forming in my brain that I know I'll have to create when I get—when I get wherever I end up. My grandfather would know what to do with that heavily shaded area in the right corner and whether we'd need to put up a retention wall along the sloped back. Something colorful by the back door, fruit trees along the sides. The ideas tumble over me one right after the other until my fingers are twitching with the need to draw it all.

"And when your sister is born," he adds, oblivious to the thoughts in my head, "you'll want to hear about that."

A sister. Family beyond the only person I thought I'd ever have. "Sure, that'd be okay."

Bauer stays out on the porch watching me until my car fades from sight. I don't think I've ever had somebody see me off before. It makes that spot between my shoulders itch, but not entirely in a bad way.

But then I can't think about Bauer or half sisters anymore, I can't think about anything anymore because I'm going to see my mom and I know she's not going to be waiting outside for me with a steaming cup of coffee.

CHAPTER SIXTY-ONE

NOW

REBECCA

I shake out my arms trying to expel some of the nervous energy that keeps coiling inside me then curl my hand around the necklace Amelia made me so long ago, the one that turned my old medallion into something completely different but no less beautiful. I haven't worn it in forever, but I need it for today.

"How much longer?" Amelia asks. She's been hovering by the door for a while now, knowing she has to leave me alone for this but not quite able to do it yet.

"Any minute now." I squeeze the pendant hard. "It's just time, right?"

She nods. "You have my car keys?"

"I have car keys, shop keys, and I've locked up dozens of times before. I'm good."

But I'm not really good and she knows that. My mom is on her way here. Because I asked her to come. Except it wasn't so much an invitation as a demand. She has no idea why but she agreed and there's no backing out now for either of us. My heart flutters, a panic trapped beating against my ribs as Ethan's words pass through my mind. *If your mom can't say it, don't spend your whole life trying to make her give you what she can't. Don't be like me, okay?* She won't ever say anything on her own, I know that, but I can't stay silent anymore.

"I'm real proud of you. And we're here for you whatever happens. Mathias said we'll ruthlessly exploit you as a live-in babysitter if you decide to move into the guest house, but we'll knock off a bit of rent too, so it'll be an almost fair trade."

"If it comes to that."

She waves a hand dismissively. "Which it probably won't."

"'Cause this whole conversation will go perfectly and years' worth of pain and damage will all go away in an instant?"

"Exactly." Then she presses her fingers to her lips. "Love you."

"Love you too."

"Try not to break anything important if you crash," she says when Mathias honks from the driveway. "And you're picking me up at 7:30 a.m. sharp tomorrow or you will be all kinds of fired."

I blow out a breath when at last I'm alone in the shop.

And then I wait.

I'm about to start working on the ring again, anything to keep my focus off what I've set in motion, but then there's a knock on the door, soft but steady.

I hurry over to pull it open and Mom sweeps in, eyes scanning over me like she's expecting to see something other than what she finds: me with my hair pulled back and my work apron and gloves on, maybe a smudge on my cheek.

And then she does something.

It's subtle, but I see it.

She exhales.

She's nervous too, maybe even more than I am.

I'm not ready for words yet though, so I stare at my workbench, at the wires still soaking in pickling solution waiting for me, and pull them out to wipe them clean, the strong, vinegary sent burning my nose. I shape the metal wire in the ring bender and then use some nonmarring pliers to finish the shape.

She steps closer, watching me work. "What is that you're making?"

"It's going to be a ring." Her ring, I hope. I reach for another wire to bend.

"Oh? But it's got an opening?"

"For now." I reach for my flex and brush a little where the ends bend together, give it a quick blast with my little torch, touch a tiny piece of hard solder to the joint with a pair of tweezers, and another shot of heat and it's ready to go back in the pickling liquid. I keep going, unable to reconcile the way my chest swells with warmth and aches with cold as she watches me finish.

"It looks like my mother's pendant," she says, oblivious. "I had no idea you could do all this."

The cold inside me crystallizes at her words. This place and these skills brought me back from an edge she hadn't even known I was teetering on. I continue to work on the ring, moving easily around the shop. "Amelia's a good teacher. And it's easy to learn something you love."

She blinks at me then. "Love?"

Warm and cold. They collide and a tornado of emotions coil inside. I let out a breath as steadily as I can, and glance down at the now-finished ring before holding it out to her. "I think I'm technically supposed to give this to John or his best man. I don't really know."

She takes the ring from me, frowning.

"He asked me to make your wedding band, so I did." If she hears the way my voice tightens with those last words, she doesn't show it. I don't tell her I told him no at first or that even now I'm sure she's wishing he'd asked anyone else. I watch her turn the glinting metal around in her fingertips. "I designed it after Grandmother's pendant and the pearl ring from—"

"My aunt Marilyn," she finishes for me. "Yes, I can see that."

That's all she says though. I can't tell if she hates it or if she's angry. I can't tell anything and the longer she stays silent the more my insides spin, gathering up old words and slights, pulling them all together until my skin is all that keeps the cyclone from lashing out.

With jerky movements, I reach into my left pocket and pull out a folded piece of paper, extending it to her, as well. "And that's my acceptance letter to Cal State Northridge."

She glances from the ring to the paper, so calm when I am a storm. "I don't understand."

I have to fight an impulse to snatch both the ring and the paper from my mom. To take it all back and smooth it all over, to not cause trouble even when it means that I'm the one who suffers. I don't want that anymore. I don't want it for her either, but if she wants me gone then I'll go. Just not to California.

"I don't want to go away to college. I want to stay here, continue working with Amelia and maybe one day have my own shop. I love it and I'm good at it and even if I wasn't in this wheelchair it's what I would pick for my future."

My mom's perfectly groomed brows draw together. "But Cal State is all we've talked about since—"

"The accident?" I feel lightning flash behind my eyes. "No, it's all you've talked about. I was crying myself to sleep every night knowing I was never going to walk again and my own mother could barely stand to look at me because I'm the reason Dad died."

The letter shakes in her hand. "I have never said that."

But she had. In every averted glance, every late night, every college brochure, every shut-down conversation. She'd said it again and again, so loudly it echoed through the entire house. "It's true, isn't it? You blame me." A single tear falls, then another. "If I hadn't been so stupid and selfish, he'd still be here?"

Mom takes a step toward me, but I hold up my hands to stop her. "Don't." If she tries to touch me now, I'll be more than the hurt lashing around inside me, I'll rip apart. "I just—" I wipe my face dry "—I just need to know if you can accept me staying here. Amelia and Mathias have a room for me if you can't, but I'm not going to go to Cal State." I drop my gaze to the letter half crumpled in her hand. "I don't want to keep hurting you if that's what me being here is doing, but I'm not going to give up everything I want either. I don't think I should have to do that." Her eyes are swimming when she glances down between her two hands, the ring and the acceptance letter, between the choices I've given her.

"You don't have to say anything right now. You can let me know your decision before the wedding."

She stays silent as she follows me outside so I can lock up. When she tells me she'll see me at home, it feels like maybe the last words we'll ever say to each other.

CHAPTER SIXTY-TWO

NOW

ETHAN

It's close to a perfect California day when I pull up outside my mom's apartment complex. Blue skies, a breeze that carries with it the fresh salty taste of the ocean. I could even turn off the A/C and stay comfortable. But the sweat clinging to me has nothing to do with the weather.

The neighbor I paid to be my lookout is smoking on his balcony and hops over when he sees me. He takes his money and points me toward her apartment as though I haven't been parked out front and staring at it for two straight days.

I adopt Rebecca's nervous habit and swipe my palms over my thighs as I draw closer, somehow losing years until I raise my hand to knock, feeling eight years old again. I have that same nervous energy skittering through me.

I've never done this part before, come for her. I was the one always waiting. It's not gonna be the same. She hasn't been scanning windows and listening for cars. She's not waiting for me at all, in fact she might not even open the door.

That realization sucks the force out of my knock, making it soft and timid. I have to repeat the gesture three more times before I hear a man's voice grumbling that he's coming and a minute later the door swings open. I recognize the features of the man who scowls at me, but just barely. The Jensen I remember had a boyish grin and waves of tousled blond hair, not these sunken cheeks and wispy ponytail. He looks a good twenty years older than I know he is, and like none of those years were kind. Seeing Bauer again that first time had been its own kind of shock. Jensen is too, but in the opposite direction.

"What?" he says, stepping out into the light and revealing that the perpetual tan I remembered has given way to wan paleness.

"Jensen?" I can't help but add a questioning note to my voice. It has to be him and yet, there's something gut punching about seeing him like this and it has everything to do with the person I actually came to find. What would somebody think seeing my mom after ten years?

Jensen's scowl shifts to wariness. "Do I know you?"

"No," I say, because he really doesn't. Unlike Bauer, I doubt he'll even remember me. "I'm looking for Joy."

At the mention of my mom's name, he drops his hand from the door and turns to go back inside. "Joy." Then louder, "Joy!"

I hold my breath waiting for her to appear. Even now I want that moment of happiness to transform her face and send her running to me. I want her to be happy that I came for her the same way she always came for me.

But it doesn't happen like that. I have no trouble recognizing her when she peers around the corner; even scowling like Jensen, there's no face I know better. There are no drastic changes either, they're the same ones I've seen chip away at her features for years and they don't shock me even though they would if I were anyone else. I just see my mother, alive, and in that moment, it's enough.

"Mom?"

She doesn't run to me; she stays right where she is in the hall and tugs the sides of her cardigan around her. "Ethan? What are you doing here?"

"What am I doing—?" I can't keep the surprise from my voice. "Mom, I've been searching for you since the day I found out you checked out of rehab."

"No, you're not supposed to be here. You're supposed to be there, with them. They said they'd take care of you." Then her eyes dart past me. "Are they here too? 'Cause I'm not going back to rehab. I'm not."

"Grandma and Grandpa aren't here. Just me."

"He's not staying here." Jensen walks in the living room and plops down on an old lounge chair before lighting a cigarette. "You can go, but he can't stay."

"She's not staying with you," I say, through clenched teeth, just as my mom says, "He's not staying with us."

I shift my gaze to her almost reluctantly. I don't have to say her name; she's staring right back at me when she takes half a step forward. "I'm fine. Better than fine. Jensen's helping me. You remember Jensen?"

Jensen blows a ring of smoke in my direction before grinning. "Looks like Mommy doesn't want to go with you."

Fury sends a spike of adrenaline surging through me and I relish the flicker of fear on his face as I start toward him.

"Stop." My mom steps in between us. "I said I was fine."

It takes every bit of self-control I have not to push past her and take years of fear and anger out on the smug piece of shit across the room. I don't know how I do it, but I look down at her instead.

"Mom, you're not fine." And then because she doesn't seem to be hearing anything I'm saying, I add, "*I'm* not fine."

That stops her. Her bloodshot eyes pass over me, head to toe, searching. "What? What's wrong with you?"

The weight of that question shudders through me. "A lot, Mom. Why didn't you call me?"

"You were fine."

This time I do raise my voice. "I wasn't fine. I've never been fine. You know that. That's why you sent me away so many times." But even as I say it I know it's not true, or at least it's not the only reason. The fight goes out of me then, deflating like a balloon until I don't even register that Jensen is there anymore. "I hurt a lot of people trying to find you, people who care about me. All because I thought it was my job to protect you. Every time you left me I thought it was because I failed, not you, me." I jab all my fingers at my chest. "You let me live in my worst nightmares for weeks and now that I've finally found you, all you can do is tell me to go back because you're not done getting high?"

A tear slips down her cheek as she lifts a hand to my face, but I push it away and swallow as my throat tightens. "Why couldn't you want me more?" It's a little boy's question and one she won't answer now any more than she could then.

She's crying harder now. "I'm trying."

I shake my head. "No, you're not. Trying is rehab. Trying is coming with me right now. You're not fine, and if you try to tell me that one more time…"

She shuffles back a step, then another, eyeing me like I might make a grab for her and drag her away whether she wants to go or not.

But I can't do that. I won't.

I've spent my whole life trying to make her stop, first as a child watching her fall prey to her addictions, then as a self-appointed jailer trying to protect her from them. And even there I failed. Maybe I could find a way to stay with her now, and maybe she thinks I could too based on the way she keeps moving back. I could watch her better this time, never leave her alone for a second. I could make my every waking moment about this singular purpose, and it might even work for a little while.

But not forever. Eventually there would be a moment I would miss. She'd slip away again and I'd be right back here searching for her, worrying for her, mourning for her and blaming myself. I would give up everything and I would still lose.

I take my own step back. "It can't be my fight anymore, not if I'm the only one fighting." She did more than make mistakes with me growing up, and I'll be making one right alongside her if I don't do this right now.

"What does that mean?"

"It means I love you, Mom, and I'll be here when you want to stop more than you want to use, but I don't want you to come back for me anymore."

And then I walk away from her, my face crumbling as she cries after me to come back.

I sit in my car in a random parking lot, parts of the conversation with my mom swirling through my mind as Old Man butts his head against my unmoving hand. Every time I close my eyes I see her tearstained face as, for the first time ever, I was the one who left her behind. Old Man purrs in soft fits beside me sounding like a car engine that isn't going to start. I glance down at him, envying the simple and clearcut life he has.

"What now, huh?" I murmur, petting him and being rewarded with louder staccato purring. "What am I supposed to do now?"

My cat blinks at me, arches his back into a deep stretch, then turns his head to stare out at the road ahead.

I stare out with him, at a brilliantly blue sky that would make the most beautiful painting, and I start my car.

CHAPTER SIXTY-THREE

NOW

REBECCA

I run into Neel in my kitchen the morning of the wedding, forcing him to press up against the fridge to protect the armful of flowers he's carrying for the ceremony later today. All morning there have been people in and out bringing flowers (courtesy of Good & Green), setting up tables and chairs, and stringing lights across the backyard.

Before I can awkwardly decide what to say to him, he does a cute bit of slapstick for my benefit trying not to drop the flowers and pretending that we'd almost collided rather than stopped a few feet from each other.

"Nicely done," I say. "Not even a single petal fell."

He bows. "I like to think I'm more than just a pretty face." He shakes his hair back. "Besides, Eddie's threatening to turn me into a reverse flower girl if he sees any petals down before the ceremony."

I laugh softly. "But will you get a decorative basket to put them in?"

EVERY TIME YOU GO AWAY

"Good point. I should ask."

Feeling suddenly uncomfortable, I glance down. "I'll get out of your way here."

He slides around in front of me. "Actually, do you have a few minutes?"

I look up, unsure of what he means. "Yeah?"

"Oh good. Okay." He lets out such a big breath of air it ruffles the flowers he's holding. "'Cause here's the thing, it turns out there's something worse than a one-sided crush on your friend that ends with you asking her for space. You want to know what it is?"

"Wha—"

"Space!" He says it comically close to my face before drawing back so I can laugh and he can smile. "It didn't make it hurt less, it just made me miss talking to you, seeing you, hanging out with you." He circles his free hand at me. "You. So, yeah, I'm still gonna have to work a little on the not wanting to kiss you thing, but I figured I can just keep reminding myself that you don't like *Gangs of Wasseypur*."

My lips twitch. "I never said I didn't—"

He cuts me off and raises his voice over mine. "Ah, ah— see, it's helping already."

I laugh again and it's a sound of pure happiness because today of all days I need the people I love closest to me. "I guess now I can tell you I'm not the biggest musical fan either."

Neel nods and gestures for me to keep going. "Good, yes. I don't like you at all right now."

I like him so much right now my heart could burst. Whatever else happens with my mom, I am so, so glad to have my friend back. "I'll see what else I can come up with."

Neel opens his mouth to respond when Eddie comes around the corner.

"What are you doing? You still have half a truck of flowers to unload."

"I think the word you're looking for is *we* as in *we* still have half a truck of flowers to unload."

Eddie gives him a tight-lipped smile. "That's yours and Ethan's job. Not my problem he's not here." Then he snaps his finger and points outside. "Now show me some hustle."

I give Neel a sympathetic look as Eddie leaves. "Sorry Ethan's not here." More sorry than he knows.

Neel rocks back on his heels, averting his eyes. "That's fine. I, ah, I actually talked to him."

"You did? When? How is he?" It's impossible to play off the question as casual so I don't even try.

He hunches both his shoulders. "Oh, um, well. Good, I guess? Sorry, but I kind of have to…" He lifts his flowers higher.

"Right. Sure, I should go change too. But later? Can we talk or maybe hang out this weekend?"

He gives me a huge, reassuring grin. "Maybe not a romantic movie in the park, but yeah. And for today, with everything, I'm here for you. You know that, right?"

My smile isn't as steady as his, but I nod and when he gives me a hug that mostly avoids smothering me with flowers, I feel as ready as I'll ever be for what comes next.

I take more time than necessary putting on my bridesmaid dress, twisting back my hair, making sure my makeup is perfect. I listen to all the footsteps passing in the hall, all the people it takes to pull off even a small wedding. Not my mom. I know the cadence of her footsteps and she never once comes near my door.

We haven't spoken since she came to my shop and I basically told her I wasn't going to leave. I don't know if she's planning to ignore me until after the wedding and then ask me to turn over my key. Even imagining that scenario, my chest hurts like somebody kicked it. I rub at the phantom pain, so distracted that I don't hear anyone approaching until my door opens.

My mom steps in wearing a simple white silk sheath. She looks as lovely as I've ever seen her with her long neck bare and tiny pearls peeking out from her swept-up curls. In a perfect world, I'd be able to tell her how beautiful she is, but I don't have any words as our gazes meet in my mirror.

"I wanted to check if everything was alright with your dress."

I look down at the short, strawberry-colored dress that fits me perfectly. I made sure I'd have no distractions for this day. "It's fine. Thanks."

I draw in a breath when she nods, expecting that to be the full extent of our conversation, but instead of turning to leave, she takes another step, one that brings her right up to me. The air pushes against my lungs as I wait for her to say something else, anything else, but she's silent as she sets a ring box down on the vanity table beside me.

I feel it hit the surface, an impossible weight that pins me down beneath it. It's as though all the air has been pressed out of my body.

She's giving it back.

She doesn't want the ring I made.

She doesn't want me.

I've known it for a long time, but I've never truly felt her complete rejection until this moment. I didn't really let myself hope for a different outcome, but I couldn't have imagined it hurting this much.

My chin quivers as my head bobs. "Okay," I say, barely making the sound that comes out of me a word. I gave her a choice and she's making it. I reach for the ring, but her hand covers mine, trapping it beneath.

"The ring you made is beautiful. I'm glad I got to see you make it and how talented you've become. I didn't realize that this meant so much to you. You never said..." There's a reproach there, but it's slight and easily turned the other way.

"You never asked."

She goes very still. "No, I didn't." Then she pulls her hand away, freeing us both from the contact we're not used to. "I know I'm not the parent you would have chosen to keep. And I understand that. I'm not the one who's good at this."

I shake my head at her. "Good at what? Emotions? Me?" She squeezes her eyes shut, but I'm done letting her shut me out. If she's not rejecting me then what is she doing? "I've tried to be so perfect, so easy. I tried to hide all the pain and everything so you wouldn't have to deal with any of it. I never even thought about what I wanted until recently because I didn't think it mattered anymore."

She flinches but her voice is soft. "I know. That made it so much worse. I didn't know how to help you. He did that, not me. I don't have that." Her hand spreads across her chest. "I've never had that."

My eyes narrow even as my vision blurs. I've heard versions of this my entire life; she wasn't the hands-on parent, wasn't the warm, loving one, so it's not fair for me to ask for more than she can give. And maybe it's not. Maybe she's giving all she can, but right now it feels like an excuse. I'm not asking her to sweep me up in her arms and hold me, or cry and comfort me over losing Dad. I've accepted the fact that we'll never have those moments, but that can't mean we don't have anything.

"I did try to connect with you when you were little," she continues. "But he was always so much better and he and I both knew it. He wasn't trying to be cruel by nudging me out, but it happened. He had this effortless way with you that I couldn't begin to understand, and so, time and again he'd step in and tell me it was okay to let him handle you, discipline you, comfort you. And he was right. I would have said the wrong thing, made things worse." She holds herself very still as she talks as though steeling herself for my reaction. "I told myself you didn't want me to attempt to make up for his loss with something so obviously inferior. So I didn't try." Her voice shakes as it cuts off before she can try again. "I don't know how to be what he was, but I read articles and found therapists, I sent you to vocational rehab, made up spreadsheets for all the best colleges for wheelchair users. I've been working for years to make sure you wouldn't worry about tuition or anything else you might need. I was so focused on that that I didn't always notice the rest. But I'm trying now," she adds with an almost desperate note in her voice. "After the engagement party, I started to see how things here could be better for you."

I think about the new table and ramp—those were her

reactions to the fiasco that was the engagement dinner, not words or even emotions, solutions. John told me in the shop that maybe she was reaching for me too in her own way; this must be what he meant.

"Mom, I'm… It's good that you told me some of this, but I don't know that it's enough for me." I can't hide the note of surprise in my voice. "I've spent years hoping for a moment with you and to feel loved and forgiven. And you just kept pushing me away, hiding out at your office—" I let out a weak laugh "—I don't even know where that is anymore."

She blanches. "You know about my office?"

"Yes, because I went there. I wanted to see the photos of us with Dad from Disney but there was somebody else's name on the door. You never said a word because we don't talk about anything. Ever. And now it's your wedding day and you're telling me that Dad didn't let you learn to be a parent when he was alive so that's your excuse for not being one after he died?" I shake my head feeling lighter and lighter the more I say. "It's not enough. Everything that happened feels like too much. And I needed more. I still need more. I deserve more."

I glance up at her, expecting to see a withdrawn expression on her face and maybe even a touch of relief, but not this.

Not the nodding.

"I know."

Tears sting my eyes. "You know? Then why? All this time I kept trying and you pushed me away. You had to know what I thought…" Didn't she? Or were we so far away from each other that she never considered or cared about what I might be feeling? "I'd rather have you say it to my face that you blame me than keep hiding away like—"

Her eyes snap open. "No, Rebecca, never." Her hand returns to press down more firmly on mine as though she needs something to hold her up. "He was always the one who dealt with you, not me, but that night he was exhausted and so I said I'd go get you. But he wouldn't let me, kept insisting that it would be better if it was just him since you two could always talk about anything." Her fingers twitch and then with an almost visible effort, they curl around mine. Not easily or without awkwardness, but she's trying to do what she thinks I want in the moment.

And I see it, feel it, slight though it is.

"But it wasn't my fault or his."

Tears run down my face as I watch her, free arm wrapped around her midsection just like mine is wrapped around me.

"And it was never yours."

She says it with such conviction that my whole body racks with a sob. It's gotten harder this summer with Ethan to hang on to my guilt, but I knew I'd never be able to purge it completely while I felt my mom blamed me. "I should have told you that from the first, but I was so caught up in my own grief that I pretended not to see yours. I thought college away from here would be the best thing for you, so that's what I set out to get for you. When you got accepted to Cal State I decided to let the lease go on my office."

Her words make me choke back a cry and I blink to clear my eyes. "You did what? Then where have you been working?"

"My car a lot of the time. John's home office when I could, and restaurants when I had to meet clients." Her chin quivers as she traces the tears on my face. "I wanted you to have a good life and I never thought you could have that here with me, that you would ever truly want that. But if you do—"

I glance at our linked hands when she cuts off. "You'd want me to stay here, with you and John and Layla?"

"I've already been looking at bunk beds."

I sniffle, my body caught between a laugh and a cry. "Is that a joke?"

Her eyebrows nudge together. "No, I drew up a whole plan for the bedroom. I think a trundle would be better than bunk beds but only if that's what you want. And we don't have to stay in this house anymore either. If you're certain you don't want to go to college, then we have the money to find a bigger place. John's already been collecting listings. He said we can start looking the second we get back from our honeymoon."

Something warm and bright flickers to life inside me, a faint glow that pushes back old shadows and lets light into forgotten corners. Tiny memories and relit moments that I'm seeing from new angles. We are so very different, but we both loved him.

She never blamed me.

She's been hunched over a laptop in her car.

She looked at bunk beds.

And she wants me to stay.

I wriggle my fingers and she drops my hands at the first hint that I want her to let go. But I just turn my hand and reach for hers again. It's not easy but I do it, and then I hold out the ring box to her again.

"So you want the ring I made?"

"Of course. John's brother has it now. Why, did you…? Oh no!" And then she hurries to open the ring box, showing me not the ring I made, but the one that inspired it. "I thought you might want to have Aunt Marilyn's ring to wear today, and to keep yourself after."

My fingers shake as I take the delicate pearl ring out of the box and slide the delicate spray of blue pearls onto my finger. It's not a perfect fit, but I can resize it. I can make it mine. "Thank you."

"I'm sorry, I didn't realize what you must've thought." She shakes her head. "I'll try to be better about that in the future." When I don't respond, she adds more firmly, "I will get better. If you help me, I will never stop trying."

The thing is I believe her. I know she is trying. It wasn't enough before, but maybe John was right that we can start something new and big today. I wasn't sure I even wanted that anymore, but looking down at my aunt's ring, I think, maybe, I want to try again too.

"I think it would be better for me to try living with Amelia and Mathias, try being more on my own. But maybe we could still get the trundle bed here? For when I'm home with you." My heart thuds like it's ready to tear free from my ribcage. "I'd like knowing I'll always have a place to come home to."

She doesn't throw her arms around me or hoot with excitement. Dad would have done that.

My mom nods slowly before taking my hand. "I'd like that too."

CHAPTER SIXTY-FOUR

NOW

ETHAN

I let myself into my grandparents' house quietly, not so quiet that I'm trying to sneak in, but quiet enough to give them the option of pretending not to hear me if they don't want to.

The door to their bedroom creaks open before I'm halfway across the living room. My grandfather appears first, already in his suit for the wedding with his tie loosely hanging around his shoulders. My grandmother is right behind him, her makeup and hair done but still in her robe.

I glance down at my own clothes, old boots, dirty jeans, a T-shirt I got from Bauer smeared with paint and the coffee I'd drunk all night to stay awake. Not exactly wedding attire.

I let Old Man out hours ago but I am surprised to see him chowing down on a fresh can of cat food in the kitchen. I guess that explains their lack of shock at seeing me.

"I know I should have called, but I didn't and I don't have to stay if you don't—"

"Of course you're staying." My grandmother slides a step

toward me. "This is your home." My grandfather gives her a look and she adds, "If you want it to be."

I start to run a hand through my hair, realize it doesn't look any better than the rest of me, and shove it into my pocket instead. "I said a lot of stuff before." I eye my grandfather. "I can't unsay any of it."

"Then I'll talk this time," he says. "You have a right to be mad for a lot of things that happened to you growing up, for the things we chose to keep from you. If you stay, you have our promise that we'll tell you everything from now on. And you can tell us about anything you want us to know, even the things that hurt us. But you also need to know that we tried everything short of kidnapping you to keep you safe, and it's on me and the sins of my past that we never could. But I promise you this, if we'd known what was happening, we'd have run with you as fast and as far as we could." He lifts a hand slowly to rest on my shoulder and squeezes. "Not a force on earth could have stopped us."

I nod, a fast jerky movement.

"Ethan, can you forgive us?"

I can't look up. I don't want him to see what I can feel building in my eyes even as I say yes.

"Did you find your mother?"

I nod again and feel his hand squeeze tighter. "She's not— she wouldn't come with me. So I had to—"

His other arm comes around me, pulling me in, holding on to me the same way he did when my mom first left me here all those years ago. I struggle this time too, only not to get away.

"You had to let her go," he finishes for me.

I can't help it; I jerk as though I've been struck hearing those words. I've never had a day where I didn't think about her, worry about her above everything else.

"It doesn't mean you don't love her," my grandmother says from beside me and I feel the warmth of her hand on my back. "It's not giving up—it's understanding that you can't fight this for her. We always pray, always hold out hope. And when the day comes when she is ready to fight, you won't be the only one ready to help her."

They hold me a long time and I let them.

The suit my grandfather lends me isn't a great fit. I'm a little taller than he is and he's a little wider. Old Man likes the tie though, based on the way he keeps leaping up to bat at it.

I thought about keeping my Docs on. Grandpa offered me shoes that look like they'll fit, but I feel like my old boots still have some wear in them. And they make me think about my mom, about good days we've had and maybe even good ones to come.

Someday.

Today though, I put on the dress shoes then have to fend off my grandfather and something he calls mousse that he keeps trying to put in my hair, before hurrying next door as a small crowd of about thirty people are taking their seats in Rebecca's backyard.

I find a spot next to Amelia and Mathias. He makes eye contact with me and I give him a nod then immediately start bouncing my foot when my grandparents sit on my other side wedging me in. I crane my neck to look back for the dozenth time, but there's still no sign of Rebecca. I don't know if she talked to her mom or not, how her mom responded, or even if Rebecca's still here. If it went badly, could she bring herself to still be part of the wedding?

John is no help. He's already up front next to the minister and his brother with a nervous, excited look on his face. I'm guessing he took the whole no-seeing-the-bride-before-the-wedding thing to heart. I spin the ring on my thumb around and around. I can only look at the flowers—which are spectacular since Good & Green provided them—for so long. I start to stand up but Amelia plunks Luis onto my lap.

"Sit down, lover boy. The last thing she needs is you running through the house looking for her. Have a little faith."

Luis immediately pulls my hair, hard, and laughs.

"Cute kid," I mutter.

Amelia beams at her son. I keep bouncing my leg to get rid of the excess energy spooling inside me. I start when John's friend begins playing acoustic guitar up front. "What does that mean?" I whisper.

But I don't need her to answer because Layla is doing her flower girl walk, dropping fresh rose petals all the way down the aisle. The second she's done, Amelia and I both wrench our necks around to stare back into the house's open door. She's just as eager to see Rebecca as I am.

"Faith, huh?" I say to her.

"Shut up."

The doorway stays empty.

I've never been to a wedding before, but I know the bridesmaids are supposed to proceed down the aisle followed by the bride with her father. Rebecca had told me that her mom's parents had died years ago and her mom wasn't planning on having anyone walk her down the aisle in her father's place, so either way one person needs to appear in that doorway: Rebecca if things went okay, and her mom if they didn't.

Twenty-seconds left.

Ten.

Amelia takes Luis from me with a little nod.

I push to my—

The music changes to the processional and two people appear in the doorway.

The bride rests her hand on Rebecca's shoulder and hope-fueled smiles light both their faces.

CHAPTER SIXTY-FIVE

NOW

REBECCA

The wedding is long over when Ethan finally finds me. I saw him, of course, the moment Mom and I started down the aisle. I shouldn't have expected him to be there and yet, my gaze knew just where to look. And even though my heart beat faster, it wasn't from surprise.

The pool is glowing light blue from the underwater lights, casting dappled light on my bare arms and shoulders. My legs dangle in the water.

I hear him halt for only a moment, seeing me, but then he's crossing the deck to sit down beside me and dropping his legs—shoes, pants, and all—into the water.

I laugh softly and smile over at him. "Bet you wouldn't have done that in your Docs."

His gaze traces my face, and I know he's seeing my slightly red eyes and hopefully a smile that looks battered but strong. "Guess you'll never know."

He moves closer so I can rest my head on his shoulder and when I seek out his hand, he twines his fingers through mine.

"You came back."

"You knew I'd be coming."

My gaze stays locked on the pool. "I didn't actually."

He stares at me. "It's over." He's studying me so intently; I know he catches the slight tremor that goes through me.

"You saw her."

He nods. "I feel like I'm floating. Like I had this anchor my whole life and I've just been set free. And I'm suddenly supposed to know which way to go?"

"What happened?"

He closes his eyes, clearly not wanting to relive it, but I think he needs me to know more.

My hand squeezes his as he tells me.

"I don't know how I'm supposed to move on from that, forget that it's happening…let go of the only thing I've ever done with my life. All I know is that when I thought about where to go after, all I thought of was you."

His gaze lifts to mine, pinning me in place with his golden-brown eyes. Warm, humid air breezes in from behind me, blowing my curls around my face and almost hiding the heat that flushes my skin.

"I'm sorry I was late."

I shake my head at him. "You didn't miss the wedding."

"I'm not talking about the wedding."

Oh. I try to look away, but he follows me, angling so that I have no choice but to see him.

That or push him in the pool.

"I've made so many mistakes and I don't want to make

any more with you. If you can forgive me, and if you want me, this is where I'm choosing to be." His gaze travels over me. "Coming down that aisle, you looked beautiful, happy."

We're still close enough that I know he feels my chest rise and fall as I inhale and then exhale. "Shhh, don't scare it."

"Is it that fragile?"

Another rise and fall. "It's new." I think about John sliding the ring—the one I made—on my mom's finger and the way I felt when he did it. "But it's good. My mom and I get a chance to rebuild what's broken between us." My finger traces the ring on his thumb, then trails up to paint clinging around his nails. I lift my head to look at him with a questioning expression on my face.

"Were you painting in LA?"

He shakes his head and then starts to stand. "Not LA. Come with me?"

I slide my chin over my shoulder to glance back at my bedroom window and imagine my mom's empty room just down the hall. She and John already left for their honeymoon, but it's late and there were a lot of things I promised myself I'd never do again after the accident. I'd never be any more trouble, never break another rule or cause anyone I loved another moment of heartache. Funny how when some of those promises conflict I know exactly which one matters.

My backyard is empty again. All the chairs have been folded up and removed, all the lights have been taken down, and the flowers gathered up and brought inside. Soon John will be moving in and my room will become Layla's. With a trundle bed for when I sleep over.

There's so much we have to work through, but for now, I'm not moving across the country. She wants me to stay.

For tonight it's enough.

Ethan hoists me higher in his arms when we reach the base of the tree house. "Don't let go."

As if I would.

It's different being up there again at night. And then it's magic when Ethan turns on the fairy lights.

Tiny glowing stars light up the walls, my wintery forest, painted moon, and sandy beach. And a last wall that isn't bare anymore.

Because he's made it into a garden.

Blooming flowers and falling leaves, arching trees with budding branches up against the bluest sky. And us. Everywhere. Silhouetted figures running in the bottom corner, slightly taller versions playing in the upper left, taller ones still splashing in a pool to the right. There's even a slightly balding cat peeking out from behind a tree.

We're biggest in the center, less shadowy but still fading out around the edges as though we haven't truly settled on our final shapes. He painted me sitting with swirling sunflower wheels on either side of my chair and a low branch for him to sit beside me. His hair is too long and mine is wild but our hands are linked in every version of us.

"When did you do this?"

"Mathias lent me the supplies and Neel had them waiting for me. I started it as soon as I got back last night and finished at around dawn."

There's too much to look at and I'm not nearly done when he starts talking again.

"I made a choice before and it was the wrong one."

I shake my head. "She's your mom."

"She is, but that doesn't mean I had to go chasing somebody who didn't want to be found and leaving the one person who needed me."

I squeeze my eyes shut. "Please don't say that. I don't want you to look at me like I'm another person who needs you, who will make you give up parts of yourself for them. That day, the anniversary of my accident and my dad's death? I wanted you, Ethan, but I didn't need you. It's not the same thing." My eyes flick back and forth between his, desperate for him to understand.

He shifts closer to me until our legs are flush against each other and all my senses are full of him, his warmth, his scent, the rough timber of his voice. "I'm not looking for somebody else to build my existence around. That's the thing I'm starting to see." He half laughs. "I don't know what I'm supposed to do with my life, but for the first time, I want one. And not a life that is another person but maybe a life that's with one." My skin tingles when his hand wraps around mine and his thumb brushes my palm. "I'm okay with not being needed, but damn I want you to want me." It's achingly slow when his other hand slides up my shoulder to lift my face. "It'd also be great if you didn't push me out of the tree house or anything this time."

I rest my hand against his chest and curl my fingers into his shirt, but this time I pull.

I taste his smile when he kisses me.

His lips are firm as they fit to mine, pressing just enough that the back of my head touches the tree behind me. He inhales and I feel the air from my lungs slip into his, causing me to clutch at him for a second before he deepens the kiss.

This is nothing like the adolescent first kiss I dared to give him in my tree house, the one that proceeded my first true taste of heartbreak. It's nothing like the nearly stolen one by his pool which felt like another promise he couldn't keep. And unlike that sadness-fueled moment in his car which is blurred with guilt and regret, the only thing driving me to wrap my arms around his neck is him.

His hands slide across my back and tighten, urging me to arch into him and the perfect way our broken pieces fit together.

I feel everything.

★ ★ ★ ★ ★

AUTHOR'S NOTE

Dear Reader,

When I first started my publishing journey, a lot of sweet friends and readers of all abilities asked me if I'd ever write a book about a character like me, a wheelchair user, and to say the idea terrified me is an understatement. For a long time the answer was always no, a pretty, polite no, but a no all the same. Not because I didn't want to, but because I didn't think I could. There is often a lot of grief and heartache associated with disability, and I wasn't sure I could bare to look as deeply into that mirror as I knew I'd have to.

Over the years I did try. I'd start and stop and start again and never let myself go *there*.

Until one day I thought of Rebecca. And Ethan. And this very broken but beautiful love story. And I couldn't let it go, or rather it wouldn't let *me* go. So I tried again.

It did hurt.

With *Every Time You Go Away*, I wasn't just imagining a character and how different experiences would have shaped them.

I have lived with a spinal cord injury, paralysis, and becoming a wheelchair user since I was seventeen. That's not to say that Rebecca's story is anything like my own—it's not (please hear that if nothing else)—but I am intimately acquainted with the emotions that come with those particular realities.

But writing this book also healed.

Because like me, Rebecca's (and Ethan's) story isn't about disability. It's about love and loss, joy and grief, struggle and success, guilt and forgiveness, and a million other things that people all over the world experience every day. More than that, this book gave me an opportunity to portray the lives of people living with disability in ways they might not often get to see, ways that I see, and ways that are wonderful and full and rich. And hopeful.

There was a time in my life early on after I became paralyzed when I felt like I was just running out the clock, putting in my time and waiting, even longing, for the day when it could be over. It was hard to let go of the life I thought I'd have and to see the goals I had set for myself as possible or even to try to set new ones when I was reminded daily how much I'd lost. It's still hard, but like Amelia says, you can't wait until life isn't hard anymore to be happy. That's easier said than done, but the end? When you get there? When hard isn't easy, but you've discovered all the new reasons to smile?

That's a beautiful thing.

So to all the friends, to all the other wheelies and readers who've asked or just wondered if I'll ever?

Rebecca and Ethan's story is for you.

With love,
Abigail

ACKNOWLEDGMENTS

For a book I never thought I'd be strong enough to write, I sure have a lot of people to thank for its existence.

Kim Lionetti, my agent who has been gently encouraging me to tell a story like this for years without ever making me feel like I had to. Thank you for your support and for understanding what a journey this was for me. My editors Connolly Bottum, Anna Prendella, and Olivia Valcarce: I could not have been more fortunate than to have the three of you working on this book with me. Aditya Desai, for loving Neel as much as I do and sharing your insight to make him even better. Bess Braswell, Inkyard's publishing director, I can't thank you enough for your tireless enthusiasm for my books and this one in particular. Brittany Mitchel, senior marketing manager extraordinaire, and the entire Harper Children's sales team, it's wonderful knowing my book is in such good hands. So much gratitude for Kathleen Oudit and her brilliant art direction for the cover and to Eiko Ojala and his stunning cut paper illustration.

All my writing friends who cheered me on and read early

drafts, Sarah Guillory and Kate Goodwin, the two best critique partners anyone could ever have. Cheyanne Young, an incredible author and an even better friend. Rebecca Rode, insightful and always spot-on when it comes to character arcs. And my amazing local author buds from AZ YA writers, I love you guys.

My parents Gary and Suzanne Johnson, my siblings Sam Johnson, Mary Groen, and Rachel Decker, my family: Ross, Jill, Ken, Jeri, Rick, the Depews, all the ones I don't get to see nearly enough, and Nate Williams—you are my family in every way that matters. I love you all beyond words.

My nieces and nephews. Grady, Rory, Sadie, Gideon, Ainsley, Ivy, Dexter, Os, Goldie, and Gabriel. You are the greatest gifts of my life. There is not a thing on this earth that I love more than getting to be your aunt.

I nearly died when I was seventeen, and for a long time after that, I wondered why I hadn't. I don't wonder anymore. 2 Corinthians 12: 9-10.